THE BRIDGE TROLL MURDERS

The Bridge Troll Murders

Hook Runyon Mystery Series
Book 5

Sheldon Russell

THE ROADRUNNER PRESS

Published by The RoadRunner Press
Oklahoma City, Oklahoma
www.TheRoadRunnerPress.com

Map by Nancy Russell
Cover Design by Jeanne Devlin

Printed in the USA

First edition published November 2017

ISBN: 978-1-937054-27-4 (HC)
ISBN: 978-1-937054-64-9 (eBook)

Library of Congress Control Number: 2017950781

Publisher's Cataloging-In-Publication Data
(Prepared by The Donohue Group, Inc.)

Names: Russell, Sheldon. | Russell, Sheldon. Hook Runyon mystery ; bk. 5.
Title: The bridge troll murders / Sheldon Russell.
Description: First edition. | Oklahoma City, Oklahoma : The RoadRunner Press, 2017.
Identifiers: ISBN 978-1-937054-27-4 (hardcover) | ISBN 978-1-937054-64-9 (ebook)
Subjects: LCSH: Runyon, Hook (Fictitious character)--Fiction. | Murder--Investigation--Fiction. |
Railroad bridges--Fiction. | Criminologists--Fiction. | LCGFT: Detective and mystery fiction.
Classification: LCC PS3568.U777 B75 2017 (print) | LCC PS3568.U777 (ebook) | DDC 813/.54--dc23

10 9 8 7 6 5 4 3 2 1

For my grandson Cole
Shangri-La awaits

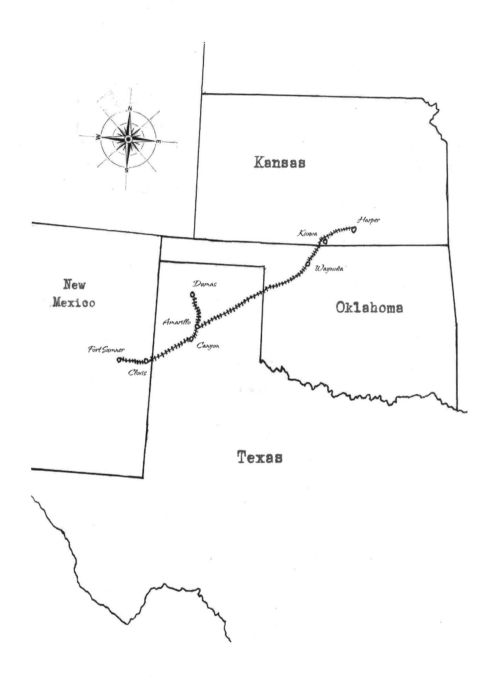

Prologue

BENJAMIN WAY TOSSED THE LAST stick of wood onto the dying
fire. Smoke twisted up through the bridge timbers and disappeared
into the blackness. He had failed to find enough firewood to see him
through the night, the jungle having been picked clean by the generations
of hoboes before him. Little remained but empty tin cans, broken whiskey
bottles, and the stench of moldy bedding.

Carved into the wood timbers were images and words left by those
before him, messages from the past, odd patterns of circles and triangles
and squares, random numbers, distorted faces, primitive and misshapen
animals. He ran his fingers over crude crosses and broken arrows; squiggly
lines, racial slurs, and obscenities; and a strange stick figure. What looked
to be an owl cocked its head and tracked him with a cold eye through the
darkness.

If only he knew what the symbols meant. Perhaps in them were messages of welcome or of warning. He leaned in closer to hear what the hieroglyphs had to say. But they were silent.

Heaving a sigh, he took out his Case XX pocketknife and began to strip
away the casing from a stick of salami. He cut the meat into thin slices on

a can lid, careful not to exhaust his meager food supply. Before partaking of his night's meal, he put away what sausage remained, cleaned the knife blade on his pant cuff, and dropped it back into his pocket. He favored the pocketknife's bone handle above all else. He had mowed yards for months to pay for the knife, knowing all the while that this day would come, the day he would leave home never to return.

Born against his will, he had had a life thus far as bleak as his birth, an unwanted nuisance even for those who bore him. He did not know why this was so, no more than they. He knew only the mark was upon him. They had broken his soul with indifference and driven him to the fringes of society. In the end, walking away had been the only option that remained.

As the last hurrah of the fire took hold, its heat rose and stung his face. At his back, the evening chill settled over his shoulders like a shroud. Somewhere in the distance, a train whistle sounded, corporeal and lusty, and a shiver passed down his spine. Fear or excitement, he could no longer tell, any more than he could identify the feeling twisting in his belly. Even in a flash of foreboding, he held no regrets. Beyond this place, beyond this night, he no longer mattered, forgotten as surely as yesterday's lunch.

Overhead, the timbers creaked, and he drew his legs up and wrapped his arms around his knees. A breeze swept in, and the grass whispered at his back. Smoke climbed from the fire and worked at the edges of his eyes. From somewhere high above the bridge, an owl hooted, signaling danger to its kind and causing the hairs on his arms to rise.

He clenched his teeth with resolve. Tomorrow, when the sun rose, things would be better. Tomorrow, he would remember all the reasons why he had left. Tomorrow, he would know that his decision had been right. The fire sputtered and paled at his feet. His shadow danced at the edges of his camp. He rubbed away the tears. He was but a boy, of no consequence, a speck in the universe. Who knew what evils waited beyond the firelight?

An ember crackled, and sparks rode the wind upward into the blackness. The circle of light closed in, and the gloom tightened about him. Something snapped from beyond the bridge pilings, a twig or maybe the contraction of the rails in the cold. His mouth went dry, and his throat tightened. The embers struggled against the darkness and then faded. If only he had gathered more wood, if only daylight would break—if only he still slept in his bed, someone familiar working in the kitchen.

He stood then. Certain. Heat rushed into his ears; blood chugged to his heart. He clenched his fists. A sudden breeze stirred the embers, first blue and then red, like eyes retreating beneath the ashes.

The blow from behind split his head like a lightning strike, collecting in electric pools under his arms and in the glands of his neck. His legs collapsed, and he pitched forward onto the ground. Fluid leaked from his nose, and ash from the fire gathered in his eyes.

A kick to his sternum shoved his heart against his vertebrae. It shuddered and quivered and struggled to regain cadence. A splintered rib pierced the softness of his lung and his chest wall. The wound gurgled and frothed. He sucked for breath, but none came, his lung an empty and useless bag. His heart trembled, and darkness drew down. His hand lay curled and blackening in the embers, while the stench of burning flesh filled the air. He did not move. He listened for a single beat of his heart, for the smallest tremor, and heard none. Felt none. An owl lifted and winged its way across the moonless sky.

Chapter 1

HOOK RUNYON TOOK OFF HIS artificial arm and laid it on the table. His caboose had been sided off the high iron next to a wheat field on the edge of Oklahoma's Waynoka yards, where he was to wait for Frenchy to tow him northeast to Topeka, Kansas. It was a new assignment, Hook having been named assistant division supervisor of security after the prior assistant supervisor had been found dead on the toilet and no one else could be located to fill the slot on such short notice.

Hook had spent his entire career on the rails, first as a hobo and then as a railroad bull. Even so, he had detected a certain reluctance in Eddie Preston, the division supervisor, about the job offer. Still, Hook had agreed to take it, figuring it was high time to see what getting paid for sitting on his ass might feel like.

He poured himself a Beam and then doubled it in celebration of his new position. Having made himself comfortable, he picked up his copy of H. G. Wells's 1897 novella, *The Invisible Man*. Reading from a rare book violated all the rules because nobody was fussier about the condition of a find than book collectors; yet, buying a reading copy struck him as extravagant, if not downright dangerous, considering the state of his caboose and the summary weight of his personal library. He could see the headlines now: "One-Armed Railroad Security Agent Found Dead Under Book Avalanche."

Early in his collecting, he had kept back just a few special editions, but somewhere along the line, less had become more, and simple interest had turned into a fascination, then a passion, and then an obsession that at times threatened his very livelihood. At one point, he had even considered giving up Beam in order to have more money to buy more books. Luckily, he had recovered his senses just in time.

Hook opened the sci-fi novel to where he had left off and moved his legs aside just enough to allow his dog, Mixer, whose reputation as a brawler was well established among other railway mongrels, under the table where Mixer settled at his feet. Hook used the term *his dog* loosely because Mixer did not belong to him, although they had shared the same caboose for many years. Mixer had simply showed up one day and refused to leave. By mutual agreement, their decision to cohabitate had always been implicit but binding: Each was to occupy the same quarters, but neither was to be responsible for the other's behavior, a matter of every man for himself, as it were.

Hook polished off his Beam and poured another. Landing an office job called for life changes of the highest order. Maybe he would buy himself a pen set to place on his new desk along with a calendar for keeping track of when he was to meet with Eddie Preston concerning security policy.

He returned to his book, pausing now and again to consider the advantages of invisibility. Catching pickpockets would be a cinch, and he could sit naked in his new office and not be seen. He could eat in the Harvey House kitchen whenever he pleased. He could scratch where it itched and wear his favorite T-shirt, the one with the holes in it. He could give Eddie Preston the finger to his face instead of to his back.

He poured himself a short one and gazed out the caboose window. The upsides of invisibility were attractive, but everything had downsides too. He would no longer get credit for stuff he did because no one would see him do it. He would have to forgo wearing his prosthesis because it would look like it was floating around by itself and that would scare the bejeezus out of people. If he died on the toilet like that other assistant supervisor, no one would ever know it. He might sit in there forever, people coming and going day and night.

Hook rubbed his face. A hard week chasing seal busters had cut into his sleep time. Taking off his boots, he reached for a cigarette and stretched out on the bunk to read. Under the table, Mixer snored, a habit of his after a hard day hunting stray cats. Being allergic to cat fur, Mixer always ended his hunts with swollen eyes and his nose whistling like a Steam Jenny, but it never slowed him down one iota.

Hook rolled onto his side, and weariness swept over him like warm water. Thank goodness Mixer wasn't invisible. There wouldn't be a cat left standing within a hundred miles. All and all, Hook figured visibility had the most advantages, except maybe for that dining thing at the Harvey House.

*****

Hook awoke to Mixer's barking. He sat up and his book slid off the bed onto the floor. Staring into the murkiness, Hook's eyes filled with water. His lungs tightened like a clenched fist in his chest, and he gasped for air. Mixer appeared from out of the gloom, whining and barking. Only then did Hook remember the lighted cigarette and realize that his mattress was afire.

"Hot damn!" he shouted, rolling off the bunk and onto the floor.

Somewhere beyond the curtain of smoke, Mixer upped the volume, his claws scratching at what Hook could only presume was the door to the caboose. Hook dropped to his stomach and crawled toward the barking, the smoke thickening over him like a storm cloud. When he could go no farther, he reached up and unlatched the door, shoving it open with his foot. Mixer dashed out over the top of him. Hook looked back at the black smoke boiling out the door.

"My books!" he yelled. Taking a deep breath, he went back in, dragged the smoldering mattress out the door, and threw it off the caboose porch. Back inside he went again, this time to open the windows to dissipate the acrid smoke and to rescue Wells from the floor.

Collapsing in the chair, Hook sniffed his shirtsleeve. It stank of smoke. He sighed. Maybe, with luck, he had gotten the fire out in time. Nothing absorbed smoke more certainly than book pages. If such was the case, his whole collection was ruined.

The smoke having cleared, he rose to close the window only to have his attention diverted by a wave of flames racing across the adjacent wheat field. The fire lit the sky, an inferno crackling and roaring as it consumed everything in its path. Hook watched, mouth agape, as smoke drifted across the countryside in a black curtain.

In that moment, he thought to repent for all the misdeeds of his life. Maybe those preachers from his childhood had been right, and the tormentors of hell had arrived to take their due. Unfortunately, his sins were numerous and varied in nature and he was not quite certain where to begin, and given that the fire had already doubled in magnitude, he thought to postpone redemption for now. Maybe another day when things were less pressing.

In the distance, he spotted a tractor crawling across the horizon, most likely manned by a farmer attempting to impede the fire from reaching his house by plowing a furrow through the wheat. The tractor had nearly completed the first pass and had turned for another run back.

Hook hurtled out the door and off the porch to help, realizing even as he did so that there wasn't a damn thing he could do for the man.

The farmer, seeing that he could not make it back through the field, leaped from his tractor and ran full tilt for the plowed furrow. The flames, fanned by a southwest wind, soon engulfed the tractor, and black smoke from the burning tires lifted a hundred feet into the air like a massive thundercloud. Embers rained down and ignited new hot spots, which quickly spread in the dry wheat stubble. When the tractor's fuel tank finally exploded, the ball of flames hurtling heavenward turned the blue sky orange.

The scream of a whistle announced the arrival of a section work train. Section hands leaped from the work cars with shovels in hand and ran into the raging fire. How they had found out so fast, Hook could not say, but the railroad was like that, a long-distance telephone line running three thousand miles across the country. Anything happened anywhere along the line, and every railroad employee, right down to the crew callboy, picked up to pass it along.

Within the hour, only a few wisps of smoke remained. The men, black with ash, made their way back to the work train. The farmer's tractor, a burned hulk, loomed in the distance like the skeleton of an ancient dinosaur. Hook watched as Curly Hoopslaw, the section foreman, made his way over to the caboose. Helix Hoopslaw was the man's real name, but not one in a hundred knew it.

"Hook," he said.

"Curly," Hook said. "Hot day, ain't it?"

Curly took out his bandanna and wiped the ash from his face. "They got the Super Chief laying by, Hook. From the top of the grade, it looked like Pearl Harbor down here."

"Santa Fe's touchy about that damn Super Chief, Curly. Guess they didn't mind sending you boys in, though."

"Not so's you could tell," he said. "How did it happen?"

"What?"

"The fire, Hook. What the hell you think?"

Hook looked up and down the track. "I could have been burned up this very minute, Curly. I'm guessing it was divine intervention saved me."

"I'm thinking divine retribution is more likely what set it off, Hook, given you ain't seen the inside of a church since Stewart fell off the boiler stack and kilt himself."

"Well, a hotbox is more apt the cause, I admit. Those dang carmen wouldn't change out a bushing for their mother's dying wish."

"Wouldn't be the first time a hotbox burned up the countryside," Curly said. "Back in thirty-nine out in Skull Valley, one set off an empty boxcar. Wasn't exactly empty, I'd guess you'd say, given that three section hands were in it sleeping on the job."

"The hell," Hook said.

"Burnt 'em to a crisp, but then, what's three section hands more or less? It's a lesson learned, though," Curly said.

"Never sleep in a boxcar while it's on fire," Hook said. "You'd think even a section hand could think that one through."

"Well, I better get that work train off the high iron. Those Super Chief celebrities will be calling the big boys by now." The engineer of the work train hit three short blasts of his whistle and bumped her back. Curly gave him a wave.

"Funny thing is," Curly said, pointing to the bar ditch, "there's a burnt mattress right down there by the fence. Looks like it could have been what set this here fire off."

Hook took hold of the grab iron and swung up on the caboose porch. He leaned over the railing. " 'Boes," he said. "You know how those bastards are always stealing stuff to sleep on."

"It's a bunk mattress out of a louse box. Might want to keep that caboose of yours buttoned up, Hook. You might be next."

And with that, Curly turned and headed down the track.

Chapter 2

HOOK RETURNED TO HIS caboose only to find that Mixer refused to come back inside for what Hook could only assume was a fear of being burned alive. He tried to coax the dog with food, but to no avail. Truth be told, Hook found it difficult not to take the dog's accusatory look personally. Eventually, Mixer gave up any show of coming inside and slinked off into the darkness, with nary a look back over his shoulder.

Hook spent the night on the floor, his jacket for a cover, and awoke to a train roaring by on the high iron. As he nursed his morning coffee, he took stock of the smoke marks on the wall. A few seconds longer, and the whole thing would have burned to the ground, books and all.

From the door, he called again for Mixer but got no response. "Damn dog," he said, reaching for his cigarettes.

He studied the package for a moment and then threw it on the table. "That's it," he said. "I quit."

The sun had risen well into the sky by the time he made his way down the right-of-way toward the Waynoka rail yards. The smell of smoke still hung in the air. Ash swirled above the field in eddies, and charred stubs of fence posts stood in testament to the intensity of the fire.

Hook patted his empty pocket for a cigarette. He figured Eddie already knew about the fire, given the nature of railroad gossip, but a call to him was required. Reporting to Eddie Preston carried all the pleasure of an ice-water enema. Without smokes, Hook figured he could not be held responsible for what he might do or say. Cutting through the supply building, he made his way over to the yard office, where he found the yardmaster gone. Pulling up a chair at his desk, he dialed Eddie Preston.

"Security," Eddie said.

"Eddie, this is Hook."

"What the hell is going on over there, Runyon?"

"Busy stamping out crime, Eddie. Listen, about my new office."

"Try stamping out fires for awhile, Runyon. My phone hasn't stopped ringing all morning. Some farmer is threatening to sue the railroad for burning up his field."

"That wasn't my fault."

"And his tractor too. He says he barely got out alive. Says all his hair's been singed off, including his eyebrows."

"How much could eyebrows be worth, Eddie?"

"On top of that, the Super Chief arrived in Chicago three hours late because of having to lay by for that fire. Three hours. And you know who was on that train? I'll tell you who: Bette Davis was on that train."

"Maybe I'll just sue the railroad myself, Eddie. I damn near burned up, and my dog won't come in. I think he's had a nervous breakdown."

You're lucky if you don't go to jail over this one, Runyon."

"I can't be responsible for every hotbox on the line."

"Curly says he found a mattress."

"A mattress?"

"That's right, a caboose bunk mattress."

" 'Boes steal those damn things right and left, Eddie."

"Half burnt and lying twenty feet from your caboose? I find that peculiar, don't you?"

"My caboose was surrounded by flames. I damn near died in that fire."

"And what if it had been Bette Davis who burned up? What then?" Eddie asked.

Hook watched the yardmaster coming across the tracks. "That would qualify as peculiar. Now, about my office."

"What office? Railroad bulls can't go around setting fires and then get an office. It don't work that way."

"I have to go, Eddie. The yardmaster needs his phone."

"I want you to get out to the Quinlan bridge. Today, you hear?"

"What for?"

"The Amarillo runs are reporting buzzards circling the bridge."

"Those runs kill more cows than a Chicago slaughterhouse, Eddie."

"And I've put an order in for Frenchy to tow your caboose to Quinlan for the time being. Someone's busting car seals and stealing freight out there. You can side off next to the track foreman's shack."

"But that's in the middle of nowhere, Eddie."

"Exactly. I don't want kids playing on those cars. We could get sued, you know."

"Right."

"And another thing, the Topeka office is sending around a forensic psychologist. She wants to talk to you, God help her."

"A what?"

"A forensic psychologist."

"What the hell is that?"

"A person knows all about criminals. They're doing a research study or some damn thing. Maybe you can learn something."

"Jesus, Eddie, I know too much about criminals already. Besides, I'll be pretty busy picking up dead cows. I'd just as soon not be dealing with some fornicating psychologist."

"*Forensic*, Runyon. Anyway, I don't remember asking your opinion. This came down from the big boys. Maybe there's more to law enforcement than herding 'boes with a short stick. In any case, she's to get whatever access she wants."

"She?"

"That's right."

"Has she ever been in law enforcement?"

"She reads books."

"So do I."

"She reads real books, Runyon, and that's the end of it."

*****

13

Frenchy eased the old steamer back and coupled her into the caboose. He waited as Hook released the caboose brake. From his vantage on top, Hook could see Mixer chasing something in the distance. He couldn't quite make out whether it was a rabbit or a cat, although Mixer's pattern suggested the former.

Happy to know his dog was back to one of his old ways, Hook climbed the engine ladder and cleared a space to sit in the steamer cab as Frenchy pulled out onto the high iron. The fireman nodded at Hook over his shoulder. Frenchy brought the old steamer up to power and gauged her stroke. Satisfied, he turned to Hook. "Heard you've been trying to burn up the country, Hook. Never knew Eddie Preston to be so pissed about anything."

"It was an act of God, Frenchy. I can't be held responsible."

"I'm thinking God wasn't within a hundret mile of that fire, Hook."

"Why does everyone assume I started that fire?"

"If it looks like a duck. . . .," Frenchy said, lighting up his cigar.

"Frenchy, is it necessary to smoke that stinking thing in here? It isn't good for my health."

Frenchy took the cigar out of his mouth and looked at it. "Some kind of hypocrite, ain't he?" he said to the fireman. "Every son of a bitch between here and California has been offended by those cigarettes of his."

"Smoking shows a lack of character, Frenchy. A man should exercise a little discipline in his life."

Frenchy flipped the ash off his cigar. "Self-discipline is something you know a lot about, I guess?"

"You don't see me smoking, do you?"

"I don't see you drinking hooch, either, Hook. Don't mean a damn thing, does it?" Frenchy stuck his head out the cab window and blew his whistle.

"Quinlan," he said, bringing the train down to a crawl.

Hook climbed out on the ladder and waited for Frenchy to back the caboose onto the siding next to the foreman's shack. After uncoupling it, with his hand held up against the blaze of the sun, Hook hollered up to the engineer.

"How far to the Quinlan bridge from here?"

Frenchy leaned out the window. "It's a walk," he said. "Why, you figuring to burn it down, Hook?"

"Not right off," Hook said. "Eddie says buzzards been flying around out there."

"Probably a cow or a section hand," Frenchy said. "Neither one's got the good sense to get off the track. You want a lift? I'm headed westbound for a short haul."

"No offense, Frenchy, but that cigar gives me a headache."

"Suit yourself," Frenchy said.

After watching Frenchy pull out and setting the caboose brake, Hook checked for level. Looked like he would have to sleep westbound or all the blood would be rushing to his head. He could not remember the last time he had been sided on level ground.

Hook climbed up into the cupola for a look around. From atop the caboose, he could see the line of freight cars and the remnants of Frenchy's engine smoke drifting away in the distance. The sun wobbled and melted into the horizon.

Climbing down, he checked his watch. Maybe he would just settle in tonight, check out the cars on his way to the bridge in the morning. He lit the lantern, poured himself a Beam, and slid a box of books out from beneath the table.

He had no electricity, no running water, and no mattress. A man of executive caliber deserved more. He picked up the pack of cigarettes, smelled them, and then laid them back down. He would give it another day. Anyway, how bad could things be? There were no 'boes, no pickpockets, and no Eddie Preston.

Chapter 3

R IA WOLFE CLIMBED THE STAIRS of the Eastman Hotel and found her room at the end of the hall. She checked the lock behind her before setting her suitcase on the bed. Opening the curtains, she rubbed the fatigue from her neck. The Waynoka rail yards lit the night sky. The roundhouse, with its myriad windows, stood in the distance like a Roman coliseum.

The drive from Boston had been long despite her new Chevy two-door sedan, a gift from her war-magnate father, a manufacturer of silver service turned mess-kit tycoon. She hoped what she would find at the end of the road would prove her trip worthwhile.

A psychology student in college, she had had an interest in human behavior that had grown while working for the U.S. Department of Veterans Affairs, filling in where needed, which was almost everywhere. The ending of the war and the onslaught of battle-fatigue cases had used up mental-health people at an alarming rate. Women such as herself had been asked to step in and help where they could. She found that she not only liked the work but that she was damn good at it. The end result had been a course of study in clinical psychology, which had led her into the budding area of forensic science. She sometimes wondered if her choice in research stemmed from having seen firsthand the impact that killing had on men. Knowing its horrors, she had struggled with what could possibly motivate anyone to kill a fellow human. She knew now there were motivations aplenty—loyalty to country and conscription; anger, she supposed; revenge; even profit; but what of those who had no obvious reason? What of those who seemed to kill for the killing? History had no shortage of just such monsters, outwardly normal-seeming humans who took life randomly and without remorse, although not necessarily without pattern or cause.

Until now, Ria had enjoyed the relative safety of the perpetual student, the luxury of not having full responsibility for her decisions. That was about to end. Ahead stood the final hurdle for her doctorate: the dissertation. Faced with the inevitable difficulties of gathering data, her confidence waned. She had fought and won on the field of academia, but now she faced the real world of law enforcement, something she knew little about.

Civil law enforcement, always fearful of the sunlight, had been unwilling to give her the access she needed for completion of her research. Her father, however, having connections in the right places, had managed to gain permission for her to use railroad security guards, better known as railroad bulls, instead. Although not the population she had hoped for, it would at least allow her to complete her research in a timely manner.

She sighed and drew the curtains closed. Everyone was so far away now, her father, her professors, her friends, all beyond reach in this desolate sliver of the American West.

Turning on the light, she opened her suitcase and laid out her clothes for the next day: matching hat and gloves, rayon slip, a bra and girdle, a jacket with nipped waist and patch pockets and matching skirt, a Bakelite bracelet, a pair of silver earrings, a handkerchief, and her strappy heels.

Slipping on her earrings, she studied her face in the dingy mirror. The years of study had failed to diminish her attractiveness, the porcelain-white skin, the full lips, the blue eyes that snapped with intelligence. She had been known to regret her looks, finding that they too often usurped her credibility as a psychologist with her fellowman.

In the bathroom, she laid out her makeup items on the sink in the order in which she would use them in the morning: eyeliner, powder, rouge, lipstick. She double-checked to make certain that nothing was missing.

She had been accused more than once of being meticulous, even obsessive, but so far, it had served her well. No detail was ever too small to be ignored, a concept highly favored in forensic psychology—and she could only hope in the field. The Waynoka yardmaster had told her that the security agent she would be looking for was a Mr. Hook Runyon, a railroad bull who had only that same day been transferred to the Quinlan siding. The yardmaster made it clear that if she wanted to catch the agent, she would have to arrive early and be prepared for anything. "He might be sober, then again, he might not," he had said. "Might welcome you with open arms or shoot you through the door. As far as I'm concerned, a more contrary son of a bitch never lived." Having worked with academics, a special brand of sons of bitches in their own right, Ria was not worried.

Turning out the lights, she slipped into bed and in the darkness studied the spot of light that cast through the window and onto the ceiling. She could hear the train whistle in the distance and the crew change making its way down the hallway of the hotel. She turned on her side and wondered if she had packed her Moleskine notebook and her Parker 51 fountain pen. She must have. After all, being prepared was what she did best.

*****

Dawn broke just as Ria pulled onto the road to Quinlan. Dust boiled up behind the car as she wound her way into the Glass Mountains, a range of mesas with soil red as blood in the far northwestern corner of Oklahoma. Gypsum caprock twenty feet thick topped the mesas, and slabs of mica winked in the morning sun. Ria could almost see dinosaurs grazing in the canyons and microraptors winging their way from mesa to mesa. She found her notebook, which she had secured next to her on the seat.

The sky, cobalt blue, swept overhead like a great sea, and the horizon fell away to infinity. She had never known such emptiness, such absence of people, of buildings, of life itself. She gripped the steering wheel as a tight turn rose up in front of her. As she maneuvered the curve, the tiny settlement of Quinlan cropped up ahead. A red caboose had been sided next to a wooden shack that sat only yards from the main railroad line.

Ria shut off the engine and waited, wondering how her journey through the ivory towers of academia could have brought her to this remote, rustic spot. When she opened the car door, a dog scuttled out from under the caboose and then ambled off into the prairie as if without a care in the world, looking back over its shoulder now and again to see if she followed.

She stepped from the car and made her way to the siding. The caboose, having been parked on a steep incline, presented a ladder so high off the ground that the first step was hip level. She struggled to secure a toe on the first rung, lost her balance, dropped her notebook, and fell backward into the dirt. "Damn," she said, getting up and dusting off her hands and the back of her suit.

On the second try, she tossed the notebook onto the caboose porch and with both hands pulled herself onto the ladder. Once up, she looked about to see if anyone had been watching her, but only the dog gazed from the shade of a distant juniper. Ria knocked and waited. No response. She thought about what the yardmaster had said and stepped to one side before knocking again.

When the door jerked opened, she jumped. "Oh, God," she said, holding her hand over her heart.

The shirtless man who stood in the doorway made no attempt to cover his arm stump. His hair lay in coal-black strands across his forehead; his face reminded her of a log that had weathered away to its core. He leveled his eyes on her. "I've been mistaken for lots of things, Miss, but never God. Who are you?"

"My name is Ria Wolfe. Are you Mr. Hook Runyon?"

"You ain't from that unwed mother's home, are you?"

Ria's face flushed. "Hardly. I'm from Boston University, and I'm here to conduct my criminal research."

"Research?"

"Yes. They said to come early."

"Boston University said to come early?"

"No, the Waynoka yardmaster."

Hook rolled his eyes. "That bastard's probably grinning in his sleep right now."

"Well, I don't know about that, but I promise I'll be as little trouble as possible, Mr. Runyon. I don't want to interfere with your work."

"Look, Miss," he said. "On a good day, and if they're too drunk to run, I might catch a 'bo hopping a freighter or a pickpocket working the crowd or a seal buster stealing apples out of a reefer car. Other than that, my contribution to Boston University and to your research in particular is going to be mighty thin."

"Not at all, Mr. Runyon. Criminal research at its heart is based on observing law officers in action to see what techniques they use and which work best. It requires structured observation and objectivity, none of which can be done while sitting in a library, much less a classroom."

Hook looked longingly back at the pack of cigarettes on the table before turning to face his visitor eye to eye.

"I can see we have a problem right off, Miss Wolfe," he said.

"Ria," she said. "Please call me Ria."

"First, I barely qualify as a law-enforcement officer. Ask any city cop between here and California. Second, I've no training and precious little education. My unwillingness to take advice is renowned, and I've been known to drop the hat first from time to time."

He reached back for his shirt and slipped it on. "So let's you and me strike a deal. Give me whatever paper it is that you need signed, and I'll sign it. You go back to Boston University, collect your degree, and I'll go back to bed. Believe me, we'll both be better off for it."

Ria lifted her chin. "I'd never falsify data, Mr. Runyon. That would be unethical."

Hook pretended to work at a button for a minute or two, knowing full well that he required his prosthesis to thread the buttonhole. Ria was still there when he looked up. He sighed in frustration. "Exactly what is this research, anyway?"

"The title of my dissertation is *The Correlation between the Application of Forensic Psychological Constructs and Case Resolution as Pertains to Capital Crimes.*"

Hook shook his head. "I can see how ethics might be involved in that, all right. Let me clear it up for you, Ria. I've never heard *railroad dicks* and *ethics* used in the same breath before, and my peers, myself included, wouldn't know a psychological construct from a cathouse."

"Investigations can't be just a matter of opinion, Mr. Runyon. Solving a crime requires detailed work conducted in a scientific and repeatable way."

"I'll swear to it," he said.

"That would only make matters worse."

"On the Bible."

"I'm afraid not."

"My mother's grave?"

"Mr. Runyon, you do understand that this study has been approved by your supervisor, Mr. Eddie Preston?"

Hook paused. "Is that a threat, Ria?"

She lifted her chin and locked her eyes on his. "Yes," she said. "Absolutely."

Hook looked first up the track and then down. He studied his bare feet, gave Mixer a little wave, and then wiggled his toes. "Come on in, then," he said. "I'll fix the coffee."

Chapter 4

HOOK POINTED TO THE room's only chair, pushed aside the bedding on the floor with his foot, and strapped on his prosthesis. He filled the coffeepot from the water cooler and set it on the stove's front burner. Water dribbled out of the spout.

"That Frenchy parks me on a hillside every chance he gets," he said. "I got one leg shorter than the other from living on the slant."

"My goodness," said Ria, who instead of sitting was taking a slow spin of the place. "All these books. You're a collector?"

Hook retrieved two cups from the cabinet. "I don't qualify as a collector. That requires money."

She picked up a book and leafed through it. "Fiction?"

"Wish I'd never gotten started," Hook said. "It's like a starving man chained up in a bakery, spending all his time yearning for something he can't have."

He gave a nod toward the closet shelf. "You're welcome to read them while you're here, providing you don't dog-ear 'em, make notes in the margins, or spill liquor on 'em."

"Thank you, but no."

"You must read something," he said. "I assume Boston University has books."

"Frankly, I find reading imaginary stories to be wasted time. I'm only interested in facts. In real life."

Hook poured their coffees, handed Ria her cup, and sat down at the table. He sipped at his coffee and slid the pack of cigarettes to the side.

"Is it possible that facts discovered is more meaningful and perhaps more convincing than facts simply stated?" he asked.

Ria opened her notebook and jotted something down. She looked up at him. "I've offended you. Sometimes I can be too blunt."

"Call me Hook, since we'll be solving crime together," he said. "And are you as blunt in your notebook?"

"Oh, this?" she said. "Mostly reminders to myself, things I might find useful when I start the writing."

Hook reached down, slipped on his shoes, and tied off the bows.

Ria watched him. "You're quite proficient with that," she said.

Hook held up his prosthesis. "Lost it in an accident. You'd be surprised what you can do when you don't have a choice."

The sun lifted over the hill and streamed in through the caboose window. She looked around. "And do you always sleep on the floor?"

"Sometimes I sleep on the table," he said. "Once, I slept on a five-inch steam pipe in the Amarillo roundhouse. They brought up the heat in the night. It took three men to unfold me."

She looked up at him, her blue eyes caught in the sunlight. "That's remarkable."

"Not so much. I heard of a 'bo once who could run down a hot shot passenger train going sixty miles an hour while rolling a Prince Albert cigarette one-handed."

"Really?"

"So they say, though I haven't witnessed it personally."

"That's astonishing."

"You don't believe me?"

"Well, why wouldn't I?"

"They say he could go to sleep in Albuquerque and not wake up until Needles, just hanging there like a bat. Said the railroad bulls didn't bother him 'cause they figured he was dead."

"And this is a true story?"

"It's hobo talk and likely a lie, though there's always a bit of truth in such tales."

Ria took a drink of her coffee. "Well, then, back to business," she said. "I'd like to follow you around as you solve your cases, make notes, interview you from time to time about the process. It's as simple as that."

"You giving this report to Eddie Preston?"

She shook her head. "The data I gather are confidential, or more accurately, anonymous."

"How do I know that?"

"I swear it."

"Good enough for me," he said.

"And what do we do today?" she asked.

"Dead cows," he said. "Eddie can't abide dead cows."

*****

Ria struggled to keep up with Hook as they walked the tracks. High heels had been her first bad decision of the day; she hoped it would be the only one. The sun beat on their backs, and the heat quivered up from the rails. She stopped to catch her breath.

"Tell me again why we didn't take the car?" she said.

Hook adjusted his hat. "No road. That's the bridge just up there where you see those buzzards sitting on the rail."

"Are you really looking for dead cows?"

"You'd be surprised how many cows the railroad kills every year. And then you got mad farmers and lawsuits to deal with. If the track isn't cleared pretty fast, all kinds of other animals show up, coyotes, buzzards, dogs. Pretty soon it's pure carnage everywhere you look. You'd think that big as the world is, critters could find somewhere else to stand besides a railroad track."

As Hook and Ria approached the bridge, the buzzards lifted, their wings flapping in slow motion as they rose into the blue and slowly banked away.

Hook stepped onto the bridge. He gestured for Ria to hold back.

"Be careful," he said. "It's a fair drop to the bottom."

25

Hook worked his way out to the center of the bridge before pausing. Easing over the side, he peered into the canyon below.

"I don't see any dead cow," he said. "But it might have fallen out of sight. We better get off this thing. It's right hard to outrun a train on a bridge."

With them both back on safe ground, Hook raised his hand to shield his eyes as he peered into the shadows of the canyon.

"I'm going down to check it out," he said. "You stay up here."

Ria dabbed at the perspiration on her forehead with her handkerchief. "I don't think so. We agreed I was to be included in every aspect of your job."

Hook shrugged. "Suit yourself, but this riprap can be damn tricky to walk on—especially in heels. Didn't they teach you anything about field work at that fancy college of yours?"

"You don't hear me complaining," Ria said.

Hook eased himself down to the bottom of the fill and then reached up and helped Ria down the last few steps. A small line of blood trickled from her ankle and into her shoe.

"You okay?" he asked.

"I'm fine," she snapped.

As they moved down the canyon, shadows leaned out like spirits, and the leaves of an old cottonwood rustled in the breeze.

Hook stopped to pick up an empty whiskey bottle and checked the label.

"Rotgut," he said. "There's a long-standing jungle here."

"Jungle?"

"A hobo hotel but without the amenities. See that big 'U' marked on the bridge piling over there?"

"Yes."

"That's a message to other 'boes. Means it's safe to sleep here."

"They have their own code?"

" 'Boes been leaving coded messages long as there's been trains. Course, you won't find that in the Boston University library."

"You might be surprised," Ria said. "I know of at least one BU professor who studies Babylonian hieroglyphs. That's practically the same thing. Symbols from a culture."

She moved closer to one of the wood pilings.

"There, that one is a simple cross," she said.

26

"Means if you talk religion at the next house, you'll likely get fed."

"And that one, the box with what looks like an upside-down comb inside it. What does that mean?"

"Watch for bad dogs in the area."

"That's amazing," she said. "And what about that one, the one that looks like a small owl?"

Hook squinted at the scratches in the wood. "Might be an owl," he said. "Might not. 'Boes ain't known for their book learning or art skills. Hobo markings can change up some from one jungle to another, so don't go setting your clock by them."

They worked their way down to the creek bed.

"Sometimes, finding the remains of a critter can be difficult," Hook said. "A forty-car train traveling fifty miles an hour can damn near vaporize a victim."

"Oh, my," Ria said, putting her hand over her mouth.

Soon, they came upon pieces of bedding, soured and chewed by rats.

"Over there," Hook said, pointing. "Looks like a campfire."

The unburned ends of firewood lay in a circle about the ashes. In the grass, he found a tin-can lid and a stick of salami with several slices cut from its end. Ants scurried about the lid as they collected the morsels of food. He held his hands over the ashes to check for warmth.

"Hasn't been long," he said, looking around. "Whoever it was took off in a hurry, I'd say. He left his food, and there's still heat in those ashes. The coons haven't gotten to that salami yet either. Doesn't take varmints long to clean up a campsite."

Hook checked his P38. A 'bo jungle, even an abandoned one, could be a dangerous place, especially for a railroad bull. A whippoorwill called from somewhere down canyon.

Ria stepped in close to Hook. "You don't think it's a dead cow, do you?"

"Whoever was here didn't know much about hobo camps," he said.

"What do you mean?"

"Looks like he ran out of firewood. He didn't gather enough for the night before he settled in. It's a must, you know. Sleeping a cold camp is a lesson that stays with a man. It had to be below fifty last night."

He eased down the bank and turned in a slow circle. The wind had fallen silent, and the bridge timbers creaked as they settled in against the heat.

"See where that grass is trampled over there?" he said.

"I see it," she said, her voice tight.

"The dirt's been disturbed just beyond. I figure something might be there."

"Do you think. . . ."

"You go on back. I'll be along shortly."

"I'm staying," she said.

Hook reached for a cigarette and found an empty pocket instead. "See if you can find me a stick I can use to clean away this dirt."

"Okay."

"But don't go too far."

"Don't worry," she said, scrambling back up the bank.

Within moments, she returned with a forked stick. Hook got on his knees and cleared away the loose dirt. At first, he thought the charred lump was a piece of firewood, but as he scraped away more dirt, a finger bone appeared, white where the flesh had burned away, and then a thumb, its nail still intact. Ria gasped.

Hook slowly pulled more of the dirt from the body. Sweat ran into his eyes, and he wiped it away on his sleeve. The smell of death rose from the putrefying body. Hook's stomach tightened.

"It's a man," he said. "Or I should say, a boy."

Matter oozed from a hole in the back of the boy's head, a lethal blow, and his chest cavity had been opened, a gaping wound running from the base of his throat to just below his navel. His shirt, still buttoned about the neck, had been sawed and hacked away in the attack. Bits of bloodied cloth still clung to his rib cage.

Ria, her breathing rapid, dropped to the ground beside Hook. She leaned into him, and he could feel her trembling.

"Deep breaths," he said. "This boy isn't feeling any pain."

Hook brushed away the offending dirt, being careful not to disturb things more than necessary. Dirt clogged the boy's mouth and nose, and dried blood filled the pocket of his throat.

Hook sat back on his heels and rubbed at his neck.

"What is it?" she asked.

He pointed to the bloodied mass in the boy's chest. "His body parts have been rearranged," he said. "There are things inside him that shouldn't be."

Ria's hand tightened on Hook's arm. "Hook, we need to go and get more help. Whoever did this could still be around."

"Just a second," Hook said, checking the boy's pockets. "I think you forget, I am law enforcement. But you have a point."

"What are you looking for?"

"His pocketknife."

"How do you know he had one?"

"He cut that salami with something," he said.

Hook eased the body onto its side, and it moaned.

"Oh, God, he's alive!" Ria cried.

"Just trapped air," Hook said. "Take it easy."

"Hook . . ."

"Right, I'm coming."

Hook pulled the boy's wallet from his back pocket and quickly checked the contents, a few small bills scorched from the fire and a half-burned driver's license. He looked up into the sky, where buzzards circled high overhead. "His name was Benjamin Way," he said. "He turned sixteen two months ago."

Chapter 5

HOOK USED A HANDFUL OF grass to erase the "U" from the bridge timber while the sheriff and his deputy pulled the body up the embankment on a stretcher. Ria waited up top with the riptrack foreman, who had brought out a popcar to transport the boy's body back to the crossing.

Hook worked his way up the riprap to find Sheriff Holcome waiting for him. Holcome reached down with a hand the size of a country ham and hoisted Hook up the last few feet to the track. Pushing back his hat, the sheriff said, "Another hour and them buzzards would've made this job a hell of a lot easier, Hook."

"Sorry to inconvenience you, Sheriff."

"I picked up some pretty rough stuff over the years, but I ain't never seen one like this. Usually them damn 'boes are too busy stealing chickens and drinking hooch to bother butchering each other."

"They couldn't get this boy dead enough, by the looks of it," Hook said.

Hook checked the sky, now absent of buzzards.

"Doesn't look like robbery. And hard to say how many there were either. Thing is, there are no tracks leading in or out. It's as if whoever did this dropped in from the sky and left the same way. Did you know this boy, Sheriff?"

"Benjamin Way. Local," Holcome said. "He was always talking about how he figured to run off one day. Damn kids got no idea what could be waiting for them out there."

"He have folks?"

"Just a ma, goes by Beth. She hangs out at the beer joint most days. You got any notions about this, Hook?"

"Maybe whoever did it had it in for him or for his ma."

"The mother turns a few tricks when things get tight. Deputy Tooney's been called out there a time or two. Other than that, she's not been no trouble. But you never know for certain what's brewing with some folks."

"You going to notify her about the boy?"

The sheriff fished out a pack of Beech-Nut and tucked a cud into his cheek.

"That's why I make the big money, ain't it?" he said, his voice muffled. "You and the young lady will be coming in for a report?"

Hook nodded.

"Must be kind of invigorating to have a partner looks like her," Holcome said. "All I got is ol' Tooney over there, and he don't take a bath but once a month."

"Good enough for this time of year," Hook said. "We'll be along in awhile, Sheriff."

*****

When Ria and Hook came out of the sheriff's office, the end-of-day sun reflected from the window of Ria's Chevy in a deep orange.

"Well," Hook said. "I should be heading home."

Ria searched her keys out of her purse. "Would you have time for a few questions first?" she asked.

"You mean now?"

"I know it's been a long day, but there are questions I need to ask while it's all still fresh."

"I'm not likely to forget much about this day," Hook said. "What did you have in mind?"

"I have a room at the Eastman. I mean, if you don't think it would be a problem. I can run you home from there."

Hook looked back to see the sheriff standing in the window. "I have a reputation to protect, you know," he said. "Going to your room ought to bolster that just fine."

Upstairs in Ria's digs, Hook sat at the small writing desk while Ria fixed them a cold drink. He took the moment for a closer look at this person who had dropped into his business from nowhere, the delicate hands, the manicured nails, the expensive suit.

"Cola okay?" she asked, turning, with drinks in hand.

"That will do," he said.

She pulled up a chair at the desk and opened her notebook. "Now," she said. "A few questions."

Hook sipped at his drink. "The stage is yours."

"What conclusions have you drawn about what happened today?"

"I try not to draw conclusions until there's something to conclude."

"You must have some ideas?"

"Ideas I have. Conclusions I don't."

"Well, an idea then."

"Could have been a jungle buzzard."

"Excuse me?"

"A jungle buzzard, a jackroller, a bindle stiff, a hobo who preys on other 'boes."

"What makes you think that?"

Hook wished he could light up a cigarette.

"The boy was attacked in a hobo jungle. That means his attacker knew the jungle was there. Most folks don't keep track of hobo jungles unless they are hoboes."

"But no money was taken?"

"Apparently not, but his knife was."

"You think someone would kill for a knife?"

"I've seen men tangle over less."

"Seems odd to me. Aren't hoboes always in need of a little cash? Why leave even a few dollars?"

"Maybe who did it was interrupted."

Ria jotted something in her notebook, before raising her head with a puzzled look on her face. "But why? And by that, I mean, why was the boy there in the first place?" she asked.

"Sheriff figures he ran away to ride the rails. Boys do that sometimes. He was green, that's for sure. He had no idea about the rules of jungle living. Fact is, kids make easy pickings when they go on the bum."

Ria soaked that in, tapping her pencil against her cheek in thought. She opened her mouth to speak and then abruptly shut it before saying, "Did you know that killers sometimes take souvenirs from their victims?"

"A little remembrance? Well, there's not much surprises me anymore," Hook said. "The boy's knife was gone, wasn't it?"

"Do you have a specific theory in mind that you'll use to reason this case through?"

Hook polished off his drink and studied his glass. "I set out to look around," he said.

"That's it?"

"Looking is a tad more complicated than you might think."

"Can you explain that?"

"Well, it depends on what you're looking for, which depends on where you've been and what you already know."

"I don't understand."

"I spent a good deal of my adult years living as a hobo. Without that, I'm not sure I would know where to start with a case like this."

"You think only an ex-hobo can do an effective job as a railroad bull?"

"I think experience is handy nearly all the time and lack of it can be damn dangerous. Whoever this guy was came upon the victim alone and in the night. It's damned quiet out there by yourself, and it takes a pretty stealthy fellow to sneak up on a man unnoticed, even on a rookie like this kid was. Whoever killed that boy was pretty good at it, I'd say."

Hook leaned back in his chair. "Now, let me ask you a few questions."

Ria frowned and shifted in her seat. "This isn't about me."

"It only seems fair."

"Well," she said, laying her pencil down. "If you insist."

"What did you see?"

"A brutal murder that can't be explained by the conflicting physical evidence alone, meaning what was taken and what was left. In short, I don't think there is an obvious motive yet."

"I didn't ask what you thought. I asked what you saw."

"I saw mutilation and humiliation. I saw that someone wanted to strip this boy of his identity and his manhood," Ria said.

Hook nodded. "Not bad."

Ria leaned in and lowered her voice. "Hook, this sort of predator—someone who kills and mutilates—has existed for eons, and I hate to tell you, but such a killer is rarely satisfied with a single murder."

Hook sat up straighter in his chair. "Go on," he said.

"Well, take Herman Mudgett back in the late 1800s in Chicago, twenty-seven murders. He liked to asphyxiate and torture his victims. He built an elaborate three-story murder castle and a maze of death traps to lure his victims in."

Ria could tell she had Hook's attention. "You can go back even farther to mythical creatures, werewolves and vampires. Why some people even believed in trolls that lured humans into underground places to kill and eat them."

Hook stood. "We saw different things, you and me. It's like those answers you're writing in that notebook."

"Excuse me?"

"The answers you get from me depend mostly on one thing."

"And what would that be?"

"The questions you ask depend on what you know, or more 'specially, on what you don't know," he said. "What I saw under that bridge depends on what I was looking for. You and me weren't looking for the same things, and we came up with different answers. Mine just happen to be useful."

Ria closed her notebook, her face blank. "I was trying to understand why something like this happened and who could do such a thing," she said. "Why butcher a young boy in the most violent way and then leave his money behind?"

Hook looked out the window. He could see the rail-yard lights glowing in the evening dusk. "And I was trying to understand what happened."

"But don't you want to understand why?"

Hook stood. "I want to catch the bastards and make them pay. Now, about that ride home."

*****

Hook waited until Ria's car lights disappeared down the road before retrieving the key from under the mat of the foreman's shack. Sitting at the old desk, he dialed Eddie in the dark.

"Security," Eddie said.

"Eddie, we've got a little trouble out here."

He could hear Eddie breathing on the other end. "Trouble? What do you mean, trouble?"

"You know, like when some kid gets butchered under the Quinlan bridge."

"Dead?"

"You're quick, Eddie. Maybe you should go into the detective business."

"This isn't funny, Runyon."

"That explains why I haven't been laughing all day," he said.

"Who the hell was it?"

"Some local, name's Benjamin Way. He was spending the night in the jungle."

"I told you to clean those jungles up, Runyon. Something like this was bound to happen."

"I had to fix that little Germany deal first, Eddie."

"Have you checked on those freight cars yet?"

"I've been pretty busy picking up bodies."

"That siding is used for making up the westbound, you know. The brakeman says they've been busting seals. He spotted someone, but he ran and jumped over the right-of-way fence. He was gone by the time the brakeman got there."

"I'll get on it soon as I can, Eddie."

"Did that psychologist lady show up?"

"Thanks for that, Eddie. Don't I have enough to do without trying to explain it to a college student every five minutes?"

"And this other deal?" he said.

"Other deal? You mean the murder?"

"We haven't established that yet, Runyon."

"Right. The kid probably cut off his own balls and stuck them where his heart should be."

"Jesus. Look, just don't rush this murder thing, Runyon. That kid might have been important."

"I think you can relax on that, Eddie. His mother is the town barfly."

He could hear Eddie thinking. "Offer her some cash to sign a release. A few hundred ought to do it."

"You're a real sweet guy, Eddie."

"Yeah," he said. "And tell her the company will pick up the funeral costs too. I mean, how much could it be?"

"I need to go, Eddie. I'm all choked up."

*****

Hook was about to close the door of the shack behind him when he paused and went back in. He found the old chicken-feather tick on the bunk in the back. He tested its softness with his hand before hefting it onto his shoulder. Clouds, heavy with moisture, drifted through the night sky as he made his way back to the caboose. The moon hung somewhere above the clouds, lighting their edges in ivory.

He lifted the mattress onto the caboose porch and had started to climb up the ladder when he heard something from down the track. Dropping low, he turned his ear into the night and held his breath to listen. Only the faint croak of frogs drifted in. He could have imagined it. Dragging dead bodies out of canyons had a way of putting a man on edge. But then it came again, this time from the line of freight cars on the siding, a sharp clink, like metal against metal.

Pulling his sidearm, he slipped down the right-of-way and came up behind the cars. He paused again to listen. It could have been no more than the tracks settling against the evening cool. But it could be a seal buster too or a 'bo waiting for the westbound. Or it could be a bridge troll, he supposed. One thing for sure: A man could get in trouble fast this far out and with no backup.

He crouched behind the wheel carriage of the end car and waited for his eyes to adjust to the darkness. He could make out six cars altogether, but no signs of life. An owl hooted from the stand of locusts behind him, and chills raced down his spine. He worked the tension from his shoulders and holstered his side arm.

When he was satisfied that all was clear, he walked back to the caboose. The air smelled damp, and a thin fog had started to settle in, silencing the night about him. Just as he climbed onto the porch, the moon broke from behind a cloud, and he could see that the door was ajar. Maybe he had left it open, but he could not be certain. He drew his sidearm, leveled it, and kicked open the door.

"Come on out now," he said.

Only the frogs down track answered back. Eyes peeled for the slightest movement, he stepped in and found it empty. Taking a deep breath, he laid his P38 on the table and searched out the lantern. Just as he lit it, something warm under the table touched his leg. He lunged for the gun, knocking the lantern off the table in the process. Kerosene spilled across the floor and then ignited, a yellow flame traveling like water across the floor. Mixer yelped and dashed from under the table. As he scrambled for the open door, he knocked Hook back against the wall.

The flames, having already grown to alarming proportions, lit the caboose like daylight.

"Damn!" Hook said, searching for something to put the fire out.

Finding nothing, he dragged the new feather tick in from the porch and threw it on the fire. Smoke bellowed up from under the mattress as the fire smothered and then died.

"Well, that's beginning to be a habit," Hook said.

He hefted the smoldering tick onto his back and headed outside, disposing of the mattress a bit farther from the caboose than last time, taking extra precautions to cover it with dirt. Afterward, he aired out the caboose and made a pallet on the floor. He set out some water and food for Mixer, uncertain when or if the dog would dare return.

Hook lay in the darkness, the smell of smoke still in the air, and counted the day's blessings: His book collection had nearly fallen victim to yet one more act of God; a mutilated body had been found under a bridge with few if any clues; a strange woman had determined to turn his life's work into a book report; and a dog with the intelligence and moral compass of a railroad official had attempted to burn him out before fleeing into the night.

He turned on his side and listened to the sound of the eastbound as she made the grade, a sound which had comforted him in the past. Tomorrow, he would rise and try again. He doubted that the boy's ma could provide much information, but if nothing else, it was a place to start.

Chapter 6

RIA STOOD IN THE DOORWAY of the caboose, her hand on her hip. "Do you know that stress can precipitate crime?" she said.

Hook looked at his watch. "I do know that. Believe me."

Ria grimaced and then stepped in and put her purse on the table.

"Take the weather," she said. "The temperature goes up, so does the crime rate."

"Heat can be irritating, so can unexpected visitors," Hook said. "Stay in this country long enough, and you'll find that out. I once saw a 'bo throw another 'bo off a moving train just so he could have his spot next to the door."

Ria slid Hook's books to the side and sat down at the table. "And then there's overcrowding, perpetual exposure to fear, filthy conditions, excessive noise."

"Noise?" he said. "Now, I can see how that might drive a man to kill."

"And, of course, socioeconomic level."

"Money?"

"Lack of money," she said.

"That's put more than one fella over the edge," he said. "I've come right close to it myself on occasion."

"The first rule of forensic psychology is to think like a criminal," Ria said.

"I do that a lot," Hook said. "In fact, I'm thinking that way right now."

Ria wrinkled her nose. "I smell smoke. Do you smell smoke?"

Hook shrugged. "Pasture fire. Happens all the time out here. Third one this week."

But Ria wasn't to be distracted. "Take that boy under the bridge," she said. "It's not beyond reason that stress factors could have been the root cause of his death, if you trace it back, I mean."

He twisted his mouth to the side. "I can see that. Some guy gets stressed out from the heat or too much noise so he opens this kid up like a side of pork, takes out his heart, and cuts off his genitals."

"Well," she said, "we just agreed stress can cause people to do things they might otherwise not do. It's possible, isn't it?"

"Let's say you're right, though I'm not prepared to concede it just yet. Let's say that's why it happened. How is this information supposed to help me catch this guy?"

"I don't know exactly, but the correlates between stress and violence are well established."

Hook searched out his shoes and put them on. "I'm going to talk to his ma today. Will you give me a lift into town?"

"I'll sit in," she said. "I think it's a smart move, actually. Mothers can be a powerful influence in a boy's life, and not always a positive one. It was Freud who first postulated the Oedipus complex as a significant developmental factor in a boy's psyche."

"The Oedipus complex?"

Ria picked up a book and studied the spine. "You know, when a young boy wants to kill his father and possess his mother sexually."

Hook lifted his brows. "Oh, that theory."

Ria thumbed through the book in her hand and said, "Developmental processes can sometimes stall, and with serious consequences. I'm assuming you want to establish if there were any residual aberrant behaviors that might have caused the boy to run away and so forth."

"I certainly had that in mind," he said. "But there's another reason for talking to his ma too."

"What would that be?"

"There's no one else but her to talk to," Hook said.

*****

They found her shack on the edge of town not far from the city dump. Smoke from the wood cookstove rose like a long braid into the morning sky. Ria stood at Hook's elbow with her notebook in hand. Hook knocked on the door and out of habit moved to the side. A barefoot woman answered. Her hair, mottled with yellow-gray strands, was swept back tight on her head with a rubber band. A cigarette hung from the corner of her mouth as she squinted an eye up against the smoke. "Yeah?" she said.

"Mrs. Way?" Hook asked.

"Ain't Way no more," she said. "It's Rossen."

"My mistake. Are you Benjamin Way's mother?" he asked.

Beth Rossen drew on her cigarette and blew the smoke out the corner of her mouth. "You the law? Look, I already talked to the sheriff."

"Railroad security," Hook said. "We're the ones who found your boy. Hate to bother you at a time like this."

"There ain't nothing I know about the boy that makes a difference one way or the other," the woman said. "Benny had a mind of his own."

"Just a few questions."

She looked over Hook's shoulder at Ria. "What's she doing with that notebook?"

"Just concocting theories," Hook said.

"Well, I haven't got around to cleaning the place up yet this morning."

"I know how that is," Hook said.

"Come in, then," she said, flipping her cigarette onto the drive. "I got business in town in a bit."

The house, two rooms with a small add-on kitchen, smelled of wood smoke and burned food. Bedding lay in a heap, and dirty clothes were strewn about. A frying pan with a charred hot dog in it sat on the counter. Next to it was an empty whiskey bottle, a jigger hanging upside down on the neck. An ice tray full of melted water rested on the coffee table. She pointed to the couch.

Ria sat down, her purse on her lap, and looked around the room. Hook continued to stand.

41

"I divorced his father when Benny was two," the woman said. "I remarried."

"I see," Hook said.

"Benny and his stepfather never saw eye to eye."

"And where is his stepfather now?" Ria asked.

"Dead. Fell headfirst right out of that rocking chair over there and never said another word. By then, nothing made no difference anyway, far as Benny was concerned."

"What do you mean?" Hook asked.

She shrugged. "Everything Benny did turned to trouble. He wouldn't have it no other way. Sometimes I'd come home, and he'd be sitting on the porch roof just staring out into space. I had to carry it all myself, you see. He wouldn't wash a dish or pick up his shoes or do a damn thing. He hauled in bugs and mice and critters I ain't never heard of. I was afraid to go to sleep at night."

"Was he in trouble with the law?" Hook asked.

"School trouble, mostly. He wouldn't do no studying, and then he started skipping. The school didn't want him around no more. No one did. Sometimes the neighbors complained about him being on their property. I guess they feared him stealing or something worse. I tried to talk to him, but he wouldn't listen. He'd just walk off like I wasn't even there."

"He had fifty dollars in his wallet," Hook said. "Do you know how he came up with it?"

The woman's eyes got hungry. "The sheriff didn't say nothing about no money."

"I'm sure he'll get it to you once the investigation is over," Hook said.

That seemed to satisfy her. Hook asked again where the money might have come from. She said, "Benny got to running with the wrong crowd at school. Seemed like he had more money then. Sometimes he wouldn't even come home to sleep at night. Once he bought some fancy cowboy boots, turquoise pulls. I asked him where he got the money, and he said he'd earned it unloading cement bags for the hardware store. But I don't think he did. I think he'd been stealing stuff with them boys."

She took a handkerchief out of her pocket and blew her nose. "Even when he had money, he wouldn't buy no groceries or pay no bills. I guess I could have starved to death, and he wouldn't have raised a hand to help."

"Benny didn't know his real father, then?" Ria asked.

"Not so it mattered," she said. "He was young when we divorced. Benny was a real mama's boy then, hanging on my skirt tail, sleeping in my bed. When I remarried, he didn't say a word to no one for nearly a month, and the only place he would sleep was under his bed. He hardly ever talked after that."

Ria glanced up at Hook. "Boys can get overly attached to their mothers sometimes."

"Do you know of anyone who would want to kill him?" Hook asked.

"Just about everyone, I guess. I considered it myself from time to time, truth be known. Benny had a way of getting a person's heat up."

"And what about these boys he ran with?"

"Boys from his school. Dirty-mouthed no-goods too."

"You remember what they looked like?" Hook asked.

"Both tall, as I recall. One had red hair. The other boy had a scar ran clean down the side of his face. I asked him what happened, and he said a jackrabbit kicked him."

"Do you know their names?"

She shook her head. "Never heard Benjamin say."

"Well, thank you," Hook said. "Sorry about your boy. The railroad's offered to pick up the burial costs. It's not much. No obligations, of course."

She looked down at her feet and studied the blackened nail of her big toe. "A simple funeral is more than he was going to get."

Hook and Ria went to the door. Hook turned. "If you think of anything, call the yard office. Someone will get hold of me."

Hook sat quietly as Ria drove them back into town.

When she hit the city limits, she said, "Where?"

"Back to the caboose," he said.

"Don't you want to locate those boys?"

"Not yet," he said.

"But they could know something or they could be involved. Maybe they killed that boy themselves."

"You have any plans for tonight?" he asked.

"Well, no. Not especially."

"I do," he said. "I'm figuring you'll be wanting to come along."

Chapter 7

THAT NIGHT HOOK COUNTED eight loaded freight cars on the siding with three empty cattle cars on the tail. Smoke from the diesel engine wafted down track as the westbound backed in on the siding.

"Come on," he said to Ria. "We can slip up from behind and get in that end car. It's empty, and the door's open."

"Are you going to tell me what's going on or not?" she asked.

"We've been losing freight off this siding. That boy had fifty bucks in his wallet. You have any idea how hard it is to come up with that much money around here, especially when you're a kid? There's a reason his ma was so anxious about who was going to get it. There's some pretty valuable stuff shipped on this line. With the right fence, there's plenty of money to be made."

"You think those boys were stealing freight?"

"I figure to find out. Keep low. The brakeman will be checking downline shortly."

"Won't he spot us?"

"Brakemen ain't known for walking any farther than is necessary. He'll figure there's nothing on the tail but empty cars."

"But won't he scare the thieves off?"

"My guess is that they know his routine. They probably wait until he's made his check, then come in fast and grab what they can before the train pulls out."

The whistle blew, and the engineer brought her back in a crawl. Hook and Ria slipped down the right-of-way. Hook knelt and motioned for Ria to use his knee for a step up into the cattle car. Once in, she reached down to help him. The car smelled of manure, and moonlight shot through the slats, creating a mosaic of light and shadows.

"I'm going to take a look out the door," Hook whispered.

Ria grasped his arm, her fingers cool. "Be careful."

Hook eased his head out. The siding had a slow curve that allowed him a clear view of the entire length of cars, and he could see the running lights on the engine. The brakeman climbed down from the cab and switched on his lantern. Hook ducked back in.

"What is it?" Ria asked.

"The brakeman's checking the line now," he said. "Let's move to the back of the car just in case."

They waited in the darkness. Ria moved in close, her breath warm against Hook's arm.

After a few minutes, Hook said, "I'm going to take another look."

When he returned, he knelt next to her on the floor. "He's on his way back to the engine. Those boys will be making their move soon if they're going to. I plan to give them a welcome."

"Hook," she said. "What about me?"

"You stay here and keep quiet. I'll come back for you."

Hook peeked out the door again. He spotted two boys coming out of the brush about halfway up the line. One boy carried a bolt cropper, the other, a large gunnysack. The minute they were occupied cutting the car seal, Hook dropped and then moved up the back side of the cars. He would have to make his move fast.

Halfway to the engine, he dropped to the ground to take a look under the cars. He could see their feet and hear their voices. When the door rolled back, he swung up on the grab iron and climbed to the top of the car. Peeking over the side, he watched them in the moonlight as they dragged merchandise from the railroad car.

46

He could draw his weapon, but from this vantage, they could easily duck out of his sight and be gone. Maybe if he dropped on them from above, he could take them by surprise.

Hook crouched on the edge of the roof to calculate his drop. Suddenly, the whistle blew, and the engine bumped out slack. Hook teetered for a moment, like a giant bird preparing to take flight, before catapulting over the side. He hit the ground feet first but then careened head over heels into the bar ditch, knocking the wind out of himself. He struggled to refill his lungs. Meanwhile, the boys, with their sack in tow, ran full speed down the right-of-way.

Hook sat up just as the train bore down for the high iron. Her engine rumbled, her smoke bellowed, and the cars clacked by with gathering speed. Her weight and power hummed down the rails and settled in Hook's stomach. He managed to stand and clear his head just as the last cattle car rattled by. Ria stood trapped in the car with her arms extended through the slats of the door. Hook thought he saw her give a helpless little wave as the train sped off into the night under a full moon.

*****

Hook sat in the section shack and dialed the depot operator in Waynoka.

"Waynoka depot," the operator said.

"Who's this?" Hook asked.

"Banjo Wilson," he said. "Who am I talking to?"

"What's the first stop for that westbound just pulled out of Quinlan about twenty minutes ago?"

"I guess I didn't hear your name," the man said.

"This is Hook Runyon, Banjo. Who the hell you think it is?"

"You could be a damn arson for all I know," Banjo said, chuckling.

"Well, I ain't. You going to tell me or not? I'm in a bit of a hurry here."

"She stops in Woodward, Oklahoma, for wheat. She'll have to lay by for the eastbound there. And might I suggest you take up smoking again?"

"Who said I quit?"

"This is the railroad, Hook. Everyone between here and California knows you gave up the smokes, and might I add that clean living just ain't all that helpful to your temperament."

"Well, thanks for the medical advice, Banjo. Just send your bill to my caboose, will you?"

Hook found Ria's keys in the ignition of her Chevy, and he quickly hit the gas for the Woodward spur. His knees burned from digging up half the right-of-way as he came off that boxcar. It had been a bad day all around. He'd missed catching those seal busters, and now he had a fornicating psychologist on the loose. If anything happened to her, Eddie would ban him to salvage duty for the rest of his life.

As he made the curve into town, Hook could see the train still parked by the grain elevator. He located the cattle car and found the door hasp jimmied with a bridge nail.

"Ria," he said. "Are you in there?"

"Hook? Hook, is that you?"

He winced at the fear in her voice. "It's me. Hang on, I'll get the croppers and cut you free."

*****

Lifting her to the ground, he said, "What the hell happened?"

She ran her hands through her tangled hair. Dirt had gathered on the tops of her shoulders and in the creases of her neck and face. "When the car began to move, I ran to the door to jump out."

"Yeah," he said. "Good plan."

"Then I saw those boys running down the tracks toward me. So I went back in and hid. By then, the car was clipping along pretty fast, but I decided I better jump anyway."

"Go on."

"Just then, I heard something on the roof, someone moving the length of the car."

"Who?"

"I don't know. It was dark, and I didn't want to push my luck, so I drew back into the shadows. The train had gained speed by then, real fast, you know. And then whoever it was on the roof came over the side like a shot, like a monkey in a tree. He knew exactly what he was doing. The car was swaying from side to side like an ocean liner, but it didn't seem to bother him one bit."

"What happened then?"

"He dropped something through the door hasp. And then he climbed back up without so much as a word. I couldn't get out. I was trapped."

"You didn't see who it was?"

She shook her head. "The light was at his back, you know, but he was tall and thin."

She paused. "Hook?"

"Yes."

"I think he rode on top of the car the whole way, just waiting. Maybe it was the troll. I mean, if you hadn't come. . . ."

Hook put his hand on her back; he could feel her heart racing. He tried to reassure her. "Probably just some of those boys. They can have a pretty dark shade of humor. Come on. Let's get you home."

Ria looked doubtful, but she followed Hook to the car. She sat in silence as Hook drove, a novelty that Hook knew could not last long.

"Hook," she said finally. "If it was a joke, it wasn't funny. I've never been so frightened."

"I jumped an oil tanker in the Chicago yards one time," he said. "That damn train was too slow to get anywhere and too fast for me to get off. Three days later, they hauled me off the top of that tanker. They said I was naked as a newborn."

"Naked?"

Hook nodded. "The wind flapped all my clothes off, except my socks and my shirt collar, though I don't remember it that well myself. I was in a state of shock."

He could see her smile in the dash lights. "I bet you weren't the only one," she said.

"Well, it could have been a couple hours, though it seemed like days. Maybe I wasn't naked exactly, but the wind did take my hat spinning."

Ria folded her hands in her lap. "Did I cause you to lose those thieves?"

Hook looked at her and grinned. "Wasn't your fault," he said. "I had one of 'em wrestled to the ground, but the other one jumped me from behind. Anyway, I have a another idea."

He pulled up to the caboose and shut off the engine.

"You do?" she asked. "What idea?"

"It's too soon," he said, climbing out of the car. "I need to sleep on it."

"Then I'll see you tomorrow?" she asked, sliding over into the driver's seat.

Hook turned. "Look, Ria, maybe you should consider going on back to Boston. These things can turn ugly in a hurry sometimes."

She started the car and switched the lights on. "I was told I'd have complete access. My research here isn't finished."

Hook looked down the track. "I might need a car," he said.

"In the morning?"

"I'm not sure yet. I'll call."

"That's a promise?"

He turned to go, pausing. "I have lots of faults. Lying isn't one of them."

Chapter 8

WWHEN HOOK WOKE the next morning on the caboose floor, both legs had gone dead asleep. He dragged himself over to the chair and pulled himself into an upright position. His knees bore scrapes from his dive off the boxcar, and a dark bruise had formed on his right ankle.

He searched out his clothes, kicked the bedding under the table, and put on his prosthesis. Just as he started the coffee, something scratched at the door. Hook opened it to find Mixer looking up at him.

"Hungry, aren't you?" Hook said. "Well, come on."

Mixer stuck his head in and sniffed around but refused to enter.

"How about I leave the door open?" Hook said. "I agree, the place could use a good airing."

Mixer wagged his tail and came in. Hook fixed him a can of tuna. The dog gobbled it down, pushed the can around the caboose a couple of times, and then disappeared out the door again.

After cleaning a few things up, Hook took a walk down the spur to search for anything that might have been left behind the night before. He saw footprints where the two thieves had cut off into the locust grove but could find no prints that might have led to Ria's boxcar. After lunch, he walked to the foreman's shack and found it unlocked. He knocked on the door.

"Yeah?" the section foreman hollered from the back room.

"Big Al?" Hook shouted. "That you?"

Everyone called the foreman Big Al, and his son, who worked in the supply room, answered to Little Al. Big Al claimed it had to do with the size of their tools, something that Little Al categorically denied.

"It's me," Big Al said, coming out of the back room. "Some son of a bitch stole my mattress."

Hook shook his head. "I swear, Big Al, can't trust anyone nowadays."

Big Al slid his suspenders over his shoulders and gave a good pull at his crotch to disengage his britches. "You'd think having security parked on your doorstep might discourage the bastards," Big Al said.

"Need to use your phone," Hook said, refusing to rise to the bait.

"I don't own it," he said. "Got to go. Men waiting. You might look out that caboose window once in a while, Hook, to see who might be stealing my goods. I'm not keen about sleeping on the floor."

"I can sleep on a concrete sidewalk and wake up chipper as a cheer-leader," Hook said.

"Lord help me," Big Al said, shutting the door behind him.

Hook dialed Eddie and watched through the window as Big Al pulled off in the company truck.

"Security," Eddie said.

"Didn't wake you, did I, Eddie?"

"About time you checked in," Eddie said. "I got this call from Wood-ward, see. Some dame riding in a cattle car. What the hell is that about?"

"How should I know, Eddie. I can't check every cattle car that comes downline. Listen, I need a favor."

"Every time I do you a favor, it comes right out of my ass."

"I'd like you to call Vital Statistics in Oklahoma City. Get me a pedigree on Beth Rossen and on that murdered kid of hers, Benjamin Way."

"What the hell is this, Runyon? You can't make a phone call?"

"I get the runaround, Eddie. This kind of procedure takes someone with clout, a big shot like yourself. You can reach me here at the Quinlan shack."

"I got other things to do, Runyon."

"Not a problem. I've got an hour or so."

When the phone rang, Hook picked it up and took Eddie's report. "Thanks, Eddie. No, no one has filed a lawsuit. Right. No sweat, Eddie. Next time, I'll make the call myself."

He hung up and dug out the phone book, a raggedy thing covered with Big Al's greasy fingerprints. He dialed the school, reaching the principal's secretary. "This is Hook Runyon, Santa Fe security agent," he said. "Could you tell me if you had anyone who skipped school this week?"

He waited while the woman checked her attendance records.

"We had an eighth-grader who broke his arm in a bike accident," she said.

"No one else?"

"Sissy Reynolds threw up on her desk, but her mother picked her up."

"Sorry to have bothered you," he said, hanging up.

Hook leaned back in his chair and studied the dust particles that stirred in the beam of sunlight shooting through the window. Picking up the phone book again, he looked up the number for the Eastman Hotel. The front-desk clerk put him through to Ria's room.

"Yes?" Ria answered.

"Do you think you could pick me up?"

"What time?"

"This evening, say, around seven or so."

"After dark?"

"Yes."

"Why so late?"

"I'll tell you then," he said. "And bring a jacket. It can get pretty cold when the sun goes down."

*****

Ria and Hook pulled down the street from Beth Rossen's house, and Ria killed the motor. A single streetlight lit the city dump beyond the knoll to the west.

"Why Beth Rossen?" she asked.

Hook cracked his window. The night smelled of trash smoke, and a pack of dogs barked off in the distance.

53

"You recall her description of those boys?"

"Well, let's see, one was a redhead."

"Right. And the other had a scar," he said.

"I think that's correct."

"I got a fair look at those jokers stealing freight. First of all, they were not that young, certainly not as young as Benjamin, and neither one fit the descriptions she gave."

The streetlight cast a glow in Ria's eyes.

"Maybe someone else from the school?" she said.

"I called the school," he said. "The only student absent that week was an eighth-grader with a broken arm. That means Benjamin Way has been in school."

"You think Beth Rossen is lying?" she asked.

"Remember that empty whiskey bottle in her kitchen?"

"Not really."

"Glenfiddich single malt."

"I don't understand."

"That's not a whiskey that boozers can afford to buy, not unless they're damn flush."

"You think she's involved, then?"

"I think she might be fencing stolen property," he said. "If she is, she'll be getting rid of the goods soon enough."

"And we know this because . . .?"

"That whiskey bottle was empty," he said. "She'll be needing money."

Ria fell silent, her arms looped through the steering wheel as she rested her chin on top. She turned. "You think those thugs killed the boy under the bridge for some reason?"

"Maybe he knew something, saw something he wasn't supposed to see. Maybe he crossed the wrong guy."

"That boy was not just killed, Hook. He was mutilated. In my mind, that's not something you'd expect from young boys—even criminal ones."

"There's a reason we send the young to war," Hook said. "They're capable of about anything you can imagine, given the right situation."

"What about his mother? That would mean she's lying about her own son. What mother would conduct business with someone who has just butchered her child?"

54

"I thought about that and made a few calls," Hook said.

"Oh?"

"Beth Rossen never had any children. Benjamin is the son of her first husband all right, but she isn't his mother."

Ria sat back in the seat. "That changes things," she said. "Blood ties aren't everything, but they're close. They have eons of evolution going for them."

Just then the light came on in the back room of the house. A shadow moved past the window, and then the light went out. The front door opened, and Beth Rossen stepped out. She wore a coat with the collar turned up and a head scarf tied under her chin. She walked to the street, paused, looked in both directions, and then turned down the road leading to the city dump.

"That's her," Hook said.

"What's she doing?" Ria asked.

"There's only one reason to go to the dump this time of night."

"To meet someone."

"Exactly. I'll wait until she's reached that knoll up there and then follow. Maybe I can get all three of these cookies at once."

Hook eased the car door open. "You stay here," he said. "They could be armed."

"Oh, no, you don't," Ria said. "I have full access, remember?"

The city dump had been scooped out of a sand hill covered with sage and mesquite. Fires smoldered from beneath the mountains of trash, and smoke hung in the air like fog. The damp smell of decay scented the night, and rats scurried from pile to pile, their tails looped over their backs.

Hook took Ria's arm and pulled her down next to him. "Over there," he said, whispering.

Beth Rossen stood in the dim glow of the streetlight. She lit a cigarette, and smoke curled up into the light. Suddenly someone stepped from out of the darkness. He had a gunnysack slung over his shoulder. Ria's hand tightened on Hook's arm.

"That's one of them," Hook said. "Looks like they're cutting a deal. I'm going to circle around where there's cover and come in from over there. If something should go wrong, you get out of here fast. Understood?"

Ria nodded. "Understood."

Hook slipped off into the darkness, circling in from the back. Piles of garbage rose like canyon walls, and the stink of melting refuse clung in his nostrils. When he spotted Old Lady Rossen, he knelt and froze.

A figure stood next to her with the gunnysack open. Rossen looked in, and her voice rose. She retrieved money from her purse and handed it to the young fellow, who looked around before shoving it into his pocket.

Hook slipped the safety off his weapon, leveled it, and stepped out.

"I've got a gun on you," he said.

Rossen squealed, and the young man spun around into the darkness of the refuse piles.

"Stop!" Hook yelled.

Beth Rossen shoved her arm into the sack just as the crack of a rifle shattered the night. She fell to the ground with her hands over her head. Hook scrambled for cover behind an old washing machine, his heart pounding.

From high up on the knoll, the single burst of a siren howled and then died away in a growl. Emergency lights spun on, red columns of light skimming the ground. Headlights flashed, and a car pulled down the hill toward him. As it approached, Hook could just make out the police symbol painted on the side.

Deputy Tooney got out and stood behind the opened door. Hook could see Ria in the back seat.

"Runyon," Tooney said. "Come on out."

Hook holstered his weapon and stepped out. Tooney, a rifle in one hand and a flashlight in the other, stepped from behind the door. He wore a khaki uniform, and his badge gleamed in the headlights.

He cuffed Beth Rossen before lifting her up off the ground. Cursing, she struggled to free herself. Shining his flashlight on her face, Tooney drew back his shoulders, and she quieted.

"Damn, Tooney," Hook said. "Did you have to shoot?"

"Figured she was going for a gun in that sack," Tooney said. "Wasn't sure you saw her, and then with that bum wing of yours. . . ."

"I had her covered," Hook said.

Tooney picked up the sack and dumped the contents onto the ground. Ten cartons of Lucky Strike cigarettes fell out. He pointed his chin into the darkness. "Too bad you let him get away," he said. "I'll run this gal in for questioning. I figure they won't be stealing no more in these parts."

Ria got out of the car and came around into the glare of the headlights.
"You okay?" Hook asked.

"I . . . I'm okay, but I think I need to quit hanging around you."

Tooney walked Beth Rossen to the patrol car and put her in the back.
He returned to where Hook and Ria waited. He clicked off his light and
worked it into his belt.

"We been watching this old babe for a good long while now," he said.
"She kept coming into money unexpectedly, like, if you know what I mean."

"You should have let me know you were tailing her," Hook said. "It's
railroad property she's been fencing."

"The goods in that sack don't appear to be railroad to me," he said. "If
they are, they'll be returned in due time. I'm declaring this is a crime scene,
and I can't have folks just walking about destroying evidence."

"I'm a law-enforcement agent," Hook said.

Tooney adjusted his hat. "Some say that," he said. "But since this unfortunate incident took place in the city limits, our office will be handling
the case."

"I expect to be kept informed," Hook said.

"Maybe you should be a little more grateful, Runyon, given that the old
gal might have been out to plug you."

"I doubt she would have managed that," Hook said. "And what about
those other two, the thieves who got away?"

Tooney smiled. "Anyone breaks the law around here is in serious trouble, and I don't give a damn who they are. Now you two are witnesses, so I
guess you'll be sticking around?"

Ria looked at Hook and then back at Tooney.

"You can be sure of that," she said.

Chapter 9

HOOK AND RIA SAT IN THE CAR in silence. Hook reached into his pocket for a cigarette. "Damn," he said.

Ria turned. "Excuse me?"

"Nothing," he said. "Listen, if you have time, I'd like to take another look under that bridge."

"Now?"

He nodded. "A man never gets the full sense of something the first time around. It's necessary to mull it over awhile, to sleep on it. I'd like to take another look."

"Okay," she said, "but the forensic evidence has all been gathered. That's what you should be concentrating on."

"If you don't mind, indulge me. Park at the caboose, and we can walk in from there."

*****

Mixer staggered out from under the caboose as they pulled in and promptly marked all four of Ria's tires.

"Thanks for that, Mixer," Ria said.

"That's Mixer," Hook said. "It's a high honor you've just received."

"Pardon me?"

"It's Mixer's merit system."

"Mixer's what?"

"Mixer's scorecard for quality of character and the like. It's one hundred percent accurate too."

"And how does this system work, dare I ask?"

"Four tires is the best possible score, given the spare tire is not readily available for marking. Four tires means your character is of the highest magnitude, beyond reproach. Why, I would put my very life in the hands of a four-tire rating. A one-pointer, on the other hand, is a sign of the lowest caliber, lower than a railroad official, and someone best avoided or monitored carefully at all times."

Ria paused, her eyes snapping. "And what if he marks no tires at all?"

"None whatsoever? That would be a rare event indeed. So rare, in fact, that it's never been known to happen. In my experience, no person has ever been so despicable as to receive a no-tire rating. That's not to say it couldn't happen, I suppose."

Ria lifted an eyebrow. "Come on, Mixer, let's get out of here. It's getting dangerously deep."

Hook and Ria walked the track in silence, only the sound of bedding rock under their feet. The rails shimmered under the moonlight, and a distant coyote lifted a wailing howl in the lonely night. As they reached the bridge, Hook stood and looked down on the canyon, a deep gorge scoured out by floodwaters and the ever-present winds. The canyon twisted and turned its way through the countryside with determination. No signs of civilization marked its beginning or its end.

Hook knew that 'boes, often victimized by town rowdies, were likely to seek isolation for their night's rest. The Quinlan jungle provided that, as well as all the amenities required for a comfortable stay: firewood, water, and a grade steep enough to slow trains for hopping.

Hook took Ria's hand as they worked their way down the riprap. At the bottom, he squatted and examined the terrain.

"It's the only way down," he said. "And it's plenty rough. Would be downright difficult to sneak up on a man coming down that rockslide."

He walked the perimeter of the jungle, stopping from time to time to study this or that. "Not a sign anywhere," he said.

"Sign?"

"No tracks in or out. It's like whatever got Benjamin Way had dropped from the sky."

"And as we know, that's highly unlikely."

Hook looked up into the silhouetted bridge timbers and the track deck high overhead. "He had to come from up there, dropping on top of that boy like a panther in the night." He pointed to the latticework of timbers that filled the expanse above them. "And he had to go back the same way."

"It seems such an unlikely scenario to me," Ria said. "How could one climb that in the middle of the night without falling?"

"Why bother in the first place?" Hook said. "Bindle stiffs can smell out money and whiskey a mile off. They can smell the lack of it even better. No one would have figured that boy had much of value."

Working his flashlight out of his pocket, Hook shined it on the array of hobo icons carved into the cross timber.

"It's marked safe haven right there in plain view, a symbol sought out and trusted by most hoboes that I know. I've seen it a thousand times along these tracks, relied on it myself, more than once. Yet this was no safe haven, not on that night."

Hook paused and studied the symbols more closely. "That owl scratching or whatever it is looks fresh to me. Done in a hurry, I'd say, and doesn't it seem a bit personal?"

"What do you mean?"

"I don't know exactly, less ordinary, a lack of sameness shared by all those other markings. 'Bo codes ain't much for flourish one way or the other. 'Boes figure to live and die the easiest way possible."

"And I still don't think those young men were involved in this either," Ria said. "The blow to the head was vicious—not to mention the ritual nature of the mutilation. I just can't see them being that evil."

"It would take someone athletic and strong to climb those timbers, though," Hook said. "They are far apart and not easily managed, especially going back up. There's no dropping from one level to the other. It's straight uphill with no place to park in between."

Ria took his flashlight and shone it up through the bridge structure.

"Someone agile, too. Young men are agile, if nothing else," she said.

"But not as strong as you might think, least not over the long haul. Endurance, I'm talking. A man will outwork a boy over a hard shift nine times out of ten. I've seen boys fade before the five o'clock whistle more than once in my life."

"I don't know what you see, Hook, but I'm telling you there's something evil going on here, not just violent but evil. There was nothing gained by what took place that night to that boy."

"I find man most nearly always has a reason for his actions, but I admit to underestimating on occasion how diabolical man can be."

"Maybe madness is the price we pay for intelligence," Ria said.

"I'm not sure that what we're seeing here is intelligence in action. There's no doubt but what man can blame something other than himself for just about anything comes along."

"Like what?"

"There's always God's will or destiny or even just plain bad luck, but it's a rare man steps up and admits it's his own damn doings."

"You're a hopeless cynic, Hook."

"Born that way. Guess maybe it was God's will," he said.

Ria shook her head and smiled. "So do you think old Beth Rossen would have actually shot you if the deputy hadn't shot first?" she asked.

"We'll never know for certain, I suppose. You'd be surprised who's capable of killing, given the right circumstances."

"Over a few cartons of cigarettes?"

"I'd kill for one right now," Hook said. "Anyway, most folks can do bad things if they get scared enough. Benjamin Way was on the run. Maybe he knew something he shouldn't have known."

"It strikes me as unlikely," Ria said. "We can't ignore the fact that the poor boy's body was mutilated, and mutilation does not rise from greed or even fear alone."

"I admit to not having the high education of some folks who will remain nameless, but I have lived these rails a good long while now and on both sides of town. There are any number of ways of making a point, cutting a man into pieces being a particularly effective one."

"Well," Ria said. "I would have to defer to you on that, but I'm thinking that what happened under this bridge cannot be defined by usual motives."

Hook rolled his eyes.

"Look, Hook, all I'm suggesting is that there are people out there whose thinking defies rational explanation and common sense. At first glance, they can appear quite normal, above average in many ways. They can be charming, rational, and keenly aware of social tenets. But their relationships are shallow and their sex lives inconsequential. They're sadistic and have no remorse, even for the most heinous acts. Put all these things together, and you have one of the deadliest predators on earth."

"Sounds like a woman I once dated back in Albuquerque."

"Now you're making fun of me," Ria said.

Hook took one more look around the hobo camp.

"What's a person like that doing under a bridge in the middle of nowhere killing a young hobo?"

"Why not?"

"It doesn't matter who he kills?" he said.

"Maybe not in the way you're thinking."

"That's an awful lot of words to describe a murder—I'd like to think there is a simple motive for what happened to Benjamin Way. If only because I have found that is usually the case when it comes to murder."

"It's a lot of things, Hook, but simple it's not."

"Well, I've had a fair amount of practice in being wrong and am prepared to be so again if necessary. Now, maybe you could take me to the depot so I can call all this in to Eddie. I'm sure he has something he'd like to contribute to the situation as well."

*****

Ria drove into town, most of the occupants of which had long since gone to bed. She pulled up in front of the depot and shut off the engine.

Hook watched Banjo Wilson through the depot window. Banjo had earned his name because he could hum "The Water Is Wide" through his nose and make it sound exactly like a claw-hammer banjo.

Banjo peeked out the window and then opened the depot door. "Hook," he said. "Eddie Preston called. He wants you to call him back. Says it's an emergency."

"What emergency?" Hook asked.

"You know I don't talk to Eddie Preston no longer than is necessary. You'll have to call him your own damn self," Banjo said, going back in.

"You want me to wait?" Ria asked.

"Let me find out what's going on," Hook said. "I'll be right back."

Hook dialed Eddie, while nearby, Banjo hummed, "Foggy Mountain" in the luggage room.

"Santa Fe Security," Eddie said.

"Hook here. Banjo said you called."

"I swear, Runyon, the whole railroad could go down before you get around to calling in."

"Well, I'm here to save the railroad now, Eddie. What do you want?"

"There's been a derailment, belly down, north of Harper, Kansas."

"That's Ludie Bean's territory, Eddie."

"Ludie's out there. He needs a hand, so to speak."

"Funny, Eddie. You need two bulls for a derailment? What the hell's on that train?"

"Thing is, she's sitting on that old truss bridge over the Chikaskia River."

"Jeez, couldn't they find a better place to pull a hoptoad?"

"Quit whining and get on out there, Runyon. Pay's the same, ain't it?"

"Look, Eddie, I got a murder on my hands here. On top of that, Deputy Tooney tried to shoot up that Beth Rossen tonight."

"Dead?"

"Close enough, Eddie."

"Well, let the locals handle it for now. I need you at that derailment, pronto."

"Not so fast, Eddie. I'm supposed to go in for a statement. The sheriff here is funny that way."

"I'll call him. You can make a statement later. Anything else?"

"How am I supposed to get there this time of night?"

"There's a rattler due in there in about fifteen minutes. She's got a louse box on the tail."

"All right, Eddie. It's your railroad."

"Oh, and one other thing," Eddie said.

"What?"

"That engine jumped through the trusses and is hanging over the side of the bridge. Ludie says nobody can get out there to do a thing."

"This isn't a problem for security, Eddie."

"It is now. The engineer and fireman are trapped in the cab. The river's at flood stage, and you know how that Chikaskia can roll."

"All right, Eddie. I'm on my way. Any more good news?"

"It's still raining," he said.

*****

Hook stood at Ria's car window. "I got a problem," he said. "There's been a derailment, and I'm hauling out of here on a freighter in a few minutes."

"I'll go with you," she said.

He shook his head. "This isn't a criminal matter. Anyway, there is no place for you to ride, and someone has to show up at the sheriff's office. Eddie's supposed to clear it for me until I get back."

"What do you want me to do in the meantime?" Ria asked.

"Nothing," he said. "Clear?"

She nodded. "How long will you be gone?"

"Depends," he said.

"You'll call when you get back?"

"Yes," he said. "When I get back."

*****

Hook waited on deck as the old freighter pulled in. Soon as the caboose came along, he snapped the grab iron and pulled on board.

Leaning out, he waved off the engineer, who bumped out the slack. As they passed through the crossing on the outskirts of town, the wigwag signal swung to and fro, and the bell clanged out its warning. The engineer blew his whistle, and the clack of the wheels filled Hook, as they always did, with that sweet sense of escape.

He turned to go in when the glint of headlights caught his eye. It was Tooney's patrol car parked alongside the road, and for a moment, Hook thought he saw someone sitting in the front seat next to Tooney.

Chapter 10

LATER THAT NIGHT AS the freighter pulled into the Harper depot, Hook swung off the caboose into boot-top water. He held his jacket over his head against the downpour. Lightning danced, and thunder rumbled off in the distance.

The operator looked up from his desk at Hook's question. "You can catch a ride out with the track crew now if you hurry. They brought in a truck about twenty minutes ago and are loading back there at the tool shed."

"Thanks," Hook said. "Any headway on that hoptoad?"

"Hell, no," he said. "They got her cocked out over the Chikaskia River like a teeter-totter. Ludie said if a bird shits on the glimmer, the whole engine will go to the bottom."

Hook dabbed the water off his face. "Heard anything on the weather?"

"Forty days and forty nights," he said.

"Where's Ludie now?"

"At the bridge. Likely sitting in the louse box eating his lunch, if I know Ludie."

"Thanks," Hook said.

Hook found himself a spot under a tarp and out of the rain with the other men as they drove the muddy road out to the bridge. No one talked as sheets of rain whipped the night into a frenzy.

When they pulled in, Hook dropped from the truck bed to take stock of the damage. The truck lights barely penetrated the downpour, but they did so just enough for him to make out the line of hoppers jumbled down the tracks. He found Ludie in the caboose with a blanket around his shoulders.

"It's a damn mess," Ludie said. "That river's lapping the bridge and rising by the minute."

At six foot four and three hundred pounds, Ludie made an intimidating figure. He towered over most other men and as such was seldom challenged by them. He had used this advantage to quickly establish himself as a hard-nosed bull, a notion solidified after he locked shut a stock car half full of sleeping 'boes. The men had nearly frozen to death by the time the train reached the Chicago yards, where they were lined up and checked over by the company croaker. Ludie's reputation as a mean son of a bitch was established overnight, and he had done little to discourage it since.

If his size gave men pause, Ludie's lack of body hair, basically a complete absence of it, made him repel both men and women alike. His flesh had a shine like snakeskin that accentuated his ball-bearing eyes. His lip line left only a slit for a mouth, which served to confirm a deep-seated contempt for anyone other than himself.

Ludie enjoyed his authority but hated manual labor more than any man alive. He had caught his share of criminals, but never by pursuit. His capacity to conduct surveillance was renowned—a hibernating bear could not sit any more unmoving for days on end. Once on a man's trail, he was known to settle in and wait the target out no matter how long it took.

"What about the engine crew?" Hook asked.

"The engineer and the ash cat are out there enjoying the view," he said. "The sons of bitches took that old bridge too fast, jumped track, and shot through the trusses. She's probably hanging by a wheel truck. It's a wonder they ain't bouncing down the Chikaskia River bottom on their way to New Orleans by now."

Hook looked for a place to sit but decided it was too much trouble to clear a spot. "Why doesn't someone go out and get them?" he asked.

Ludie slid a hand over his shiny head. "They called in on the two-way before it conked and said that the cab door's jimmied up. They can't get out."

"Has anyone tried to go out there?"

"Climbing out on that engine to pry open that cab door could send the whole thing into the Chikaskia. I didn't sign up for drowning, and this rain ain't took a breath all night."

"What about a crane?"

Ludie shook his head. "You ain't reaching that engine short of a skyhook," he said. "I figure this rain's likely to stop someday. Until then, I say wait her out."

The rain swept the caboose window in sheets, and thunder rumbled down the right-of-way.

"So why did you call me?" Hook asked.

Ludie sucked at a tooth. "I didn't," he said. "Must have been Eddie Preston's idea. Far as I'm concerned, you can just turn around and go back to your own territory."

Hook reached into his pocket where he usually kept his cigarettes. "Damn rain," he said. "Think I'll go have a look-see."

"I figure a one-armed bull don't swim so well," Ludie said. "You got kin you want me to notify?"

"I do a hell of a sidestroke," Hook said. "Anyway, maybe I can get close enough to see something."

"Suit yourself," Ludie said.

While the track crew, rain soaked and cold, remained hunkered under the truck tarp like coons in a hole, Hook walked to the bridge, water dripping into his collar and down his back. Four of the hoppers had jumped track. The one nearest the bridge had bellied onto her back and cracked open like an egg. Wheat had oozed out and now swelled in the rain.

On his approach, Hook paused to assess the situation. Two hoppers had made it onto the bridge before she jumped and now served as the counterbalance to the engine, which had torn through the truss and shot slightly upward from the railing. The engine still idled, and diesel smoke climbed slowly into the night.

Hook wiped the water from his face and stepped out onto the bridge. The river rumbled, and the bridge trembled beneath his feet. He balanced himself against the hopper and worked his way farther out. Froth churned up between the ties, and the smell of mud and fish hung in the air.

When he was nearly to the engine, he stopped. The ties had sheared away from the force of the derailment, and the river now opened up in front of him in a muddy torrent. He could see the engine, an EMD FT, around 1944, by the looks of her. The cab door appeared to have crumpled like an accordion when it snagged on the truss, and the window had shattered out. Hanging like a loose tooth on the front, the glimmer shot a column of light into the dark web of overhanging tree limbs.

Hook's foot slipped on the slick rail, and he grabbed for the hopper ladder to catch himself. His pulse ticked up. Falling into the torrent below would be the end of a side-haul amputee. He pushed back his hat and let out a whoop to the men in the cab, his voice falling away in the downpour. He hollered again, and a hand poked out of the broken window and waved.

"Don't worry!" Hook shouted. "We have a plan to get you out."

The hand waved again, but without conviction, and then retreated into the cab.

Hook had lied. The one thing he did not have was a plan. He could crawl out on top of the engine, but not without risk of sliding into the river, and he could not be certain what movement might send the engine over the brink. Debris had gathered on the piers, increasing the pressure on the structure.

He had to admit that Ludie was right for once. Only a skyhook could rescue these guys. He held his hand against the rain and studied the overhanging walnut tree. Just maybe he had a plan, at that.

He worked his way off the bridge. Lightning cracked overhead, and the rain deepened around him as he headed back to the caboose. He hustled the track crew inside and laid out his plan. Ludie sat at the table, his jaw locked.

"There's a walnut tree hangs out over the river," Hook said. "We'll have to get over to the far side, but I think a man could be lowered down. We could haul them up one at a time."

Ludie rolled his shoulders. "That's bunk, Runyon," he said. "We need to just wait her out. It ain't going to rain forever. When the river drops, we can collect them then."

Lightning lit up the caboose. Thunder gathered on the horizon and rolled out across the prairie.

"The river's rising, not going down," Hook said. "Half the ties are ripped away, and the trusses are damaged. Limbs and trash are gathering up on the pilings. The whole thing could go down at any moment. I don't think waiting it out is much of an option."

Ludie stood. "I ain't climbing no tree," he said. "Since it's your idea, maybe you ought to be the one to do it."

The track foreman said, "Christ, Ludie, the man's only got one arm."

"That ain't my problem," Ludie said. "He takes a job and earns his pay just like the rest of us."

"Here's the deal," Hook said. "We'll lay out some planking to cross over to where the bed's torn out of the bridge. Once on the other side, I'll take the rope up the tree and half-hitch it over the limb. I'll tie off, give a whistle, and you boys can lower me down. What do you think?"

"How we going to get the rope back down for the next man?" the foreman asked. "It's blowing sideways out there."

"Tie on a weight. Looks like a straight drop to the engine to me."

"Anchor Ludie on the end of the rope," the track foreman said. "Take more than a diesel engine to drag him into the river."

"I ain't hauling folks up and down trees," Ludie said.

"You boys bring rope along?" Hook asked.

"Oh, hell, yes," the foreman said. "Enough for hanging yourself and three or four others if need be."

"Then let's get out there," Hook said. "I got business waiting."

*****

Once they made the other bank, the track foreman gave Hook a knee up into the tree crotch and handed him the rope. Hook looked into the limbs of the walnut and then down at the men who had lined up for the tow. Ludie had staked out a dry spot to rest under a large cedar.

"Someone will need to follow me up to manage this rope," Hook said.

"I'll do it," the section foreman said.

"Okay, but don't come out there until I've landed on the engine. You stay off that limb much as possible. She might not hold two men. I'll whistle when I'm ready to be lowered."

"Okay," he said.

"One other thing, if I fall into the river, call Eddie Preston and tell him I said he's a first-rate son of a bitch."

The men laughed and shook their heads. Hook worked his way up, using his prosthesis for balance. His legs and right arm he used for hoisting himself to higher limbs. Halfway up, he paused to rest. He peered into the rain and could just make out the men below hunched against the downpour. Above him, the engine glimmer shot into the top of the tree like a beacon light. When he reached the overhanging limb, he pulled slack and looped it over his shoulder. Suddenly the glimmer went out on the engine, and the world plunged into darkness. He could hear the rush of the river below and smell the smoke drifting in from the engine.

He straddled the limb and edged out, the limb's diameter diminishing with each forward slide of his body, now bowing and dipping with the slightest movement. He paused to gather his courage, and the sounds of the river settled in his stomach. Lightning streaked across the sky, its tributaries crackling away into the blackness. Below, the windows of the locomotive lit yellow like the eyes of a giant cougar and then went black once more.

Hook half-hitched the rope over the limb, tied it around his waist, and then whistled between his teeth. When the slack had been taken up, he lowered himself over, closed his eyes, and let go. He dropped a couple feet before stopping, twisting first one way and then the other. He whistled once more, and the descent commenced, a slow twist down through the blackness. He struggled to locate the sound of the engine, which had shifted directions again and again in the rain and wind.

Hook imagined himself lowered into the boiling water below, unable to disengage from the rope. He imagined the water closing over him, sweeping him away in its current like a fish on a hook. He imagined his lungs filling with the muddy water, and his life ebbing away in the black depths of the river.

When his feet touched the engine's roof, relief surged through him. Reveling in his reprieve, he had failed to whistle for a stop. The rope slacked, and he began a slide over the side of the cab. Instinctively, he grabbed for something, anything, and snagged the air horn with his prosthesis. He whistled as loud as he could, and the feed of the rope stopped.

Leaning over the side of the roof, he tapped the cab with his prosthesis. Moments passed, and then a flashlight blinked on, followed by a head sticking out the window. Hook recognized the engineer as Slick Housely, a name bestowed because of his ability to slither down an engine ladder without using his feet.

"Holy day!" Slick said. "There's a damn rail dick sitting atop the engine."

"Can you climb out the window?" Hook asked.

"Hell, yes, I can," the engineer said. "But it looks safer in here."

"Anyone else in there?"

"Just an old bakehead," he said.

"Who is it?" Hook asked.

"Chance Reece. We could just leave him. Who the hell would care?"

"Can't litter up the river with old ash cats," Hook said. "Send him on out while the boys are still fresh."

Chance was an aging fireman prone to gambling away his paycheck before making it home on paydays. Hook could feel the tremble in Chance's hand as he hoisted him atop the cab and tied him off. Hook whistled him away and watched as Chance disappeared into the darkness overhead. Soon the rope appeared with a rock tied to its end. Hook reached down for Slick and pulled him atop the cab.

"Ain't you got a train pass, Hook? It's a wet ride up here."

"Too damn dangerous to ride inside with you," Hook said.

Slick clung to the air horn while Hook secured the rope around him.

"Tell those boys up there not to dally," Hook said. "There's debris building on those pilings, and this son of a bitch could give way any second."

Hook sat in the blackness waiting for the rope to return. The surge of the river hummed through the bridge timbers, and lightning danced overhead. Suddenly the bridge jolted, a shock that set his ears to burning.

He lifted onto his knees, and it came again, a shifting of the structure. Hook stopped breathing and searched the blackness for the rope.

The bridge timbers groaned like an old man rising from his chair, and then they cracked like gunshots as the weight and force of the river splintered them away. Hook slid sideways, his prosthesis screeching across the roof of the cab. At the last second, he snagged the air horn and pulled himself erect.

He could just make out the rope dangling out of the darkness, and he lunged for it, catching the rock with his good hand. He wrapped the rope about himself and whistled for a tow up. Just as he lifted off, the bridge slumped sideways. The engine moaned and rolled onto her side. Water spewed into the air and rushed into her cab as she slid away into the depths of the Chikaskia.

*****

As dawn broke, the shivering men stood on the riverbank with their hands buried in their pockets. Where the bridge had once stood, only a few jagged pilings now protruded from the water. They could see the truck in the distance and the dim glow of the lantern from the caboose window.

"What the hell we do now?" Ludie asked.

Hook turned. "Why don't we just wait it out, Ludie?" he said. "That river will go down sooner or later."

Ludie walked to the edge of the water and then back. "Why don't you just walk into town and send out a truck?"

Hook rubbed at his shoulder where he had got tangled in the rope.

"Ludie," he said, "it ain't like me to get my temper up, but I'm thinking it's you who's going to walk to town. Otherwise, I'm going to whip your ass and leave you for dead."

Ludie cocked his arms and clenched his fists. "You ain't that mean," he said.

The crew gathered behind Hook, and the track foreman stepped up beside him. "Maybe he is and maybe he ain't," the man said, "but what he doesn't finish, me and the boys here will."

Ludie's cheeks bulged in and out like a bullfrog. He looked at Hook and then at the others before turning down track for town.

Chapter 11

RIA LAID HER EYELINER aside and picked up her face powder. Looking into the mirror, she dusted her cheeks and forehead and followed with a dab of rouge. Pulling her mouth tight over her teeth, she drew the outline of her lips and filled it in with her lipstick. She brushed her hair to the side and checked out her profile. Only then did she see the bruises on her wrists when Deputy Tooney had pushed her into the patrol car, instructing her to keep quiet.

The image of Beth Rossen sprawled on the ground with her dress hiked to her panties flashed before Ria's eyes. Tooney had been in a hell of a hurry to rush her off to jail . . . and a lot less interested in catching the other thieves.

Ria opened her purse and counted her money. Living in a hotel and eating in restaurants had taken its toll on her finances, but she should be okay for another week. If an emergency came up, there was always her father.

She sat on the edge of the bed and leafed through her Moleskine notebook. First thing, she had to go to the sheriff's office and fill out the report about last night.

Too bad she had yet to gain access to a large police department for her research. To date, Hook Runyon had provided precious little useful information. As far as she could determine, he had no structure or identifiable techniques for solving a case other than holding his finger in the air to determine the direction of the wind. His approach came down to intuition, a large dose of ego, and a little experience thrown in for good measure.

Although she did not dislike him altogether, she did find him abrupt, undisciplined, and at times defiant. He lacked proper manners and could be condescending when it came to her work. On the other hand, there was no denying his animal magnetism and a certain streak of sensitivity just beneath that gruff exterior. Picking up her purse, she searched out her car keys and walked to the door. Hook had certainly taken off in a hurry, too big of a hurry, leaving her behind to deal with the sheriff. Perhaps his sudden emergency had been no more than a ploy to ditch her. Well, if that turned out to be the case, she would have to let her father deal with it. His influence reached into many quarters, and she had no doubt that he could bring plenty of pressure to bear if need be.

She stood at the door and listened to a westbound train pulling the grade south of town. She had to admit that having not heard from Hook made her a bit uneasy. Even though he lacked polish, he had always been forthright, and she did not want anything to happen to him.

*****

Sheriff Holcome pointed to the folding chair. "Sit down, Miss Wolfe. You know why you're here?"

"Yes," she said.

"We've gone eight years without any major problems in town and then this death," he said. "That hasn't happened since the Freeze family committed suicide by driving off the Cimarron bridge in the middle of the night."

"How can I be of help?" she asked.

"Maybe you could just tell me what happened, and we'll go from there."

"Hook Runyon and I were watching Beth Rossen's house—staking it out, I believe you call it."

"And why is that?" the sheriff asked, pulling his chair closer to his desk where he could write.

76

"Hook—Mr. Runyon—discovered two boys looting the freight cars at the Quinlan siding. He thought Beth Rossen might be involved in the burglary, as a fence for the goods."

"Ah, boys. We've had some trouble at the county shed too, you know, tools, gasoline, things like that. I'm sorry to have interrupted, Miss Wolfe. Did Hook have evidence that Beth Rossen might be involved?"

Ria crossed her legs and noticed that the strap to her high heel had come loose.

"It's not always clear where Mr. Runyon's ideas originate," she said.

"I've noticed that myself," the sheriff said. "Please continue."

"Beth Rossen left the house and walked to the dump. We followed. She met up with a boy there. He handed a sack to her in exchange for money."

"Can you identify the boy?"

"No. I couldn't see much at that distance. Mr. Runyon asked me to stay out of sight while he circled around for a better look. When Mr. Runyon stepped out with his weapon pulled, the boy took off. About then a shot rang out, and everyone hit the ground."

"And who fired the shot?"

"Deputy Tooney, I assume. Shortly thereafter, he drove up and put me into the patrol car, a bit sternly, I might add." She showed him the bruise on her arm. "We then drove down to where Mr. Runyon and Mrs. Rossen were."

Sheriff Holcome got out of his chair and walked to the window. The seat of his pants was shiny from wear.

"The sack contained cigarettes," he said. "Now, Miss Wolfe, this is an important question, and I want you to think about it before you answer."

"All right."

"Did Beth Rossen reach into that sack before the shot was fired?"

Ria replayed the scene in her mind. She looked up. "Yes," she said. "She reached into the sack and then the shot followed."

"And was there a weapon in that sack?"

"No," she said.

"Then would you conclude that Hook Runyon might have been in some danger of being shot by Beth Rossen?"

Ria fastened the strap on her high heel. "I suppose it could have been construed that way. She could have pulled a weapon and fired before he got to her. I wonder how Deputy Tooney saw she was reaching for anything, though, much less a gun, I mean, he was a considerable distance away."

"Well, you can't take chances in this business, I suppose. Is there anything you'd like to add? Anything you've overlooked?"

"That's how it happened, as I recall it."

"Fine," the sheriff said, returning to his desk. "If you would sign here, please."

Ria signed the paper and stood. "Is that all?"

"Beth Rossen has been released on her own recognizance. Deputy Tooney felt the evidence for burglary was too weak to charge her. Where can you be reached?"

"At the Eastman, at least for the foreseeable future," she said.

"I'll be talking with Mr. Runyon when he returns from his emergency," he said. "In the meantime, I'd ask you not to discuss your statement with him or with anyone else, for that matter."

After leaving the sheriff's office, Ria returned to her room at the hotel, where she spent the afternoon organizing her notes. She then constructed a letter to the chairman of her dissertation committee, explaining that although her data collection was slow, she had gleaned some valuable information concerning the problem-solving strategies of untrained law-enforcement personnel.

Afterward, realizing that she had yet to eat, she searched out the local café and took a booth near the back. She looked up from her menu to see Deputy Tooney coming across the room toward her.

"Miss Wolfe," he said, hooking his thumbs in his gun belt.

He smelled of cheap cologne and tobacco. She had not remembered him being so short, square, and heavily centered. His eyes reminded her of a koi she had once seen frozen in a garden pond. He slid into the seat across from her.

"Deputy," she said.

"Got a minute?"

Ria adjusted her leg so that it no longer touched his knee. "I was just ordering my dinner," she said. "Is it important?"

"You been in to make that report yet?"

"Yes," she said.

The waitress appeared, and Ria ordered a ham sandwich.

"I guess you saw that old lady might have been going for something the other night at the dump, didn't you?"

Ria looked at her watch. "The sheriff asked that I not discuss my statement with anyone."

"Holcome's a stickler for the rules, but he's running a little slow in his old age. Thing is, sooner or later a cop pisses off nearly everyone in a small town, even if it's just over a traffic ticket. Some of these bastards would like to see me get it in the neck, if you know what I mean."

"Last night wasn't exactly about traffic tickets," she said.

He bobbed his head from side to side and dropped the corners of his mouth.

"Made the paper, front page," he said.

"Congratulations."

"I could have killed her if I'd had the notion. I've shot and skinned plenty of deer. Head shots too. Damn good practice. Nothing gets up from no head shot."

"I suppose not," Ria said.

"Savage Model 99," he said.

"Excuse me?"

"My weapon of choice, though I'm also good with a hunting knife."

Ria flinched. "Oh. That's nice to know."

The waitress brought her sandwich and scratched out a ticket. Ria, her appetite having waned with the talk of head shots and deer skinning, pushed the plate to the side.

"Didn't mean to rough you up last night," Tooney said. "I mean, pushing you into the car and all like that. Had my blood up."

She looked at the bruises on her arm. "It's all right," she said. "Shooting at someone must be very intense, even if it's an old lady."

"I usually don't reach for no weapon, not unless I have to. I can handle most stuff myself, but that old lady could have been fixin' to blow that rail dick into the ground."

"I'm sorry, but the sheriff said not to . . ."

"Right," he said. "I hear you're doing research about law enforcement."

"Well, yes," she said. "That's correct."

"You ain't learning nothing from no rail dick like Hook Runyon," he said. "Everyone knows he spent most his life running from the law. Now, take me. I've been through real cop training. I got ways of taking things underhand, if you know what I mean."

"Like what, may I ask?"

"Like my palm sap, for instance," he said. "I can stop a fistfight midair with that baby."

"Palm sap?"

He reached into his pocket. "Fits over your hand like this, see. There's a slab of lead right in the palm of your hand. Slap a man upside the head, and he drops like a shot pig. Sometimes I just crack an elbow or a shin or bust up their knuckles to get their attention. Used right, you could push it right through a man's chest. Thing is," he said, dropping it back into his pocket, "no one even knows you got it on most of the time. They just figure you carry a jackhammer punch. Builds a man's reputation, if you know what I mean."

Ria studied the tabletop. "Yes," she said. "I can see where it might."

"I don't tell just everyone about that sap," Tooney said. "Say, maybe you'd like to go out shooting with me sometime or hunt a few rattlers up in the Cat Hills?"

"Thanks, but no. I'm here to work," she said.

He slid out of the booth and dropped his hand onto his sidearm. "Thing is," he said, tipping his hat, "when you run with Tooney, ain't no one going to bother you. No, sir, you're safe as home when Tooney's on duty."

With that, he turned and sauntered out the door. Ria watched him go, and a chill passed through her. She took her compact out of her purse and checked her lipstick in the mirror.

When the waitress took her money at the cash register, she stuck the ticket onto a nail and handed her back her change.

"Sorry about the deputy spoiling your lunch," she said. "But don't pay no mind to him. He hits on all the women he don't shoot."

Ria smiled wryly and dropped her change into her purse. "You wouldn't happen to know where the county barn is, would you?"

"Oh, sure, Honey. It's just west of the creek, a prefab sitting back in them elms. There won't be nobody there this late, though."

*****

A full moon bobbed onto the horizon and lifted into the night sky as Ria parked her car in the trees. From there, she could see the road leading into the county shed but not the shed itself. She dropped her keys into her pocket and pushed her purse under the seat. A short walk should put her in viewing distance of the shed. She had come on a hunch, an educated hunch. Criminal behavior, when reinforced with success, tended to be repeated, like any behavior.

There had been some close calls with those boys, but even adrenalin-charged near misses could serve as behavior reinforcement. This was particularly true of youth who tended to be more impulsive and less cerebral. These boys fit the bill on both counts.

Hook had warned her against interfering in the case, but then, this did not qualify as interference, not exactly. This was a simple exercise in observation, a test of a hypothesis. If it turned out to be correct, she would turn the information over to Hook.

Once in position, she could see the shed and the security fence that encircled the compound. All manner of road equipment was parked inside. Crickets chirped from down on the creek. An hour passed and then two as she waited. The evening cooled; Ria turned the collar of her coat up against the chill. At first, she thought it just a breeze whispering along in the cottonwoods, but then she saw them, two boys dressed in sweatshirts and stocking caps. They crouched at the fence and took stock of the night. One clamped his hands together and hoisted the other to the top of the fence. He then slipped back into the brush out of sight.

Ria scrunched down and held her breath. Where the hell were the cops? If she could figure this out, why couldn't they?

Ten, fifteen minutes went by before the boy inside the compound returned. He tossed something over the fence and then climbed over. She could hear their voices rising in excitement as they took count of their loot.

And then they were gone. She waited an hour to make certain they were not returning before she moved from her hiding spot. What she had witnessed under the Quinlan bridge had made her cautious. Even though these were just boys, they might be involved in something a lot more dangerous than she knew.

When confident they had gone for good, she made her way back to her car. She paused to listen before stepping into the clearing. Her heart thumped in her ears, and perspiration broke on her forehead. The car door was ajar.

Suddenly someone broke from the brush nearby and headed back east toward the railroad tracks. She attempted a better look, but it was dark, and he was fast. His stride was long and deliberate, and he was soon out of sight. Perhaps he was one of the gang of boys, the lookout, maybe. But why had he not warned them of her presence, then? Maybe he wasn't with them at all but watching them instead. And then a thought came to her, causing a chill to race down her spine. Maybe he wasn't watching them at all but rather her instead.

She slipped back into the shadows and waited there for some time, trying to remember if she had left the car door open herself, screwing up her courage to return to the car. How long that took, she couldn't be sure, but the first light of dawn had broken by the time she pulled into the Eastman Hotel parking lot.

Chapter 12

HOOK DROPPED FROM the work train just as the funeral procession for Benjamin Way passed on its route to the cemetery. There were four cars in all, two of which belonged to the funeral home.

Deputy Tooney stood guard at the intersection, the red light on his car whirling. Once the procession had gone through, he climbed back in, lit a cigarette, and watched Hook through his open window as he drove off.

Hook found Banjo digging a banana out of his lunch box.

"You always eat on company time?" Hook asked.

Banjo peeled the banana back. "Some of us do real work for a living, and a real working man has to keep his strength up."

"Right. I need to give Eddie a call."

"Maybe you're too uppity to learn anything from working folk, Hook, but I got information you ought to hear."

"And what, I wonder, would that be?"

"Diesel engines rarely float," he said, grinning. "And they don't run on the river bottom worth a damn either."

"Maybe you ought to stick to playing your nose, Banjo, so it doesn't get broke."

Banjo chuckled and turned back to his desk.

Hook dialed security and kicked his feet up.

"Eddie Preston," Eddie said.

"Hook here. I'm back in town."

"Don't expect a parade, Runyon. You know what an EMD FT costs the company? You couldn't pay for one in a lifetime."

"Yeah, I'm safe, Eddie. Thanks for asking."

"I sent you up there to do a job, not to shove an engine into the Chikaskia."

"We rescued the engineer and fireman, Eddie."

"I heard," he said.

"Anyway, that's Ludie's territory."

"Ludie needed the help."

"You can say that again. Why the hell would anyone hire a three-toed sloth for a rail dick?"

"We take what we can get, Runyon, believe me. You get that Quinlan thing cleared up?"

"I've been dangling from a rope over a flooded river, Eddie. It slipped my mind."

"The press is picking up on that killing out there," he said. "And then with that deputy shooting at that old lady, all hell's broken loose."

"I'm not in charge of Deputy Tooney."

"I want things wound up, see. The big boys are climbing up my ass."

"Right, Eddie."

"And what about that psychologist?"

"Thanks for that, Eddie. She's a lot of help, teaching me all about Sigmund Freud and everything."

"Who?"

"Freud. He's a psychoanalyst."

"Don't be a smart-aleck, Runyon. Everybody knows about *Fraud*."

"*Freud*, Eddie."

"That's what I said. Damn, Runyon, you're like a three- year-old."

"Freud believes that boys want to make out with their mothers and kill their fathers."

"You need to clean it up, Runyon. Living on the bum has turned your morals into a shithouse."

"Nice visiting with you, Eddie, but I have to run. Banjo's playing 'Onward Christian Soldiers' on his nose and out of tune at that."

*****

Hook hung up the phone and watched Banjo pitch his banana peel toward the trash can, where it hung up on the lip of the can.

"Anything headed out Quinlan way?" Hook asked.

Banjo checked the board. "There's a caboose hop headed for Mooreland. Bobtail's running her over for the section-gang foreman."

"Bring her in, Banjo. I need a ride home."

When the bobtail rolled in, Hook swung up on the caboose grab iron and then waved off the engine. The caboose, a model far newer than his, sported electric lights, cushioned seats, and a nice bunk, complete with reading light.

He climbed into the cupola and kicked back for a rest. The sun warmed his back as they clipped down the high iron. The Glass Mountains lifted out of the prairie, their gypsum caps flat as box tops. Mica sparkled in soil red as blood, and mesquite trees clung to the cliffs with bony fingers.

As they approached the Quinlan siding, the engineer brought her down. Hook climbed from the cupola, dragged the mattress out of the caboose, and tossed it over the back railing. Soon as the foreman's shack came into view, he dropped off the ladder at a trot.

He had no sooner gotten his new mattress situated on his bunk than someone knocked on his door. He found Ria Wolfe standing there with Mixer at her side.

"Your dog is out here," she said. "He refuses to leave."

"Not my dog. He just hangs around," Hook said.

"How long has he been hanging around?"

Hook shrugged. "Thirteen, fourteen years."

Ria rolled her eyes and moved her purse to the opposite shoulder. She raised her hand against the sun.

"Well, he gave me another four-tire rating. May I come in?"

"I was just tidying up. One thing I can't stand is an untidy caboose."

"I think he's hungry."

"That's a safe bet," Hook said.

85

Ria stepped in, but Mixer balked at the door. "He's afraid to come in," she said.

"Just leave the door open. He's a bit neurotic."

"Neurotic?"

"It's a psychological term," he said. "It means emotionally unstable. Like, Mixer is neurotic when it comes to closed caboose doors."

"Yes, I know what neurotic means," she said, blocking the door open with one of Hook's boots. "I just never heard it used to describe a canine."

"You never met Mixer," he said.

Ria shook her head. "Really, Hook, how's one to ever know when you're serious?"

"Not even I know that," he said. "Sit down."

She took a seat at the table and got out her notepad. "About this emergency of yours that left me dealing with the police on my own. . . ."

"A little derailment problem," he said. "Look, Ria, you and I both know there's nothing you can learn from an old railroad bull like me. Maybe it's time to close that notebook of yours and go back to your studies."

She laid her pen down. Mixer sidled in next to her, keeping an eye on the door the whole time. "I defer to your experience on most things, Hook, but not when it comes to my notebook and my studies. Frankly, you know nothing about either."

Mixer sniffed Ria's hand, and she cupped his chin. "Oh, my," she said, looking Mixer in the face. "What happened to his whiskers?"

"He's never been much for pretty," Hook said.

"They're all curled up like he's been too close to a fire."

Hook studied Mixer. "Too bad he can't talk," he said.

Ria picked up her pen and clicked it against her teeth. "Perhaps there are some things you could learn from me, if you'd listen."

Hook pushed books aside and took up his seat at the table. "I've learned things from the most unlikely people," he said. "Once, I had a five-foot 'bo black both my eyes."

"What did you learn from him?" she asked.

"Size and heart are two different things. Now, what is it you're wanting to say?"

"I spotted those boys stealing again," she said.

"Oh?"

"The county shed. I staked it out. I saw them."

"How did you know they would be there?"

She leaned in and tapped her forehead. "Psychology," she said.

Hook picked rope hemp out of his prosthesis hinge and stacked it in a little pile on the table. "I'm listening," he said.

"Well, when I was making my statement to the sheriff, he said that someone had been stealing tools and gasoline from the county shed. Reinforcement theory suggests that rewards, particularly rewards that are randomly given, can cause a behavior to be repeated over and over, you know, like a rhesus monkey, even at the risk of an occasional punishment. Sometimes just the sheer rush of adrenalin can serve as reinforcement in itself. The theory fits our boys: loot, the chase, the escape, more loot. Anyway, who else might it be?"

"Almost anyone," he said. "Every delinquent in town takes a run at the county shed sooner or later. So you went there, even though I asked you not to interfere with the case?"

"I didn't see any harm in just checking it out. I had no intentions of interfering."

"You saw them breaking in?"

"Yes. I waited until they were gone before returning to my car." She paused. "There is one other thing."

"Oh?"

"I also saw someone running, a man, I think."

"One of the boys?"

"Maybe. I don't think so. I didn't get a good look, but he was tall, you know, and fast."

"Which way was he going?"

"East."

"Toward the tracks?"

Ria nodded.

"May have been a 'bo. You're pretty close to the rails there. In any case, those boys may have figured out that they had been spotted," Hook said.

"It occurred to me that he could have been following the boys. Maybe he was planning to do to them what he did to Benjamin Way," Ria said.

"It's hard to know what a man's thinking from this distance," he said.

"Maybe it was the troll, Hook. It could have been, for all we know."

"First, for the last time, there are no such things as trolls. Still, it's possible, I suppose, it could be the culprit we're looking for. In any case, you'd do well not to take such chances in the future."

Ria laid down her pen and looked out the window of the caboose. "There's something else that's been bothering me."

Hook rearranged his books and slid them under the window. "Deputy Tooney," he said.

"How did you . . ."

"It's been bothering me for some time now. There are just too many things that don't add up."

"Like?"

"The sheriff said Beth Rossen was a drunk but not much trouble. If that's the case, why was Tooney following her? And he pulled that trigger pretty damn fast. He had no way of knowing if a weapon was in that sack. She could have been reaching for knitting needles for all he knew. Maybe he just wanted to shut things down before she could talk."

"You think he's been working with Beth Rossen and those boys all along? Making a little money on the side?"

"Small-town cops can earn less than the garbage man," he said. "They know the ins and outs of most everything that's going on in town, so the temptations run pretty high. Combine that with a man who has the IQ of an engine coupler, and you have Deputy Tooney."

Ria brushed at Mixer's nose and some of his whiskers crumpled off. Mixer sniffed, and they blew onto the floor, like fake snow falling off a Christmas tree.

"Tooney pumped me for information," she said. "He asked about what I told the sheriff in my statement."

"I'm not surprised."

"Then he asked me to go shooting with him."

"I'm not surprised by that either," he said.

Hook got up and went to a cabinet, found some canned tuna, and opened it. He set it down for Mixer, who licked the can around the caboose floor.

"I asked you not to interfere for a reason," he said. "I don't want you directly involved in these things. It's dangerous."

"But I am involved now, aren't I?" Ria said.

"Yes, you are. So if the word should just happen to get out that there are boxcars filled with army-surplus weapons coming through the yards, it just might flush out some of these characters," Hook said.

"And is that the case?"

"They've been switching the surplus cars onto a different line to Chicago, using the wye junction in the yard to couple them onto the tail."

"What's the point?"

"Sometimes those cars sit on that wye for quite awhile. Any thief worth his salt could figure out that it's a perfect place to break into them, and nothing tempts a thief more than free weapons. Course, I want to make it clear that I'd advise anyone who's not law enforcement to stay out of this altogether."

She pushed her hair back from her face and locked her eyes on Hook. "It explains a lot, I suppose," she said. "Maybe Benjamin Way was involved in all this too, I don't know. Maybe it got him killed, but what it still doesn't explain is the sheer brutality of his death."

"Death comes in many forms," Hook said. "And for many reasons."

"Maybe so. In any case, I think I'll check in with Deputy Tooney. I can't remember the last time I went shooting."

Chapter 13

RIA DID NOT HAVE TO find Deputy Tooney because he was waiting in the parking lot for her when she got up the next morning. One foot on the front bumper of the patrol car, he stuck a cigarette in the corner of his mouth and watched her as she approached.

"You know you're parked in a no-parking zone?" he said, lighting up.

"Really?" she said. "I had no idea."

"Consider yourself warned. Next time I'll have to take action."

"Yes, Deputy," she said. "I'll be more careful."

"I thought maybe you'd like to go down on the river this afternoon and shoot a few cans."

"I don't have a gun."

"Guns, I have," he said, dropping his hand onto his sidearm. "I'm off duty about three. I'll come by."

"I should warn you. I've not had much experience with shooting."

"Just aim and squeeze," Tooney said, climbing back in the patrol car. "Easiest thing in the world."

*****

Ria spent the day getting a start on her research design and writing an overdue letter to her father. She signed off with a backhanded hint that he might send a little money her way, that although she was doing fine, one never knew what emergencies might arise in such a remote locale.

At three, she was on the front steps of the Eastman. When Tooney pulled in, she gave him a little wave and took a deep breath. She could think of a lot of places she would rather be going than with Tooney to shoot cans.

He pushed the car door open. "Hop in," he said.

She slid into the patrol car. It smelled of liquor and cigarette smoke. Deputy Tooney sported sunglasses and had his shirtsleeves cuffed a half-turn. The two-way crackled as he turned out onto the highway.

"I need to stop by the house and pick up a little ammo," he said. "It's on the way."

"Okay," she said. "Do you shoot often?"

"Oh, hell, yes," he said. "In this business, you got to be ready. You never know when someone's going to be gunning for you."

"Must be frightening."

He turned into a drive and slowed for the potholes. "Me, it's just part of the job. Take it as it comes, I say."

"You live alone?" she asked.

"That's right. I was married once. Didn't work out. She couldn't get used to the police work. Always at me about this and that, especially the women." He looked at her and winked. "Uniforms. You know how it is."

He pulled up to a small bungalow with half the roof shingles missing and turned off the motor. The front porch leaned to the side, and one of the plank steps hung out in midair. "Ain't always lived here," he said. "Me and the wife had a brick home up on Sixth Street. The ex is living in it with the city electrician, and I'm back living in a damn shack. When I was a kid, we lived in a tarpaper shack down by the tracks in Wellington, Texas. Makes this here place look like a mansion."

"Do your parents still live there?"

"My mama does, same old shack too. One winter night they found my daddy facedown in a mudhole not a hundred yards from the house. They said his hand was frozen solid around the neck of a whiskey bottle. Guess he figured to take it with him.

"Cops work for peanuts in a small town, see. It can be just as dangerous as the city too, maybe more so. Hell, in the city, I'd have a better weapon, a faster car, and a partner watching my back. Here, it's just me—me and old Holcome."

Reaching under the seat, he retrieved a flask and held it out to her.

"Thanks, no," she said.

He shrugged, tipped the flask, and then dabbed at his chin with his sleeve on what escaped.

"Never touch the stuff until I'm off duty," he said. "Holcome gets his heat up about it. Hang on, I'll be right back."

Soon, he returned with two rifles, which he laid in the backseat of the patrol car. "The small one there is yours. She don't pack much of a kick, but she shoots smack-up straight."

He turned back onto the highway and brought the car to speed. He tipped the flask again, and water gathered in his eyes. "My ex took me for about everything I had," he said. "And me working for shit. So I just take off from time to time. Hole up, you know, drink a little whiskey and shoot cans. Sometimes I go hunting, take a deer or two."

He laughed and looked over at her. "I told Holcome if he didn't like it, he could just find someone else to work for these wages, just see if he could."

By the time they passed the dunes outside town, ancient sands deposited by the slow meander of the Cimarron River, Tooney had killed half his flask. He cut onto a dirt road that led into the valley. Mesquite cropped up out of the sand, and the smell of sage rose from the car wheels.

He pulled up at the riverbank and took out the rifles. The Cimarron, half a mile wide in some places, had only a trickle of water lacing down its bed. Tooney lined up some old tin cans and came back for another go at his flask.

He showed Ria how to hold her rifle, his whiskers raw against her cheek, his breath rancid with booze.

"Then just squeeze," he said. "Like as if you're running your finger right through the palm of your hand." He demonstrated a shot, sending a can spinning into the air.

"Now, the biggest mistake folks make is that last-second jerk. You gotta have a cool head and just bring your finger right on in."

Ria fired off a shot, jumping at the last moment and sending her bullet astray.

"You must have been in the army," she said. "I mean, someone who shoots like you."

He slid his sunglasses off his forehead and onto his eyes. "First in line to volunteer," he said, "but the bastards wouldn't take me."

"Flat feet?"

"Hernia. Big as a damn golf ball. So I says, sew the bastard up. I could shoot more Krauts by noon then these other bastards could in a lifetime. But they said the hernia might just pop back out at the wrong time and jeopardize the other soldiers."

"Too bad," she said. "You would have made a wonderful soldier, I'm sure."

"Yeah," he said.

"I hear the army has lots of surplus coming back now."

Tooney fired off another round, sending a can spinning off to the side in a dazzle.

"I heard that myself," he said. "I'd sure like to have one of those army rifles with a scope and all. I bet you could knock 'em off their pins with one of those."

"Hook Runyon says there are freight cars coming through all the time filled with surplus ordnance. He says they switch them out at the wye junction, mostly at night."

"I bet a man could pick some up cheap in the city too," he said.

"Hook says most that army stuff is just like new."

Tooney polished off his flask and slid it back under the seat. After a few more shots at the cans, he said, "You want to take another go at it? I got plenty of ammo."

"No, I better be getting back. I'm expecting a call from my father."

When they pulled into the Eastman parking lot, Deputy Tooney stopped the car and dropped his arm around her shoulder.

"Maybe we can go snake hunting up in the hill country," he said. "Takes a warm day to bring the rattlers out sunning. I have a snake catcher and everything."

Ria slid for her door. "Yes, another time," she said. "Snake hunting sounds like fun."

She watched the deputy pull out of the parking lot, his tires squealing as he gunned the patrol car onto the road.

Shooting cans with Deputy Tooney was like lifting a wet rock and having a multilegged critter crawl up your arm. It called for a shower.

*****

Ria waited until dusk before driving out to Hook's caboose. Together, the rail-yard bull and the East Coast academic sat inside with the door open and watched Mixer dig a hole in the right-of-way, the dirt kicking up between his back legs and into the air.

"What's he doing?" she asked.

"It's better not to know," Hook said.

"So I met with Tooney," Ria said. "Shooting lesson. If we're ever invaded by beer cans, I'm ready to go."

Hook held up his prosthesis. "I have to be so close to hit anything, it's just as easy to whack 'em over the head."

Ria looked through the fading light at him. "You've never said much about what happened to your arm."

"Well, I could tell you I was wounded in the war, got a Purple Heart and all that. Fact is, I lost it in a car wreck."

"I'm sorry," she said.

"Probably just as well. I was headed down the wrong track at high speed. There's something about leaving your arm behind that gives you pause long enough to take a look around. Now, about this shooting lesson," he said. "Did the topic of army surplus happen to come up?"

"Tooney's eyes lit up like headlights," she said.

"I figure to stake out that wye junction, see if he takes the bait. Maybe catch myself a thief."

Ria dug through her purse and took out a stick of gum. She folded it into her mouth while watching Mixer trot down the tracks.

"You might catch yourself a thief," she said, "but I'm not sure you'd have your killer."

Hook cracked a window. Somewhere off in the distance, he could hear a series of barks telling him that Mixer had picked up a trail.

"What's your point?" he asked.

"Tooney's dull-witted, a pathological liar, and a womanizer. Unfortunately, none of that is against the law."

"Which is a good thing," Hook said. "Half the country would be locked up otherwise."

"In my opinion, he might well be involved with the burglaries, but I'm less certain about the killing of that boy."

"Someone killed that kid," Hook said. "Tooney had plenty of opportunity and just maybe a motive."

"I'm not saying it's not possible. I am saying that I think it's unlikely."

"Because?"

"Well, his wife left him and took all his money in the process. He's working a job that doesn't pay enough for him to live. But his biggest problem, in my estimation, is that he's an alcoholic. He's desperate for money, and he has inside information about folks who would be willing to steal, all of which makes him an excellent candidate for burglary but not necessarily for murder, especially the kind that transpired under that bridge. In my opinion, he doesn't have it in him. He is not sick enough inside to do what that killer did to that boy."

"I can't disagree with any of that, providing you know what transpired between him and that boy, and I'm not sure you do."

They sat quietly for a moment.

"So I'm going with you tonight, right?" she said.

"Bad idea."

"Look, I set this thing up for you. I expect to be included in the closing."

"Okay, but you'll have to keep that damn notebook shut."

"Anything else?"

"We'll need a car."

*****

They parked the car in a stand of trees overlooking the wye junction. The lights in the rail yard grew brighter as the night darkened. Switch engines bumped and hauled over the myriad tracks, thundering off into places unknown. An hour passed, and the Super Chief slid in from the north, its passengers peering out into the darkness from the observation car.

When a switch engine rumbled in, her brakes screeching, Hook stood. "That's the car with the surplus," he said.

The brakeman stepped down and signaled for the engineer to bring her back onto the wye. He uncoupled the end car, pulled up on the ladder of the next car, and swung a go-signal with his lantern. Soon, they had disappeared into the yards.

The night fell silent, and the yard lights shone on the lone boxcar left behind. Shadows eased out from the trees, and the smell of diesel oil rode in from the distant yards.

And then Hook spotted them, two shadows slipping in from the trees. They cut the car seal and rolled back the door. Ria's breath shortened.

One of the boys climbed aboard and threw supplies out to the other one, who then carried them back up the hill and into the woods. Just then a whistle announced the return of the switch engine. When her glimmer broke down track, the boys rolled the door closed and headed for the trees.

"We're going to lose them," Ria said.

"That ordnance is too heavy to carry afoot," Hook said. "I figure they're waiting for someone to pick it up. If you're right about Tooney, he should be along soon enough."

Chapter 14

I T WAS LATE, AND THE YARDS had quieted when Ria reached for the car keys. "Wait," Hook said, taking her hand. "There's something moving out there."

Ria stared into the darkness. She could just make out Tooney's patrol car coming down the right-of-way. The headlights were out, but the emergency lights were on. "It's Tooney," she said. "What do we do?"

"We'll let him make contact with the boys first, and then move in while he's busy checking out his take."

When Tooney's car door opened, the interior light flashed for a moment, and Ria caught a glimpse of the deputy. Her stomach tightened.

"He's pretty good with a gun," she said, "and he's not going to be happy to see us."

"I think I can get to them without detection by way of the back side of the boxcar."

"But there are three of them," Ria said.

"It's all about surprise. If something should go wrong, get Holcome."

"You're not leaving me here by myself," she said.

Hook shook his head. "Do you ever do what you're told?"

"Do you ever quit giving orders?"

"Well, stay behind me and don't make a sound."

Following the shadows, they worked their way around the back of the boxcar. Tooney's voice lifted with the breeze, and someone near him laughed. Hook motioned for Ria to stop.

The boxcar towered above them. The ties smelled of creosote. Wheat, spilled from the jam and bump of hundreds of hopper cars carrying the grain from Oklahoma farms to the big cities up north, had attracted birds and other critters. Droppings from their feasting littered the area.

Hook took out his sidearm. He turned to Ria and pointed to the route he would take. He signaled for her to stay put.

She nodded and moved up to the wheel truck for cover. Hook circled wide, pausing again and again to assess his position. From the trees came a curse, and then a match flared.

Ria hunkered down, the smell of weeds and sage pungent in the night. She figured Hook was nearly there, and her heart tripped. It was one thing to read about crime, quite another to be knee-deep in criminals.

At what point she realized that a rat had dashed out of the weeds straight for her, she could not be certain—perhaps when its little toenails scuttled over her foot or when its warm tail trailed light as a string behind it. Her yelp was spontaneous and irretrievable. For a moment, she thought it had come from someone else. Not until she heard bodies crashing through the darkness did she comprehend that it was she who had probably just killed them both.

Hook appeared from out of nowhere. "For Pete's sake, are you okay?"

"I couldn't help it," she said, her arms clasped about her. "It was a rat!"

"Damn," Hook said. "I dropped my sidearm in the weeds. Go for Holcome. I don't want to lose these guys."

Hook looked back and saw the three men emerge from the woods and split off from one another at a dead run. He took off full throttle behind them. Dozens of tracks, lit with the first light of dawn, led into the rail yard. Hiding places abound in a rail yard but none better than the roundhouse, so he cut for the turntable where he would have some cover and maybe a better view.

On the turntable structure, Hook climbed to where he could see into the roundhouse. It was like looking at a bicycle wheel on its side, with all tracks leading to the center. Inside, engines idled, like slumbering cats, over concrete pits. Windows stretched upward, three stories high, and great steel plates covered the unoccupied pits.

He crouched in the shadows to listen. Smoke from engine stacks swirled high above in search of exhaust ports, and the lights shimmered through the haze.

He checked his watch. The shift change had drained the roundhouse of workers, its vast emptiness amplifying the slightest of night sounds. Arches and doorways adorned the roundhouse recalling the interior of a Gothic cathedral. Overhead, pigeons chortled and strutted, and the wail of distant whistles drifted in from the high iron.

Hook waited and watched the open bays. Without a weapon, there was little to do but hope that help arrived soon.

The second the pigeons took flight, sweeping in a flutter out an open bay, he realized he had overlooked the turntable control cabin behind him.

"Raise your hands," the boy said, his voice breaking.

Hook lifted his arms. "I only have one hand, boy," he said.

"Move on in there under the lights," the boy said. "I know how to shoot this thing."

Hook climbed the remaining way over the turntable and into the roundhouse.

"That's far enough," the boy said.

Hook turned to see his own P38 leveled at him. In the dim light, he could not be certain if the safety had been unlocked or not.

"You better think about this," Hook said. "Up to now, it's only burglary, providing it wasn't you who killed Benjamin Way under that bridge."

The boy wiped at his nose with his sleeve. "I ain't killed no one," he said, "but I damn sure know how."

Hook started to lower his arms, but the boy circled to the side.

"Keep them up," he said.

Hook eased toward the boy.

"Sure, I got 'em up," Hook said. "I can see you mean business."

The boy stepped back onto the steel plate covering the engine pit behind him. The sound of his foot on the plate rang hollow and uncertain. He looked down at his feet and then at Hook, realizing in that moment that the plate he stood on clung by a hair to the edge of the pit. When it came

101

off, the boy yelped and dropped from sight, the plate clattering in on top of him. Hook waited to make certain the boy was not going to climb back out with his gun ablaze. In the distance, a police siren rose from the quiet of the night. Hook peered over the side of the pit and saw the boy lying in the fetal position, blood seeping from his head and into the oily water that had gathered in the bottom from idling engines.

Holcome and Ria arrived first, followed by the city ambulance. By the time the boy had been lifted out of the pit and was placed on a stretcher, the sun shone through the roundhouse windows, lighting up the gloom.

Sheriff Holcome picked through the boy's billfold while Ria stood at a distance watching with a concerned look on her face. "Looks like he's from over Woodward way," the sheriff said. "Just a damn kid on the loose, I suppose."

"Is he going to be all right?" Hook asked.

The sheriff shrugged. "They're taking him on into the city. That steel plate did a number on his head."

"Any word on the other two?" Hook asked.

Holcome shook his head. "There's trains out of here by the hour. They could have been on any one of them—together or alone. The city council's going to be up my ass about Tooney. I'd like for you and the girl to come with me over to the wye junction and see if his patrol car is still there. She can pick up her car while you're at it."

"All right, Sheriff," Hook said.

"You might want this," the sheriff said, handing Hook his P38. "Don't mean to be telling you your business, Hook, but things will go along a hell of a lot better if you don't give your weapon away."

"Thanks for the tip," Hook said.

"Anyway, the safety was on," the sheriff said. "You were never in danger of being shot."

They found Tooney's car where he had left it. In the trunk were several items that had been taken from the Quinlan siding. A search of the woods turned up the surplus ordnance that had been abandoned when the three thieves had fled. It looked as if Tooney and the other boy had made a clean break of it.

Sheriff Holcome leaned down so he could see through Ria's car window. "Hook," he said. "You'll be needing to come in and sign a statement on that shooting sometime. There's sure to be a hell of an investigation now that Tooney's implicated in this other matter, and I'll need statements about what happened at the wye tonight."

"Will be in soon," Hook said.

*****

Ria started the car and turned down the right-of-way, edging past Tooney's patrol car, which had been parked at an angle across the road.

"Where to?" she asked.

"Depot," he said. "I'll have to call this in to Eddie."

They rode in silence, breaking it only after Ria pulled into the depot and shut the engine off. "About last night," she said. "I nearly got us killed."

"Well," Hook said. "It didn't help matters with me handing my sidearm over to the boy."

"I don't know what came over me," Ria said. "I felt that rat, and I screamed without thinking."

"I did that once when a yellow jacket crawled up my pant leg."

Ria looked over at him. "What did you do?"

"Dropped my britches and shot him with my P38."

"No, you didn't," she said.

"Well, I gave him a hell of a pistol whipping."

Ria smiled. "Do you want me to take you out to your caboose when you're finished here?"

"Thanks, but no need," he said. "I'll catch something going that way."

"I've been thinking that maybe you're right. Maybe it's time I went back to the university," Ria said. "I'm afraid I'm not so good with this field research thing."

Hook opened his door. "You care to run over to Woodward tomorrow after we get the statements finished for the sheriff? There's a used bookstore downtown where I do some serious book hunting."

"But the investigation," she said. "Won't they be expecting you to follow up?"

"Sure," he said. "And that's exactly what I'd do if it wasn't my day off. Anyway, I need a lift over there."

"All right," Ria said. "Tomorrow, then."

*****

With the disconcerting sound of Banjo humming "She'll Be Coming Round the Mountain" in the john, Hook dialed Eddie's number, taking a peek into Banjo's lunch box while the phone rang.

"Security," Eddie said.

"Just calling to let you know I caught one of those boys who's been seal-busting out to Quinlan."

"I heard," Eddie said. "I get a call from the sheriff over there, see, and he says that kid's head was busted open like a ripe melon."

"The kid took a dive into an engine pit," Hook said. "He did it his own damn self."

"You know what the papers are going to do with this?"

"He had a gun on me," Hook said.

"It was your gun, Runyon."

"I don't think so, Eddie, but guns look pretty much alike, what with barrels and triggers and all."

"The sheriff said that Deputy Tooney and the other boy got away."

"Appears so," Hook said.

"I guess they're looking for another kid to cut up?"

"I didn't get a chance for an interview, Eddie."

"Why ain't you out hunting that killer down, Runyon? That is your job, isn't it?"

"Because I don't know whether the suspects went left or right, Eddie, and my helicopter's broke down."

"I'm getting flack from the big boys, see. You got more bodies out there than the Russian front. I need results soon, you hear?"

Banjo came out of the latrine with toilet paper hanging out of one nostril.

"Right, Eddie."

"And another thing, the engineer on that hop to Mooreland reported that someone stole the mattress out of the caboose."

"Who would steal a caboose mattress?"

"I don't know. Maybe someone without one who hitched a ride in the caboose."

"Look, Eddie, I got to go. Banjo's got a nosebleed," said Hook, hanging up the phone.

Chapter 15

HOOK LOOKED OVER AT Banjo. "What the hell happened to your nose?"

"That's my trumpet mute," Banjo said.

Hook pushed his hand through his hair. "Jeez," he said. "It's not that appealing, Banjo."

"It's a trumpet mute; doesn't matter what it looks like. Anyway, sometimes I forget it's in there. I hear you've taken to pushing kids into engine pits now, Hook."

"How you know that?"

"It was on the two-way 'fore you got your pistol found."

"I swear, railroading is like working with a bunch of old gossips. Everything I do beats me back to the caboose."

Banjo took an overly ripe banana out of his lunch box. "Why didn't you push old Tooney in too? That son of a bitch's been on the take ever since he hit town."

"Why didn't you say something earlier, Banjo? Could have saved me a lot of trouble."

"I got my job, and you got yours," he said with a shrug.

"You have anything going out my way?"

Banjo checked the board. "There's a dingdong making a mail run to Mooreland later."

"Don't you have something where I don't have to ride in the cab and listen to the engineer the whole way?"

"Well, there's the Super Chief in at eleven. Maybe we could kick Clark Gable out of his sleeper. That way you could sip martinis and take a little beauty nap on your way home."

"See if that dingdong will make a slow, Banjo, and don't expect that mute to help your music or your looks."

"I don't know what I'd do without your help, Hook, seeing as how I've been doing fine without it for most my life."

*****

By the time Hook swung down off the doddlebug engine, sunset had lit the horizon into the color of a ripe peach. He walked from the foreman's shack to the caboose, the weariness of the last twenty-four hours rushing in like a flood. He paused where Mixer had dug a new hole. Giving in to his curiosity, he scraped the dirt back with his boot toe, finding a leather glove with one of the fingers chewed off.

"Damn it, Mixer," he said to himself.

He lit the lantern in his caboose, only to discover the new bunk mattress missing. He threw his hat across the room, and it slid under the table. In the process of retrieving it, he bumped his head.

"Damn," he said, rubbing his noggin.

He poured himself a Beam and looked at the pack of cigarettes. He thumbed the box of matches he kept near the lantern and then put them back. He picked up the cigarettes and smelled them.

A whine at the door announced Mixer, and he got up to let the dog in. Mixer balked at the doorway, however, refusing to come inside until Hook propped the door open.

Mixer's whiskers had started to grow back from the fire and now looked somewhat like a worn-out hairbrush. The new stubble made him look alert and clean cut. Hook opened a can of tuna and watched Mixer spin the tin in a circle on the floor with his tongue.

"Where the hell you get that glove?" Hook asked him.

Mixer's response was to unfurl his tongue, like a pink ribbon, as he cleaned his muzzle on the way out the door.

Hook returned to the table and his books. Although he considered himself a collector, he did not collect in an official way. That took money, big money. Instead, he satisfied himself with Americana, modern firsts for the most part, and he collected what he enjoyed reading. He had put together a healthy collection of Raymond Chandler's stuff and hoped to find *The Big Sleep*, the 1939 N.Y. Knopf first edition, to fill out his collection.

His collecting depended on luck and low prices. Still, it added something to his life, not that he could define it, not that he wanted to. Sometimes it was enough to just enjoy something without explaining why.

Digging out some old bedding from the closet, he rolled it onto the floor, blew out the lantern, and lay down in the darkness. In the distance, the eastbound raced downgrade toward town, her whistle screaming and her wheels thundering. He thought about the day's events, clicking through them one by one. Damn little had gone right by any standards, which begged the question of his excitement and anticipation for tomorrow.

*****

Ria stood in the doorway of the caboose, her hair, black as night, clipped back with silver barrettes. She smelled of gardenias and held a sack in her hand. "Glazed doughnuts," she said, holding up the sack. "Hungry?"

"Well," Hook said, smiling. "I had burned toast in mind."

He put the coffee on while Ria browsed through his books. Mixer appeared and even ventured inside to greet their guest.

"I'd give him to you," Hook said, handing her a coffee, "but he doesn't belong to me. Maybe you'd like to borrow him for a couple years?"

"Poor thing," she said, patting Mixer's head. "It's a wonder he doesn't get killed around all these trains."

"Mixer? I don't think so. He can run under a moving boxcar, kill a cat, and come back under the same car without so much as a scratch. Course, what with his whiskers out of whack, he's off his game a little."

Ria sipped her coffee. "Well, that's just amazing, Mixer," she said, giving the dog another pat.

"More coffee?" Hook asked.

"No, thank you. I'm ready for this book-hunt thing."

The sun beat down hot, as it can only in the Southwest, ribbons of heat quivering skyward from the highway as they set out. Hook gave instructions on what to look for at the bookstore, as far as titles, condition, rarity.

"Doesn't sound so hard," Ria said, slowing the car for the approach into town.

"They call them rare books for a reason," Hook said. "But a man in my financial condition doesn't try to collect what the big boys collect. That's a game only money can win. Still, it's a hoot to make a find, even if it's just to fill out a series or complete an author's works."

The owner of the bookstore greeted Hook as an old acquaintance, and soon Hook was lost in the stacks. An hour passed, then two, and finally Hook emerged with an armload of books. He found Ria waiting in the car.

"Sorry," he said, sliding in. "You should have said something. I'm afraid I lose track of time when it comes to book scouting."

"No problem," she said, backing the car out. "You're in better book-scouting shape than I am."

They stopped for lunch at a local landmark that had a garage door for one wall, with original southwestern paintings covering the other three. They ordered fried catfish with hush puppies and lemonade as they waited for their order to arrive. Hook caught Ria watching as he picked up the saltcellar with his prosthesis.

"You'll get used to it," he said.

"Oh, sorry," she said. "Didn't mean to stare."

"I'm as used to it as one can be. You get a lot of attention with one of these. It serves me well, though I would never want more than one."

"I have a surprise for you," Ria said, reaching into her purse.

"Oh?"

"I found this back at the store."

Hook took the book and turned it over in his hand, Raymond Chandler's *The Big Sleep*, 1939 N.Y. Knopf first edition, complete with cursive title and boards of black with a blue band.

"I'll be damned," he said. "You found one."

Ria raised her glass, her eyes shining. "Bargain price too."

"I've been looking for this forever," Hook said.

"Goes to show you what a new perspective can do," Ria said. "I found it in a stack next to the desk that had yet to be catalogued. I must say the whole thing was rather exciting."

Hook studied the title page. "What do I owe you?"

"My pleasure," she said. "You didn't say a word of complaint about my blunder the other night, and I appreciate it."

After the late lunch, they drove back to Hook's caboose. Clouds towered into the sky, their bellies aflame with the setting sun. Ria shut the car off and turned to face him.

"I enjoyed the day," she said. "More than I thought I would, to tell you the truth."

"Better than shooting cans?" Hook asked.

"Considerably," she said.

"Would you care to come in? It's early yet."

"Well, I don't know."

"Look, Ria, I'm not one to go where I'm not invited, if that's what you're thinking. But maybe you'd prefer a little company over an empty hotel room."

Unsnapping a barrette, she pushed her hair back and clipped it up again. She looked at him through the fading light. "I think a little company would be nice," she said.

Hook fixed them drinks and talked some more about his books, pointing out where her find fit into the scheme of things. He talked about his past, his days on the rails, and how he had struggled to bring his life back on track after the car accident. He talked and talked as she watched him through the lantern light.

"Hook," she finally said. "I heard what you did at the Chikaskia bridge."

"Oh, that," he said. "Eddie wasn't happy about losing that engine."

"Are you ever afraid?"

"I don't fear men," he said. "In the end, they're no more than me, and that isn't much."

She took his hand in hers and drew her fingers over his palm.

"Are you afraid of me?" she asked.

He studied her through the dim light, the slight pout of her mouth, the tilt of her chin, the eyes that looked straight into his soul.

"Yes," he said.

"I want to stay with you tonight," she said.

Hook's throat tightened. "I'm sleeping on the floor, Ria."

She turned down the light and watched the black smoke curl up and out the chimney. She took his hand and brushed her lips against his fingers.

"I know," she said.

Chapter 16

HOOK AND RIA SIGNED THEIR statements in the sheriff's office and then waited for Sheriff Holcome to tally out the last of the stolen items. "There," he said, looking up. "That accounts for the sum total as far as I can make out."

"Thanks," Hook said. "Have you heard anything about the boy in the hospital?"

Holcome pushed back his hat. "Still unconscious, more or less," he said. "Doc said he opened his eyes once. Didn't like what he saw, I guess."

"Nothing on Tooney or the other boy?" Hook asked.

"Figure those two hopped a train and beat it out of here," he said.

"It's a rare snake that doesn't leave a track in the sand," Hook said.

"This is one I'd like to catch up with," Holcome said. "I take it personal when a man I trust with my life leaves me in a lurch."

Ria picked up some of the stolen items. "I'll take these out to the car."

When she had gone, Sheriff Holcome said, "Hook, I find myself a little shorthanded, as you know. I've been thinking maybe you'd like to take on the deputy's job, seeing as how there's a vacancy."

Hook gathered up the remaining loot. "I'm proud to be asked, Sheriff, and no one I'd rather work with. Thing is, I wouldn't be much for town work. The rails are all I know."

"If you change your mind, I could use a man knows how to stick with a job until it's done."

Hook found Ria waiting outside with the trunk open. She helped him load the last of the stolen goods. Hook slid in on the passenger side and waited for her to start the car.

"The sheriff wanted to talk to you?" she asked.

"Appears there's a deputy's job open."

She pulled into the street. "And you said no?"

Hook rolled down his window. "I'm just a rail bum doing what I have always done, except now I carry a sidearm and wear a badge. The city council would have me strung up in a week."

"I'm not so sure about that," she said. "Where is it you wanted to go?"

"Depot. I can store this stuff in the baggage room until they get it straightened out and we find the rightful owners."

After they had unloaded, they headed to the office, where they found Banjo half asleep at his desk. Hook shut the door hard enough to sit Banjo up in his chair.

"Hope I didn't disturb you," Hook said.

Banjo pulled at his whiskers and gave Ria a straight look.

"This is Ria," Hook said. "My associate."

"I remember. Young lady," Banjo said, "I normally ain't one to interfere in other people's business, but do you know who you are running with?"

"I do know better," she said, "but he can be quite persuasive."

"There's nothing a yard dog won't say or do to get his way, you know," said Banjo.

"I've heard that," Ria said.

"They've been known to push kids into engine pits and run diesel locomotives to the bottom of the river. Some say they even set fires, if it comes to it."

"That will do, Banjo," Hook said. "I put some stolen goods back there in the baggage room. They're all accounted for just in case someone thinks they can help themselves."

"It's a comfort knowing the strong arm of the law is at work."

"Banjo here can play music on his nose," Hook said. "He considers himself a celebrity, which he thinks gives him leave to say anything that comes to mind."

"His nose?" Ria said.

"He has trouble keeping it tuned, what with it growing bigger every day. Now it sounds more like a tuba than a banjo."

Banjo rolled his eyes. "That boss of yours called."

"Eddie Preston?"

"That's the one," he said. "He has his shorts in a wad."

"What about?"

"I don't ask Eddie questions," Banjo said. "It's like sticking your finger in wet paint and then wondering why the hell you did it."

Ria took up residence on the bench by the front door while Hook dialed Eddie. "Banjo said you called, Eddie."

"Why ain't you ever where I can get hold of you?" Eddie said.

"I live in a caboose without electricity and as far out of town as you can get me, Eddie. I guess you'll have to send up a smoke signal next time."

"The big boys are in a stir."

"What about?"

"Oh, nothing much, just that we got a diesel engine on the bottom of the Chikaskia, a kid with his brains leaking out of his head, and a rogue deputy on the loose, not to mention a boy cut up into pieces under the bridge. All the while you ain't nowhere to be found."

"I'm only one man, Eddie."

"Now we got a switch stand covered up on the Capron spur."

"A switch stand?"

"That's right. Covered up so there's no way of knowing which direction the switch points are set."

"Covered up with what, Eddie?"

"That's why we got yard dogs. Get on out there before we have a major hoptoad on our hands."

"All right, Eddie."

"There's a doubleheader coming through there in an hour. Be on it."

Hook hung up with a scowl on his face.

"What's going on?" Ria asked.

"Someone's covered up a switch stand. Probably some kids fooling around. I'm catching a doubleheader out in an hour," Hook said.

"Is it dangerous?" Ria asked.

"Some hotshot might hit the switch too fast and derail."

"I'd like to go with you."

"No place to ride but the engine," he said.

"We could take my car."

Hook looked at his watch and then at the car. "Let's go," he said.

By the time they reached Capron, dusk had settled in. They pulled onto the right-of-way at the crossing outside town and made their way to the switch point. Fence posts cast shadows over the road and flicked past the window as the sun sank below the horizon. Ria negotiated a curve and stopped for a wash cutting across the road. "This is as far as we can go," she said.

"I think that's it up there," Hook said. "Do you have a flashlight?"

"In the glove compartment."

Ria walked next to Hook as they made their way up track. He paused to pan the area with his light.

Suddenly Ria stopped. "Hook," she said, pointing. "Look."

The body of a boy was impaled on the switch stand. His shirt had swept over his head and shoulders, covering the stand. Hook knelt and pulled the shirt back. "It's his end for sure," he said.

The switch stand had entered the boy's chest and exited his back, taking with it a fair piece of his spine. Ria pointed to a series of 'bo symbols that had been scratched on the switch signal.

"What do they mean, Hook?"

"Mostly that the train has to slow here and that it's a good place for 'boes to hop a train," he said.

"Look, isn't that the head of an owl, like the one under the bridge?"

Hook examined the scratching and frowned. "Maybe it's an owl. Maybe it isn't. Hard to say."

He took the boy's billfold from his pocket and laid the contents out under the beam of the flashlight.

"It's Busey," he said. "Tooney's running mate."

He lifted the boy's head. There was a wound in back. His eyes, now indifferent to the cruelty of his death, had retreated into his skull.

"Tooney did this?" Ria asked.

Hook reached for a cigarette. Having none, he clicked off the light, the horror before him still vivid in his mind. "He could have slid off the top of a tanker car or a dozen other things and landed here," he said. "It's down-grade, and trains hit a pretty fast clip through here."

"Fell off or was killed and then pushed off?"

"He could have hit his head on the way down. I've been there myself a time or two," Hook said. "A tanker sits pretty snug at first, but then the train picks up speed, and the wind starts dragging you over the side. Then the cold turns your hands to ice, and you don't know if you're hanging on anymore. It's a short haul over the side from there. Luckily, I never had a switch stand waiting for me."

"But why just the boy? Where's Tooney?"

"Hard to say. Maybe he pushed the kid off, figuring he might slow him down. Maybe not. Maybe he hopped a different car. If nothing else, we know what direction at least one of them was headed."

"What do we do now?"

"The body has to be moved off the switch."

Ria looked up at him. "Moving a body violates crime-scene protocol," she said.

"This is a working railroad," Hook said. "A train jumps track because of this switch, and there could be a hell of a lot more bodies than this one to worry about. Grab his feet. We'll lift him off."

"Hook," she said. "I don't know."

"Get hold," he said. "It's got to be done."

On the count of three, they lifted the body but failed to clear the stand. The corpse settled back on the stand and assumed its slump.

Ria dropped her arms to her side. "I can't do this, Hook," she said.

A distant whistle sounded, and the faint light from a train glimmer broke down track.

"We have to," he said. "Get hold now, and don't quit until it's done."

The glimmer grew brighter, and the rumble of the approaching train rode down the rails. Hook counted off, and they both groaned as they hoist-ed the corpse high enough to disengage it from its mooring. Hook rolled the body clear of the track and adjusted the switch.

Ria stood, frozen. Hook pulled her away just as the train thundered by, the wind from the cars whipping dirt into their faces. They watched in silence as the caboose clacked away into the night.

"We made it," he said. "Come on. Wellington is just down the road."

Ria turned and looked at him, her face drawn. "Hook, look," she said, quietly. "His chest cavity has been opened, and there are body parts inside that shouldn't be there. He was dead before he came off that tanker. Do you think Tooney . . ."

"Did this? I don't know, but I do know he has to be caught."

Ria walked over to the boy and then back to Hook.

"I know where he is," she said.

"Where who is?" he asked.

"Deputy Tooney," she said. "I know where he is."

Chapter 17

AFTER REPORTING THE MURDER, Hook had Ria drive straight to the depot in Wellington, arriving with the new day. "If Tooney's at his mother's house, he won't stay long. He knows we'll show up sooner or later."

Ria pulled up at the depot and shut off the engine. "He said he grew up in a shack close to the tracks."

"Pete, the operator, has lived here his whole life. He should be able to help."

Pete looked up as they entered the station office and pushed his pencil behind his ear. "Hook Runyon," he said. "What you doing over the border? Won't you get arrested?"

"Nice seeing you too, Pete."

"I ain't loaning you no money, Hook. I never got that five dollars back I loaned you three years ago."

"I think you must be mistaken, Pete. I'm keen to pay my bills on time."

"Oh, sure," he said. "Three years is right timely, isn't it?"

"Like to jaw as much as the next man, but I'm in kind of a rush. I'm looking for a fella. It's my understanding he grew up around here."

"What's his name?" Pete asked.

"Deputy Tooney."

Pete kicked his feet up on the end of his desk. "I don't believe I ever knew a fella by the name of Deputy before."

"Do you know a Tooney or don't you?"

"I know lots of folks named Tooney," he said.

Hook looked at Ria, who watched with her brows furrowed. "Can you believe they put these guys in charge of keeping trains apart?" Hook asked.

"His mother is supposed to live close to the tracks," Ria said. "Maybe you could help us find her?"

"I figure I could come up with something for a pretty lady like you," he said. "Tooney, you say?"

"That's right."

"There's a Mildred Tooney off the roller-mill spur north of town. She rides a three-wheeled bike everywhere looking for stuff to sell. She had a boy, as I recall. I ain't seen him in years. Mighty glad of it too. He'd steal a man's gold teeth right out of his mouth."

"Sounds like him," Hook said.

"His name was Jude Tooney, though. Not Deputy."

"For Pete's sake, man. Is Ludie Bean around?"

"He's been staying in a crew car out in the yards. In fact, that's pretty much all he's been doing. Guess he wore himself thin rescuing that train crew out of the Chikaskia."

"Right," Hook said. "If you see him, tell him this Tooney guy could be dangerous. He might want to keep his eyes open for a change."

"I'd feel obliged to do just that if I had my five dollars back."

Hook took his billfold out and counted out the money. "I'd run you in for blackmail if I had more time."

"By the way," Pete said, grinning. "Bakehead said someone's been settin' fires up and down the line."

"Don't believe everything you hear, especially from no fireman, Pete."

"Well, guess you'd be right about that. Kind of a coincidence, though, that arsonist having one arm and all."

*****

Hook and Ria drove by the roller mill, a multistoried structure adjacent to the grain elevators and the rail spur. During World War II, the mill had turned out Honey Bee wheat flour twenty-four hours a day and then loaded it into boxcars and shipped it out to the East Coast to help the war effort; its output had dwindled to a trickle in recent years.

On the second pass by the mill, Hook spotted an old tar-paper shack not far from the tracks. An enormous elm had grown up in the front yard and nearly covered the shack with its limbs. Ria parked up the street far enough away so as not to alert anyone.

"There's only one way to do this," Hook said. "I'm going to the front door. You keep an eye on the back. If you see anyone leave, give me three short honks."

"Three honks," she said, pausing. "Hook, I'm frightened."

"Me too," he said.

He made his way through the tangle of weeds and trash that littered the yard. An old sofa, blooming with black mold, sat on the front porch under an overflowing mailbox. The screen door was bellied out and rattled on its hinges when Hook knocked. He stepped to the side and waited. Arthritic fingers slid through the door crack.

"What do you want?" a woman said.

"I'm looking for Jude Tooney," he said.

"You got the wrong house," she said.

Hook stuck his foot in the door and eased it open with his shoulder. The old lady wore a flour-sack dress and had skin the color of tanned leather. "I know he's in there," Hook said. "You tell him to come along now before someone gets hurt."

Suddenly there were three short honks from Ria's car horn. Hook turned just in time to see Tooney running from behind the house and heading full tilt for the roller mill.

"Damn it!" Hook said. He jumped from the porch and cut an angle across the yard. By the time he reached the roller mill, Tooney had disappeared through the side door.

Hook, his weapon drawn, cracked the door. Beams of sunshine seeped through opaque windows, and a couple of mill workers, lost in a cloud of wheat dust, shoveled grain into an auger. The clamor of belts and chains boiled up from the vast chambers of the mill.

Hook slipped past the men and made his way to the elevator rail that ran up the wall to the top of the building. A one-man platform inched up the side through the open expanse of floors. Noise drifted down from grain chutes and gears. When the platform lurched to a stop at the top, Hook waited until he figured it was cleared, then pushed the green button on the wall. The slack popped out of the elevator cable, and the platform commenced a slow descent. When it had stopped at his feet, Hook climbed on and closed the gate, a single iron bar, the only thing between him and the yawning innards of the mill.

He pushed the button again, and the platform clanked upward. The floors fell away, and his stomach tightened. Chutes, bearing tons of grain to the top, vibrated and thumped, and plumes of dust boiled from their joints. Wheat dust stung Hook's eyes and gathered on his shoulders. He looked down to see the bottom floor spiraling away, the workers now looking like ants in a den. The little platform rose upward like a kite in the blue.

When it creaked to a stop at the top, Hook pulled his sidearm, crouched, and scanned the area for Tooney. Light struggled through the dusty windows like silent layers of debris from an ancient tomb.

He heard the noise above him, but too late. Tooney crashed across his shoulders with his full weight, and Hook sprawled onto the floor, his gun skidding off to the side. Tooney clawed for his own sidearm, but Hook caught him with an elbow to the groin. Tooney grunted and fell to his knees, his gun plummeting over the side of the elevator platform and into the abyss.

Hook scrambled out of reach as Tooney got up. Tooney wiped wheat dust from his face with his shirtsleeve. His eyes, filled with hatred and fear, locked onto Hook.

"I've been wanting to do this for a long time, Runyon," he said.

Hook squared off, his feet set. "What's stopping you?" he said.

Tooney stepped in, and Hook stuck him with a blow to the throat. Tooney staggered back and honked for breath. When he'd recovered, he came in with a roundhouse. Hook ducked and landed a cross punch under his uplifted arm. Wind and saliva blew from Tooney's mouth, and his legs wobbled.

Tooney shook his head clear, backed off, and reached into his pocket. He slipped something onto his hand. He spit and rolled his shoulders.

"I'm going to crack you like an egg, Runyon," he said.

Hook took the moment to gather up his reserve. Tooney stepped in, one fist at his ear, the other dropped to his side. Hook fired an uppercut, but Tooney slipped to the side and delivered a crashing blow to the side of Hook's head.

Hook's brain sloshed in his skull, and lights flashed in his eyes. The world flipped upside down, and his legs turned to water. He pitched onto the floor, a cloud of wheat dust billowing up around him.

When he came to, the room spun like a carnival ride. He crawled over to his sidearm and then struggled to stand. Somewhere, the elevator platform clacked away. Following the wall for support, he made his way over to where he could see Tooney disappearing through the floor below.

Blood trickled down Hook's neck, and he touched the lump on his head. He hated heights more than anything in the world, save for letting such a son of a bitch escape, so he reached out with his good hand and swung onto the moving cable. He wrapped his legs around it, locked his ankles, and descended into the chasm. Sweat ran into his eyes, and his arm burned as the platform crawled downward. If Tooney looked up, Hook knew it would be over. He hoped he died fast because counting seconds on his way to the bottom seemed an awful way to go.

When at last the platform jerked to a stop, Hook waited for the click of the door latch and then the sound of Tooney's footsteps. Hook's arm, dead with fatigue, slipped on the cable, and the prosthesis harness cut deeply into his flesh. Waves of nausea swept over him. When he could hold on no longer, he slid in free fall to the platform, landing with a crash.

When he looked up, Deputy Tooney stood facing him, both hands over his head. Ludie Bean sat on a bench behind him with a shotgun in his lap.

"Where the hell you been, Runyon?" Ludie said. "I ain't got all day."

"Ludie," Hook said, dusting himself off. "What the hell you doing here?"

Ludie took out his handkerchief and wiped the sweat from his hairless head. "Saving your ass, by the looks of it," he said. "Pete said you were headed out here. I figured Tooney would be a bit much for a one-armed rail bum. Figured right, by the looks of it."

Hook wished for a cigarette and for Ludie Bean to blow off his own damn arm, in that order.

Ria came through the door, her hair scrambled by the wind. "Hook, are you okay?"

Hook touched the rising lump on his head. "Just great," he said. "Would you go to the sheriff's office and tell him we have Tooney in custody?"

"Now?" she said.

"Now's good as any," Hook said.

Ludie hung his shotgun over his arm. Swaths of sweat spread from under his arms and the folds of his belly. "I can handle this man my own damn self, Hook, given he is in my territory."

"Last I heard, there's also a corpse in your territory, Ludie, Deputy Tooney's partner in crime. In the meantime, I have a few question for Deputy Tooney."

"He's got cuffs in his belt," Ludie said. "I suggest you use them."

"I'll get around to it," Hook said.

Ludie shrugged and got up. "He runs, it's on your watch, Runyon."

After Ludie and Ria had gone, Hook located an empty office and escorted Tooney into it.

"Put your hands on the wall," Hook said.

Tooney's lip curled. "I got no weapon, as you know, Runyon."

Hook searched him, finding the palm sap stuck in his back pocket.

"I guess this don't count," Hook said, pushing him into the chair.

Tooney didn't answer. Hook leaned against the desk and laid his sidearm next to him.

"We got you cold, Tooney, stolen goods from the Quinlan spur, army-surplus ordnance in the back of your patrol car, and plenty of witnesses to the whole thing."

"Like you never stole anything," Tooney said.

Hook continued as if Tooney hadn't spoken. "But then what's a few stolen items compared to murder?"

"I didn't have anything to do with no murder."

Hook moved to the window, leaving his sidearm on the desk.

"Let's see if I can count them," Hook said. "Start with your sidekick, Busey, the one gutted and spiked on a switch stand like a pig on a spit."

"He hopped an oil tanker. I ain't seen him since."

"Maybe you cracked him open and helped him over the side, Tooney, you know, one less witness to worry about. And then Benjamin Way, the kid you cut up under the bridge. Folks don't live long when you're around, do they? And they seem to die an ugly death."

"I got nothing more to say," Tooney said.

"Cops are none too popular in prison, you know." Hook, his back to Tooney, slipped the palm sap on his hand. "You're in deep, Tooney, over your head and no way out."

When he heard Tooney come off his chair, Hook spun just in time to see Tooney go for Hook's sidearm. Hook caught him across the bridge of the nose with the palm sap, cracking it like a limb in an ice storm. Tooney's eyes went blank, and he dropped to the floor.

Hook removed the cuffs from Tooney's belt and cuffed him to the chair. Blood dripped from Tooney's nose, which was fast doubling in size and turning the color of a fall apple.

"Don't touch my sidearm," Hook said. "I got a thing about that."

Chapter 18

RIA SAT IN HER HOTEL ROOM and looked over her notebook in surprise. With all she had been through in recent days, she had not taken a single note. After asking her to take care of Mixer, Hook had hopped a milk run to Topeka, Kansas, to verify employment references that had been backing up. He had been gone a week, and she had been left treading water. In the meantime, Tooney lounged in the county jail, awaiting his preliminary hearing.

Ria fixed herself a cola and stared out the window of the hotel. Although she had developed a grudging respect for Hook, for his work, even for his badgerlike fierceness, she had to face the fact that she had made little progress with her own research.

And there was something about the killings that she could not reconcile, something that did not fit into any of their theories, not with any of their suspects, not with what she knew of murder. If she could only establish a pattern and a motive, then maybe she could narrow it down. But she'd have to do it her way.

The differences between Hook and her were profound, perhaps insurmountable. As a psychologist, she explored, characterized, catalogued, and then remediated dysfunctional behavior. It all came down to therapy, the charge to fix what was broken. Such a mission required the conviction that things should and could be changed. Hook, in contrast, hunted men. He tracked them, subdued them, and locked them up for punishment. Ria suspected that he might also from time to time administer a little justice of his own. And clearly, he cared nothing for establishing underlying cause and effect and even less for rehabilitation.

If Hook had a construct, a set of principles that he followed, he either didn't know them, couldn't express them, or wouldn't. For him, it all boiled down to instinct and some notion that manna stemmed from experience alone. Although perhaps that made sense to him, it failed to reach the standards inherent in forensic psychology, much less for an academic paper. It left her, in fact, holding the proverbial empty bag.

The upshot was that her sole purpose in being there in the first place had come up short and had resulted in a quiet despair and uneasiness, a sense that she not only had failed in making progress but had lost ground.

Still, in the end, they both wanted the same thing when it came to finding the killer, or so Ria told herself.

She sat down at the phone and drummed her fingers on the desk. Picking up the receiver, she called her committee chairman. "It's not working," she said. "The number of cases is limited. The railroad security agent is unwilling or incapable of defining any kind of structure or process. I'm making no progress, and I don't see it changing. What am I to do?"

"Well," he replied. "Time is of the essence if you want your proposal before the committee. If it doesn't come together soon, you'll have to postpone a semester, which would also result in the selection of a new committee, none of which makes things any easier for you or the university."

"I need this," Ria said. "I can't wait another semester."

Silence fell on the other end. "I suppose you could go to the records for your data. It's ex post facto research, and your study will have less significance as a result. Perhaps it's the only choice now. It's your call."

"What records are we talking about?"

"Any repository of criminal-case resolutions, jail records, court records, penal institutions. One could conceivably use mental-institution records. Your population, however, would be restricted to the criminally insane so would have limited general applicability. Getting access to the records would also be more difficult, given you'd be dealing with medical-privacy issues. Your hypothesis would have to be revisited as well, of course."

"I see," she said.

"Keep in mind that the data collection is only the first step. Treatment and analysis are left, not to mention the write-up and oral defense."

"Okay," she said. "Thank you. Let me think this over, and I'll get back with you as soon as I make a decision."

Ria hung up the phone and went to put on her makeup, realizing that she had failed to set it out the night before, a task that she always did with regularity. But then being trapped on runaway stock cars, seeing the mutilated corpses of boys, and pulling impaled bodies off switch-point stands had never been part of her routine before either.

After dressing and making a few notes in her Moleskine, she drove down to Sheriff Holcome's office, finding him at his desk in stocking feet. He was busy polishing his boots, which he had placed atop his desk.

"Oh," he said, looking up. "Sorry. I usually don't have much business on Sundays. Everyone's dumping their troubles on the preacher instead."

"Could I have a word with you?" she asked. "Nonemergency stuff."

"Sure," he said. "Coffee?"

"No, thank you," she said, taking up a chair.

His big toe peeked through the end of his sock as he slipped on his boots. "There, now," he said, settling back. "What is it you need to talk about?"

"I am not so sure that it is clear to you what my purpose in being here is," she said.

The sheriff slid his coffee cup over and looked in it. "Well, local gossip has it that you're some kind of shrink."

"Not exactly," she said. "I'm collecting information for a scientific study. So far, I'm not making much progress."

The sheriff stood, cup in hand, and headed to the coffeepot in the corner. "Hmmm, and Hook Runyon is the one who was to provide you this information?"

"Yes, well, that was the plan."

"No offense, but you're dealing with Hook Runyon," said the sheriff. "If he has any plans, nobody but him and God knows what they are, and I'm not so sure about God."

"Exactly," Ria said. "So I've been thinking of changing my strategy."

"And my office might have something to do with this new strategy?"

She dug through her purse for a stick of gum. "Have one?" she asked.

"Ah, no thanks. Wears me to a frazzle," he said.

"I need access to records, you see, for this change in course, and I'm assuming you maintain some here in your office?"

Holcome sat down and sipped his coffee, wrinkling his nose. "This tastes just like that shoe polish smells," he said. "What kinds of records are we talking about?"

"I'm trying to identify and categorize the theoretical constructs used in the field to resolve criminal cases," Ria said.

"Theoretical what?"

"Constructs. I'm trying to find out how law-enforcement personnel go about solving their cases, from a forensic-psychology point of view."

The sheriff swallowed his coffee and slid the cup to the side.

"Most everybody I know just tries to figure out who done it," he said. "Take Hook. You'd be hard put to find him solving two things in a row the same way. Even if he knew how he did it, he'd not likely say. Just like that Chikaskia thing," he said.

"Chikaskia thing?"

"The track foreman told me Hook went right in that flooded river after that engine crew. Saved their lives too, both of them. I'd bet he ain't said a word to no one about it to this day."

Ria frowned. "Maybe if I had access to your records here, I could deduce certain patterns."

"You'd deduce a decided lack of records," he said. "Now, the folks at the county courthouse in Alva are forever writing stuff down. Maybe you ought to give them a try."

"Well, yes, perhaps so. Thank you for your time, Sheriff." She paused. "I've also been wondering about Deputy Tooney's situation."

"A broken nose and two black eyes," he said. "He'll live, though."

"Was he with your office long?"

"Sure felt like it," he said.

"And was he consistent with his case strategies?"

"Consistently wrong," he said. "I guess his constructs needed some tuning up."

"Were you surprised about the larceny?"

"Tooney groused a lot about his pay, but that's a given in this job," he said. "I'm not that surprised about him stealing, I guess. The temptations are pretty strong."

"And do you suspect him of having something to do with the deaths of those boys?"

Holcome slipped his hands into his back pockets as he considered the question.

"Tooney could shoot with the best of them and was always anxious to show it off," he said. "I can't say we have evidence of any actual killings as a result of this, though his judgment about when to shoot might well be questioned. Comes down to it, I'm not sure he had the balls for killing, if you'll pardon the expression.

"But after being in this job, not much surprises me anymore about what folks will do on any given day. One way or the other, I figure Tooney's pretty much where he deserves to be. There's a good case against Beth Rossen having possession of stolen property and Tooney's connection to her. Other than that, there's not much other to charge him with until there's some sort of concrete evidence tying it all together."

*****

Mixer, lying on the caboose porch, greeted Ria with a wag of his tail. She knelt and rubbed his head. "Hungry?" she asked, opening the door.

Mixer peeked into the caboose, sniffed a couple of times, and then followed her in. She searched the cabinets for dog food, coming up with nothing but canned tuna. She opened a can and poured him some water.

She stepped over Hook's bedding, which still lay strewn on the floor, and heat rose in her neck. She had been impulsive that night, even stupid, but then some things were just worth it and not meant for regrets.

When Mixer had finished his meal, she said, "Come on, boy. Let's close up here."

She shut the caboose door and leaned onto the porch railing as a diesel engine pulled the grade in the distance. The tracks, lit in the last rays of sunset, streaked off toward the Quinlan bridge. "Want to go for a walk, Mixer?" she asked.

Mixer stretched and leaped off the porch. As she headed down the tracks, he circled wide once and then came in to follow at her heels. The evening felt warm, and the smell of creosote drifted on the breeze. A covey of quail exploded from out of the brush nearby, their wings beating the air. Ria jumped, her heart fluttering, as she watched them bank away into the sun.

When the Quinlan bridge came into view, she paused, trying to remember why she had come. Mixer, unhampered by the riprap, descended into the canyon and waited at the bottom for her to follow. She worked her way down, slipping and sliding on the rock. The bridge timbers cast a latticework of evening shadows, and the cottonwoods whispered, a thousand spirits high in the branches above her.

Empty whiskey bottles winked in the sunset, and remnants of makeshift bedding rotted in the mud. Chicken feathers, plumage from past butchering, had drifted and gathered in the surrounding brush. The owl-like symbol that had been carved into the timbers looked down on her with eyes blank as death. She felt the sadness that had lived here, the struggle and despair of lost souls in the dark hours of the night.

She knelt in the dirt where Benjamin Way had fallen, his image burned forever in her memory. And in recalling the indignity and humiliation of his death, she knew in her gut that something monstrous had happened in this place. She looked up into the towering structure of the bridge. For a brief moment, she thought she saw someone climbing high in the structure. But by the time her eyes focused, the image was gone. As Hook had observed, it would be no ordinary man climbing his way to the top of such a bridge, but rather someone with a rare combination of confidence, agility, and skill. But it would also take a sober one.

Could Tooney have butchered Benjamin Way stone-cold sober and then scaled that bridge? Maybe. Maybe not.

Either way, the world was a safer place with his arrest.

Chapter 19

HOOK STEPPED OFF THE train into a foggy morning. He had half expected to see Ria waiting for him on the station platform but then he had arrived earlier than planned. He had exhausted all avenues for chasing down employment references and decided to leave the rest for another go.

Why anyone bothered with employment references escaped him. In his experience, no one admitted to the truth of his past or offered references from anyone who might. An employer found out soon enough what made up a man. Keep him or fire him and move on. Then again, it had been awhile since the big boys had consulted him on hiring practices.

He found Banjo sitting at his desk blowing up a red balloon. Banjo looked up and saw Hook as the air escaped the balloon.

"Hook, will you call Eddie Preston? That bastard's driving me crazy."

"What's with the balloon, Banjo? Birthday celebration?"

"You ever listen to bagpipe music?" Banjo asked.

"Not for long," Hook said.

"Well, they blow up this big bag, see. So I figured to do the same with this here balloon. You don't have to breathe all the time that way 'cause it's already breathed up for you. And it hums, see, like having a band behind you."

Seeing the look on Hook's face, Banjo added, "I don't have it perfected just yet. I tried it with my nose first, but it blew my dentures out. I can't do diddly without my dentures."

Hook scratched his head. "I'm debating whether to run you into the loony bin, Banjo, but I don't think they'd take you."

Banjo's attention was already back on the balloon. "So I figured to use it in my mouth. The plumbing's all hooked up together, no offense, Hook. If one thing don't work, try another, I always say. That's how Thomas Edison got famous, you know."

"Thomas Edison didn't use his nose for a bagpipe, Banjo."

"That's 'cause he didn't think of it."

"Okay, I'll ask. Does it work?"

"You ever hear 'The Star Spangled Banner' played in all flats?"

"I'd as soon be dragged down track by the Super Chief," Hook said.

"No surprise there," huffed Banjo. "None of you bastards got any class, anyway."

Hook rolled his eyes and sat down at the phone. Eddie answered on the second ring. "You called?" Hook asked.

"We got a problem, Runyon."

"I've been talking to Banjo. It couldn't get any worse than that."

"I thought you arrested that Deputy Tooney so he wouldn't be killing nobody else."

"He's in county awaiting trial."

"Well, I got a call from the section foreman south of Kiowa. He says there's a foot on the tracks."

Hook looked over at Banjo, who had blown his balloon up to the size of a basketball.

"What did you say, Eddie?"

"There's a foot on the tracks, a human foot. What the hell you trying to do over there, bump off the entire population of Oklahoma?"

"Well, that just can't be," Hook said. "Tooney's bail was more than ten thousand dollars."

"The foreman says that foot's still got a tan saddle shoe on it, with a hole in the bottom."

"For the love of Mike," Hook said. "Look, that's Kiowa, and it's Ludie Bean's run. I'm wore out from chasing down references, Eddie."

"South of Kiowa ain't Ludie's run. It's your run."

"Do I get overtime?"

"The newspapers are picking up on all these killings. I've got officials lined up out my door like penguins. The section foreman will meet you at the Kiowa depot with a popcar. I want this cleaned up and fast, Runyon."

"And how am I supposed to get to Kiowa?"

"Any way you can."

✳✳✳✳✳

Hook knocked on Ria's door and waited. The door opened a crack, just far enough for Hook to see she was still in her pajamas.

"Hook?" she said, rubbing the sleep from her eyes. "Are you okay?"

"Did I wake you?"

"What's going on?" she asked, one hand clutching the top of her pajamas as if a button had recently failed her.

"I thought you might give me a lift over to Kiowa," he said.

"Well, sure. I guess I could. Come on in. Is it an emergency?"

"The section foreman found a foot," he said.

"A what?"

". . . with a shoe on it, and with a hole in the bottom. I swear, drunks would rather sleep on railroad tracks than in a feather bed."

"A foot?"

Hook shrugged. "I thought you might want to go along—it's not too far, a little something to spice up your research."

"Come in," she said. "I'll get dressed."

By the time they got started, the sun had climbed well above the eastern red cedars. Ria pulled over at a café and waited for Hook to bring back coffee. He handed her a cup through the window before getting into the car. She sipped her coffee. "Picking up a foot. What a way to start the day."

" 'Boes are forever grabbing onto an open car door and then not having the wherewithal to heft in. First thing they know, they're lying on both sides of the rail. There's a good chance the engineer didn't even know he'd ruined that 'bo's day."

As they pulled onto the highway, they both fell silent. The morning sun lifted into the sky. Ria drained the last of her coffee and handed Hook the empty cup.

"I've been meaning to ask," she said.

Hook glanced over. "About what?"

"About that Chikaskia River thing. I heard you saved the train crew from drowning."

"Engineers are like cats," he said. "Put one in the water, and he'll climb straight up your arm."

She waited for him to say more. When he didn't, she said, "I called my adviser."

"How's he doing?"

"He's fine, Hook, but that's not the point."

"What is the point?"

"I'm thinking of changing the focus of my research."

Hook rolled down his window and let the wind fill the car. "Like I told you, there's nothing much to gain by following me around all day. Did you feed Mixer?"

"My adviser says I can use records instead, like the courthouse records in Alva."

"Mixer usually doesn't talk that much, good morning or good night once in awhile is about it."

"Hook, are you even listening?"

"The courthouse would be the best bet," he said. "If they go to the bathroom up there, they have it notarized."

Arriving at the depot, Ria turned into the parking lot and waited for Hook to go in. In short order, he returned. "The section foreman's got a popcar waiting. He says it's all right for you to come along."

Ria followed him to the back of the depot and aboard the popcar. She introduced herself to the foreman, who nodded to her before pulling off. Soon they were clacking their way through a wheat field. No one tried to talk above the motor.

When the popcar finally coasted to a stop, the foreman said, "The work train's sided about a quarter mile up ahead. But this is where the tie dumper spotted the foot. Scared the hell out of the guy. He backed off the flatcar and damn near killed himself."

"A severed foot's been known to have that effect on a man," Hook said.

"It looked like it just got whacked off to me," the foreman said. "Gives me the belly creeps to think about it."

"Have any idea where the rest of the owner of that shoe is?"

"That foot could have come in on a cowcatcher from Tucumcari for all I know. Thought once to just forget the whole thing but decided you needed the work."

"Appreciate that," Hook said. "What did you do with it, the shoe, I mean?"

"Put it in a nail keg so the critters wouldn't get to it."

"Don't give it away or nothing," Hook said.

"Well, damn, and I was thinking to take it home to the wife," he said.

"We'll walk the line and be on up in awhile."

Hook and Ria waited until the popcar had disappeared down track before they started walking. Ria took one side of the tracks and Hook the other. The sun bore down, and heat waves shimmered up from the rails. Ria stopped and scanned the area.

"Exactly what are we looking for?" she asked.

"A man with no foot," he said. "And he's likely to be out of sorts."

She rolled her eyes. "Why did I even ask?" she said.

They had gone only a few hundred yards more when Hook pulled up and craned his neck, looking to his right.

"There's a concrete culvert down there," he said. "We better take a look."

Willows covered much of the swampy ground, and wild grapevines threaded through the limbs. The culvert, large enough to stand up in, covered an active creek, which trickled down the center and gathered in a small pool at the opening. Cool air bled from the culvert and smelled mossy and dank.

Hook jumped over the creek and extended a hand to help Ria across. Inside the culvert, he paused to let his eyes adjust to the darkness. They worked their way through and were nearly to the other end when Hook stopped. Sunlight shot through the branches of the trees, its mottled light illuminating the area. Hook pointed to a "U" scratched in charcoal on the wall. "A jungle," he said, his voice echoing in the culvert. "Safe haven for sleeping, according to a previous tenant."

"And right there," said Ria, pointing a little higher, "Is that an owl? Like the one we saw on the Quinlan bridge?"

Hook squinted. "That's a stretch in my way of thinking. Could just as easy be an 'M' or a couple of triangles. Hard to say."

The scene revealed itself slowly: an old frying pan in the dirt near one of the pillars, an empty whiskey bottle captured in the mud, like a fly in amber. A bindle stick propped against the wall.

"Over there," Hook said, pointing to the ashes of a cold camp. "Looks like we found our man, or what's left of him, at least."

Chapter 20

FLIES LIFTED OFF THE BODY in a buzz as Hook approached. Brain matter had spewed from a one-inch hole punched through the back of the skull. The arms, crossed at the wrists, suggested a casketlike pose. The torso had been opened and the victim's testicles placed inside the cavity. The legs, neither bearing a foot, had been primly arranged in tandem.

Ria covered her mouth and pointed to the culvert exit where a severed foot inside an old shoe lay half-buried in the mud.

"Critters," Hook said.

Ria steadied herself with deep breaths. "I wonder who he was."

"A 'bo, I figure," he said. "That's probably his bindle stick over there."

Ria leaned against the culvert wall while Hook loosened the cloth from the stick and dumped the contents: matches, wool socks, a tobacco sack with two one-dollar bills rolled up inside.

"His road stake," he said. "For emergencies." Hook knelt and studied one of the man's hands, old fingers knotted with arthritis. "He's missing a ring too, by the looks of it. See the white skin on his ring finger where the sun couldn't reach? But why not take the money?"

Ria shuddered. "I don't think it's about money; haven't since the first boy. And we know it wasn't Tooney. Maybe bridge trolls do exist."

Hook studied her in the dim light of the culvert. "I wasn't serious about that troll business, Ria. I don't much believe in fairy tales, nor do I believe a man kills without a reason."

"Fairy tales are usually based in reality, Hook," Ria said. She took out her handkerchief and covered her nose against the stench. "These body parts have been rearranged as well. But why? It's like the body has been dismembered and then reassembled, like it's been transformed into a different being."

"It's a mighty poor attempt at resurrection if you ask me," Hook said.

Ria walked to the culvert opening and breathed in the warm air. She turned.

"I don't know the reason," she said. "Maybe neither does the killer."

*****

"I'll be damned," the section foreman said. "The rest of him is in that culvert?"

"In a fashion," Hook said. "I'd like to talk to your men. Maybe they know something or seen something that could give us a lead."

"No problem, but you better get after it," the foreman said. "It's payday, and they won't be sober long. Some of these boys come out of El Paso, and they ain't much for conversation on the best of days. That don't get better with money in their pocket."

"Some say the company took on scabs down that way, what with the union strike and all," Hook said.

The foreman shrugged. "I wouldn't know nothing about that. All I know is these boys can drive spikes, and that's what we get paid to do."

Hook and Ria walked down to the flatcars where the men were laying track. Two spike drivers worked opposite sides of the rail, their elbows held close to their bodies, the snap of their wrists like the crack of a whip as they sunk cut spikes with machinelike precision.

The man who faced Hook, a powerful figure with rippling muscles, stepped back and wiped the sweat from his face with his bandanna. He was dark, black hair but with blue eyes, a half-breed maybe by the looks of him. He propped the spike maul over his shoulder, a sledge with double working heads no larger than fifty-cent pieces. He locked his eyes on Ria. Ria slipped her hand into Hook's.

"Have a minute?" Hook asked the second man.

"You got business, see the foreman," he said.

"I'm the railroad bull," Hook said.

"Congratulations."

"I need a little information."

The man looked up through thick brows. "The only one has time for talking around here is the foreman." He paused. "And you."

"Anything unusual going on around here?" Hook asked.

"Working track ain't all that unusual," the man said.

"We just found a dead man under that culvert back there," Hook said. "Thought one of you might have seen something."

"Saw a foot," the big man said. "Maybe an arm will turn up before the day's out."

"Let me know if it does," Hook said. "I could use one."

The man's expression remained unchanged as he turned back to his work. The dark one was still eyeing Ria, and he paused for the longest moment before lifting his maul. The sound of steel against steel rang out in the heat as he drove the spike deep into the tie.

"Not so friendly, is he?" Ria said to Hook as they walked away.

"Hammermen ain't known for their winning ways," Hook said. "Comes from driving cut spikes day in and day out in a summer heat so hot it could fry an egg."

While Hook interviewed a few of the other men, Ria waited in the pop-car. Having turned up nothing, Hook searched out the foreman.

"Maybe you can run us back?" Hook said.

"What about that foot?"

"Keep it cold and under wraps until this gets investigated by the locals. That fella in the culvert's going to need it back."

*****

They found Ludie Bean reading a magazine in the waiting room of the depot on their return.

"Runyon," he said, looking up. "Figured you'd be along sooner or later. I hear you drummed up a little business."

"Another three miles north, and the case would have been yours," Hook said.

Ludie stood, took out his handkerchief, and ran it over his bald head. There were mustard stains on his shirt, and he smelled of fried onions. Whiskers sprouted from the deep cracks in his huge neck, and the tufts of hair in his ears curled back on itself like wire springs.

"Eddie Preston says some extra body parts turned up out there," Ludie said.

"The rest of him is in a culvert. All the pieces are accounted for now."

"Probably a bindle stiff eating his own kind," Ludie said.

Stepping past Ludie, Hook opened the door for Ria and waited as she went out to the car.

"You been having any particular troubles, Ludie—'bo or otherwise?"

"Minister in Kiowa complained that a traveling preacher had showed up and was baptizing all the women, so to speak. Said the man was holding services down on Main Street and collecting tithes. Complained it was cutting into his own collections. Time I got there, the man was gone. The reverend apparently don't stay in one place for long.

"Gathered up a couple Yankees riding on the tail of a hotshot this week. Drove 'em out to the water tower and let them go. Told 'em to catch the next train north."

"That's an abandoned line, Ludie."

"That so?"

Hook turned to leave. "You ever hear of bridge trolls, Ludie?"

"There ain't no bridge tolls in Kansas, Runyon. Everyone knows that."

"Right," Hook said. "Have a nice day, Ludie."

*****

With the report to the locals finished, Hook and Ria drove back in the dark. Hook could see Ria's face in the dash lights. She had been quiet and somber the whole trip home. Hook regretted what she had experienced that day. Some things were better left unseen to keep them from being forever burned into one's memory.

140

Ria pulled up to Hook's caboose and shut off the engine. The motor creaked against the cool of the evening. Stars rode through the night and crowned the trees.

Hook started to get out and then hesitated.

"Sometimes I don't listen like I should," he said.

She turned. "Excuse me?"

"My shortcuts get taken for rudeness. You got something to say, I'd like to hear it."

She pulled a knee onto the seat and leaned back against the door, situating herself so that she faced Hook.

"There's something sinister going on here, Hook. I went back to the Quinlan bridge again, and I asked myself what would it take for me to attack a person in the dead of night, execute him, and then mutilate his body? What would it take for me to eviscerate him and then degrade him in such a way?"

"And what was your answer?" he asked.

"Insanity. I'd have to believe that I was no ordinary man, that I had been put on this earth to reign supreme and thus could do no wrong because of that supremacy, that I was somehow above everyone else."

Hook considered what she'd said. "It's not so hard to reign supreme over 'boes, Ria. For the most, they are men on the bottom rung starting out."

"They might only be in the wrong place at the wrong time," she said. "The killer might be an opportunist, but he also is as dangerous as any man who believes he is invincible. History has proved again and again that those are the ones capable of the most inhumane acts."

"Don't know much about history, but I've run up against a few arrogant men in my day. Don't see what that proves," Hook said.

Ria refused to be distracted. "Remorse doesn't exist for the men I'm talking about, and if I'm remembering the research correctly, usually they are someone who has been degraded and dehumanized themselves at some point in their lives."

"And so they pass it on to the next one coming up?" Hook said. "Keep it in the family, so to say."

"Exactly. The thing is they can sometimes have winning personalities. They can be charming even. They use their charm to gain whatever it is they want."

"You're thinking this bridge-troll fella is such a character?"

He could see her jaw set.

"It's possible," she said. "This guy might not even look or behave like a criminal, you know."

She clenched her fingers together and leaned forward. "And the scary part: He'll likely gain more confidence with each success. It won't be enough to just kill. He'll want to share it, to prove how shrewd and powerful he is. He'll want to relive it, to rekindle the memory of the pain and suffering that he is capable of inflicting."

Hook watched her through the darkness, her eyes ablaze with intensity. "And that's when he's likely to make his mistake?" he said.

She nodded. "Confidence turns to a feeling of invulnerability, of being so superior he's untouchable—so he gets more brazen and more taunting with each kill. And then, if the world is lucky, he gets careless."

Hook studied the full moon through the window. It rose big as a melon in the sky. He tapped his prosthesis on the dash.

"And this is what is known as a theoretical construct?"

"Yes."

"Notions is what I call them."

"Same thing with a different name."

"Then here's my notion: The victims are 'boes. They are being killed in hobo jungles, places not easily gotten to except by train. Our man has a pretty good knowledge of the rails, knowledge that comes only through firsthand experience and lots of it. He's either got to be very stealthy or his victims don't fear him or suspect him from the outset. He could be both, for all I know. And the final notion I have is that a man who knows he's likely to die if he's caught is going to put up a hell of a fight. That makes him dangerous to anyone who gets in his way."

"So where does that leave your investigation?" Ria said.

"He could be a bindle stiff, a 'bo preying on his own kind. In a way, 'boes consider themselves to be part of a larger family, and nothing can be more dangerous than family because you don't figure family to come in and kill you. What you don't suspect, you can't prepare for."

They sat in silence for some time. Finally, Ria said, "I'll be going to the courthouse tomorrow to see if I can get access to their records. I guess you're on your own. You think you can manage without me?"

"Where do you go from there?" Hook asked.

"It shouldn't take long to gather the data. I'll be heading back to the university to finish my work after that."

Hook got out and leaned back in the window. "You've a good head on your shoulders, Ria, and you're pretty damn tough too. I have a notion you'll be doing just fine in the future."

She started the car. "Hook," she said, dropping the shift into reverse. "Tell Mixer good-bye for me, will you? I'm going to miss him too."

Chapter 21

THE KNOCK ON THE CABOOSE DOOR sat Hook upright, causing him to hit his head on the table. "Damn," he said. "Who is it?"

"Big Al. How about letting me in before this mangy animal eats me alive?"

Hook opened the door to find the section foreman squared off against Mixer, who had his teeth bared. "Get on out of here, Mixer," Hook said.

Mixer slinked to the caboose steps, looked over his shoulder at Big Al, and lifted his leg on the porch railing. Hook pushed the hair back from his eyes and peered through the glare of the morning sun.

"Come on in. I was just cleaning up."

"What the hell is an African hyena doing on a caboose, anyway?" Big Al asked.

"That's a tracking dog," Hook said. "He tracks up my caboose damn near every day."

Big Al watched Mixer loping off across the countryside. "That hyena's lived with you too long, Hook. Picked up some of your ways."

"Mixer's got a sensitive nature, 'cept when it comes to cats and foremen."

Big Al stepped over Hook's pallet and sat down at the table.

Hook searched out his prosthesis and put it on. "Coffee?"

"Bad stomach," Big Al said. "Say, someone stole my gloves. Thing is, they only took one of 'em. I swear, you can't trust nobody nowadays. You ain't seen it, have you?"

Hook pulled at his chin. "Not that I remember, but I haven't been looking that hard, either."

"Damn, Hook, you sleeping on the floor?"

"Sleeping on the floor can be more exciting than you might think."

"And what's with all these books?"

"I collect them," Hook said.

"What the hell for?"

"It's complicated," Hook said.

"I ain't read a book since third grade. Didn't care much for that one."

"What brings you here, Big Al?"

"Eddie Preston called," he said, taking out a cigarette.

"Mind not smoking in the caboose? Smells up my books. I've given it up altogether, so I reckon you can postpone it five minutes."

Big Al frowned and put his cigarette back in the pack. "Nothing holier than a convert, is there? You give up liquor too?"

"Liquor can be enlightening, taken in moderation," Hook said.

"Moderation isn't the word comes to mind, Hook."

"What can I do for you or are you just here to criticize my lifestyle?"

"I got a call from Eddie Preston. Not like I ain't got enough to do. He wants you to contact him right away."

"And why would that be?"

"Appears a cattle rancher spotted a dead man sitting under the Pecos River bridge over to Fort Sumner, New Mexico."

"Damn," Hook said, pulling on his britches. "What's it been, fifteen minutes since the last body?"

"He wants you to get on down there pronto before the locals get called and they start nosing around."

"Can you take me in to the depot?"

"Suppose so. I'm headed into town now to pick up supplies."

"I might need a ride back too, if you don't mind. I'm getting too old for hopping trains."

*****

The look of the sun promised a hot day as Hook climbed into the passenger's side of Big Al's truck. He rolled down the window and caught the sound of a switch engine backing cars onto the siding in the distance. Big Al pulled onto the narrow road leading to the highway. The smell of dust lifted from the wheels filled the cab. Big Al took a cigarette out of the pack and reached for his matches.

"You couldn't wait on that?" Hook said.

"Hell, Hook, I don't see no books around now."

"Smoke gives me a headache."

"I don't like to bring it up, Hook, but this is my truck. You're just a guest rider."

"Well, then, just smoke away," Hook said. "Though some might consider it to be a display of a lack of character."

Big Al slid the cigarette back into the package. "Far be it from me to press my bad character on anyone else," he said.

"So how did they happen to find this body?" Hook asked.

"Eddie said the rancher came upon it while building a fence. Said at first he thought it was someone watching him from under the bridge. But when he got closer, he could see the body was leaned up against a concrete abutment. Said it looked like he'd been cut up or some such. So he calls Eddie, and Eddie calls me. And I'm left giving you a ride without my smokes."

"If you recall, that's a girder bridge down there. The rancher said it scared him so bad he lit out like a flushed roadrunner and forgot which way was home."

"It's not dead men who are dangerous," Hook said.

Big Al negotiated a curve and stuck his unlit match in the corner of his mouth. "I ever tell you the story about ol' Fred Becker?"

Hook steeled himself. "I've the feeling I'm about to be able to say yes."

Big Al wheeled out onto the highway and brought his rig up to speed. "Well, sir, one time Fred Becker's cows get out upriver about three mile from here, so he takes off tracking them. The tracks lead out onto the riverbed and then disappear."

"How can a herd of cow tracks just disappear?"

"Well, that's the way it was told to me," Big Al said. "Anyway, Fred walks on a bit farther to get a good look up and down the river. Damned if he doesn't step right into a quicksand bog and sink clean up to his crotch. Every time he tries to extricate himself, he sinks a little deeper."

"You saying a whole herd of cows was lost in that bog? For gosh sakes, Al, who's going to believe that?"

"Just listen to the damn story, Hook. Maybe you'll learn something.

"So when Fred doesn't come home for dinner, his wife gets the neighbor men, and they go looking for him. Well, they find him all right, but by now he's sunk up to his waist.

"They try to pull him out, but he's sucked in so tight they can't budge him. So they go back for Fred's saddle horse. When they get back to the river, Fred's sunk clean up to his armpits. They tie a rope on him and loop it over the saddle horn of his horse, but every time the horse pulls, Fred screams that they're tearing him in two."

Hook rolled his eyes. "All right, so what did they do?"

"Nothing they could do. Pretty soon Fred's sunk to his neck. He asks for something to eat, but all they have is some stale corn bread, which he refuses, saying he's had all the corn bread he ever intends to eat in this life. Just before he goes under, he asks for one last thing in this world."

Hook looked over at Big Al. "What?"

"A cigarette."

"Damn it," Hook said. "Just smoke, will you? I'd rather have a headache than listen to another story like that one."

*****

Banjo looked up from his typewriter as Hook came into the depot. One of his eyes sported a half-moon bruise the color of green copper under it.

"What the hell happened to you?" Hook asked.

Banjo pulled the paper from his typewriter and tossed it into the trash can. "A number of things happened, now that you mention it, including a railroad bull poking around in my business."

Hook took up a chair. "Kind of testy this morning, aren't you?"

Banjo hung his head. "That bagpipe idea didn't work out so well," he said. "It gets dang monotonous playing nothing but flats all the time."

"That doesn't explain the black eye, Banjo."

"So I figured to make harmonica music instead, given my range of talents, just up notes and down notes, you know, sucking and blowing."

Hook lifted a brow. "The black eye?"

"So I chose 'Red River Valley,' being it's an old harmonica standby. Turns out there's a considerable amount of sucking and blowing required in its playing."

"Let's get to the black eye, Banjo."

"All of a sudden I just fell over like I'd had a stroke. Hit my head on the desk and knocked me out cold. Damn near ran two freighters together before I woke up."

"You must of hyperventilated."

"Hyperwhat?"

"Hyperventilated."

"No, I just passed out from too much sucking and blowing. You ain't going to tell anyone, are you, Hook? I could lose my job."

"Who would believe me?" Hook said, picking up the phone and dialing Eddie Preston's number.

"Security," a voice said.

"Eddie, this is Hook."

"Hook Runyon?"

"Yeah, that one."

"We got another body, Runyon. What the hell is going on over there?"

"Big Al filled me in, Eddie. I'm on it."

"For Pete's sake, how many dead men does that make?"

"Depends on whether you count me or not," Hook said.

"Counting dead men ain't funny, Runyon. The newspapers have me bent over the baggage cart, and now their saying as how the bridge troll is killing folks, screaming as how passengers aren't riding the train for fear of being dragged under a bridge and cut up by the troll."

"Troll? Where did they come up with that?"

"I'm told a newspaper up Wichita way thought it made for a clever headline. Now it's above the fold on every paper from here to Abilene. Why does that surprise you? It's like anything on the railroad: A bloody bulletin board set up next to the time clock. Anyway, they got it, and they're damn sure using it. These killings have got to stop, and that's your job, Runyon."

"Look, Eddie, I have an idea these killings are by someone on the inside," Hook said.

"Inside of what?"

"Inside of the hobo community."

"Hoboes don't have no community or nothing else for that matter."

"Hoboes have their ways, Eddie, and whoever is killing these guys knows what they are."

"So what's your point?"

Hook searched a lemon drop out of his pocket and blew the lint off. He had been using them to stave off nicotine attacks, but so far, they had done little more than make his tongue sore. "I'm thinking I might move into the jungles for a while."

"You want time off, clock out on vacation, Runyon. I can't have you laying up in hobo jungles and drawing a salary at the same time."

"You want this troll thing stopped, don't you, Eddie?"

There was silence on the other end of the line. "How long?"

"I can't know for sure."

"What about your other duties?"

"Pry Ludie Bean off his ass. It wouldn't hurt him to pick up some slack around here for a change."

Hook could hear Eddie breathing. "First, you get down to Fort Sumner and get that wrapped up. And keep it out of the papers, you hear? I don't want no more troll stuff in the papers."

"I'm catching the next train out," Hook said.

"I'm thinking I'm making a big mistake here. You check in, and don't be destroying no railroad property."

"Right, Eddie. Maybe Ludie can finish up those employee reference checks in the meantime?"

"We'll see," Eddie said. "And don't set no pasture fires."

"Right, Eddie. Thanks for your concern about my welfare."

As Hook hung up the phone, Banjo looked up from his typewriter. "What's a troll, Hook?"

"They live under bridges, lure people in, and then kill them."

"Do they ever come into depots?"

"Only if they hear harmonica music."

"What do they look like?"

"You can smell them before you see them."

"Hell, that could be about anyone works on the section gang, Hook."

"Exactly. You got anything headed to New Mexico?"

Banjo checked the board. "Frenchy's deadheading to Roswell to pick up one of them salvage engines."

"What time?"

He checked the board again. "Should be coming through about nine."

"Can you get word to him to stop at the Quinlan spur? I need a hitch." He paused. "Would you give Eddie Preston a call and have him arrange some kind of transportation for me out of Clovis?"

"I'd as soon eat a light bulb as call Eddie Preston, Hook."

"You might be getting a package from me, Banjo. Just put it someplace until I get back."

"Where you going, Hook?"

"Back to the past."

"What if you don't come back?"

"Then open the package. Damn, Banjo, I'm glad you didn't go into brain surgery."

"Hook?"

"Yes, Banjo."

"What if that troll comes here?"

"Play your harmonica."

*****

With enough time left before Big Al was to arrive, Hook walked to the Eastman Hotel and checked the parking lot for Ria's car. Not seeing it, he went inside and found the clerk busy reading the morning paper.

"Could you tell me if Miss Ria Wolfe is in?" he asked.

"She left early this morning," the clerk said.

"Did she check out?"

The clerk folded his paper and laid it aside. "Who wants to know?"

Hook took out his badge. "Official business," he said.

The clerk rose and checked the register. "The room is still booked," he said. "Message?"

"Thanks, no," Hook said.

*****

Big Al, having decided to eat first, did not get Hook back to the caboose until late.

Hook said, "I'm gone for a few days. Maybe you could feed Mixer for me? I'll leave the door unlocked."

"How the hell do I get close enough to feed that killer dog?"

"Mixer loves anyone who feeds him, even foremen," Hook said.

"Like me to polish your shoes too while you're gone?"

"That's not necessary, but it wouldn't hurt to tidy up a bit," Hook said, climbing out.

After Big Al had pulled away, Hook laid out a small travel bag. In it, he put a railroad-systems map, one pair of old overalls, work boots, heavy coat, pocketknife, and a tin of matches. He folded two dollars under the liner in his boot for emergencies. Keeping everything to a minimum was a must, weight being the biggest enemy of all when bumming the rails.

He checked his watch. Frenchy should be coming in any time now. After setting out food for Mixer, he made his way to the tracks. The night was calm, windless, a rarity in those parts.

When Frenchy's glimmer broke down track, Hook's spine tingled a little. Freedom lay ahead, and the likelihood of danger as well. The beat of the engine struck the tempo for his heart, and in that moment, he knew no man could be more alive.

Chapter 22

FRENCHY EASED THE STEAMER to a stop, the cars clicking down her length like a row of dominoes. Steam shot from her belly and drifted off. Frenchy stuck his head out of the cab and pushed back his hat, displaying a streak of grime across his forehead.

"Is this a holdup, 'cause if it is, you're damn sure out of luck. There ain't twenty-five cents between me and starvation. The bakehead here has even less."

"If I was to hold up a train, it damn sure wouldn't be this old teapot," Hook said.

"You don't have that dang dog with you, do you?"

"He's more particular who he rides with," Hook said.

"Well, climb aboard then," Frenchy said.

Hook found a place to sit behind the bakehead and settled back. Frenchy brought her up and eased out the slack.

"Where you going, Hook?" he asked. "Or is it one of them need-to-know security secrets?"

"If it was a secret, I damn sure wouldn't be telling an engineer," Hook said. "I'm going to Clovis and then on to Fort Sumner."

"What the hell's at Fort Sumner?" Frenchy asked.

"A dead man, if you gotta know."

"Hell," Frenchy said. "If you're looking for a dead man, he's sitting right there in the fireman's seat. Save you a trip all the way to Clovis."

"I was hoping for one looked a little better," Hook said.

The fireman shook his head and turned to his gauges.

"I've been hearing about this bridge troll killer," Frenchy said. "They say he cuts off the heads of 'boes and rolls them down the track."

"It's an exaggeration," Hook said. "He doesn't roll them down the track."

"What does he do, then?"

"Much as I'd like to, I can't be gossiping about such details with railroad employees. Security is involved. Things get out, and pretty soon you got the public up in arms."

"Maybe you ought be riding the Super Chief instead of this here bullgine, you know, where you can get the proper respect required of someone of your position."

"Tell it to Eddie Preston. He's got the notion that me taking up a seat on the Super Chief might threaten to put the entire railroad into bankruptcy," Hook said.

Frenchy took out a cigar and wet it down.

"You going to smoke that stinking thing?" Hook asked.

"Why, no, I was just figuring on licking it all the way to Clovis."

"Smoking can make a man impotent, you know," Hook said.

Frenchy lit the end, blew a puff of smoke into the air, and watched it drift over Hook's head. "Can it melt iron? Speaking of which, I hear you been running with a new sweetie pie."

Hook moved closer to the window to escape the smoke. "I've been studying up on forensic psychology, if that's what you mean."

"Forensic psychology? The hell you say!"

"That's right, the latest theoretical constructs."

"What kinds of constructs you been studying, Hook, or is that one of them security secrets too?"

"About deviants, mostly."

"Deviant what?"

"You know, like boys who want to sleep with their mamas or kill people because they keep thinking about it even when they don't want to."

Frenchy gave him a funny look over the top of his cigar. "That's the dirtiest thing I ever heard, Hook. I don't know how you sleep nights."

Hook leaned back and dropped his hat over his eyes. "I sleep like an angel. Give me a shout when we get to Clovis, Frenchy. A crime fighter needs his rest."

*****

Hook found an old section truck, newly equipped with a two-way radio, waiting on him at the Clovis depot. The late noon sun cut through the windshield as he headed out for the Fort Sumner bridge. Once there, he pulled onto the right-of-way and bumped his way up to the floodplain. The bridge span stretched a quarter mile before coming to the river proper. Concrete abutments held up the iron spans and provided excellent windbreaks for cattle and hoboes alike.

He smelled the body before spotting it leaning against the abutment as if in rest. And as he approached, Hook could see a puncture wound in the back of the head, which had no doubt killed the man instantly. Pink fluid still leaked from the hole. His chest had been hacked open and his testicles placed inside the cavity like a holiday centerpiece. There was dirt on the victim's knees as if he'd been praying or begging for mercy.

Hook took a deep breath before retrieving the wallet from the man's pocket. He found no identification, but hidden behind the flap was a single dollar bill. Stuck in the plastic photo insert were the remains of a torn photo of what appeared to be a little girl's legs with white shoes on her feet.

Hook stepped away and turned his face into the breeze to clear his head before circling the area in search of tracks. He found two sets where the struggle had ensued but could see only one set in and none out.

A broken cup lay on its side next to the campfire where the struggle appeared to have been at its height. Hook figured the 'bo, like the other victims, had been taken by surprise. The last thing the poor bastard had expected was a visit from the local troll.

Hook squatted by the campfire and studied it, a small fire built right and with extra firewood for the night. A search of the abutments turned up the safe-haven symbol "U," and next to it, drawn in red Crayola, was an easily recognizable owl with its head cocked. Its steely eyes looked back at him.

Hook paused and scanned the scene, imagining himself first as the victim and then as the killer. How would he have stalked without being seen and hit without warning? Perhaps the killer came in on a train, secured himself atop one of the abutments, and then struck his unsuspecting victim. After cutting the corpse into serving size, the killer could have climbed back the same way for a hop out. That would, however, take someone who knew a bit about trains to pull it off.

Maybe Ria had it pegged. This troll, or whatever the hell he was, had once again showed no mercy and no obvious motive. He had put into action what only a sick mind could concoct. To make matters worse, he had hid in the open and lived among his victims, which made him a killer of the most sinister ilk, to Hook's way of thinking.

*****

After reporting the killing to the local police, Hook followed the law back out to the scene, where they took charge of the body and assumed the investigation. One of the cops circled the body, loaded his jaw with tobacco, and shrugged.

"You gonna question the rancher what stirred this up?" he asked.

"I'll leave the rancher to you," Hook said. "I figure he didn't see more than me, anyway."

"Well, one dead hobo more or less, no big loss," the cop said, spitting.

Before Hook could take offense, the cop said, "I'll run this through the usual channels."

That evening Hook bought a couple of smoked hocks, wrapped them in newspaper, and tucked them into his coat pocket. After that, he located a cardboard box in the baggage room at the depot and took it into the bathroom, where he changed his clothes for the overalls. Next, he studied the railroad-systems map, placing an "X" on every hobo jungle that he knew to exist along the line. He took out his billfold and badge and dropped them into the box along with the other items. He checked the ammo in his P38 clip and put his pocketknife in his pocket. He took the box to the operator and asked that it be sent back to Banjo on the eastbound.

In the dark, he walked to the edge of town to where the steep grade and crossing limit slowed even the most ardent hotshots. He moved into the weeds that grew in abundance along the right-of-way to wait. Without his badge, he had been freed from constrictions and responsibilities but had also been stripped of power and security.

The night darkened as he waited, and mosquitoes whined in his ears. The sound of the train broke in the far distance, its rumble gathering inside him as it charged through the night. When its light popped onto the horizon, his heart thumped, and blood coursed through his veins.

The engine glimmer grew bright as day, and the train roared by, the ground quaking under his feet. He ran to the track and set his pace to avoid being yanked out of his shoes by the train's momentum.

A quick look over his shoulder confirmed a grain hopper coming downline. Breaking into a dead run, he latched onto the grab iron as she came by and hauled himself aboard. He worked his way over the wheel truck and crouched in the shadows.

The train gathered speed as it moved into open country; soon they had to lay by for a Santa Fe work train coming down the high iron. Hook recognized one of the men sitting on the rear flatcar as the big spike driver he and Ria had seen outside Wellington that day. Railroaders were like a community all stretched out in a single line across country. Many was the time he had met the same man doing the same job two weeks later two thousand miles downline.

As the train drove windward, Hook pulled his coat up against the chill. The clack of the wheels beat like a metronome, and the wind whipped his hair, bringing tears to his eyes as he raced pell-mell into his past.

Chapter 23

RIA PULLED UP TO THE county courthouse and shut off the engine. After checking with the court clerk, who had to check with the county judge, she was given access to the court records.

After three hours of digging through the proceedings, it became clear that what she needed was not to be found. If she had wanted to know what went on with lawyers and the mendacity of the judicial system, it would have been a gold mine. Unfortunately, what she wanted, the inner thought processes of those directly involved in crime resolution, was nowhere to be found.

In a last-ditch effort to find something, anything, she visited the county sheriff's office in the basement of the courthouse, where she was advised that the only records they maintained were dispatch calls. In the end, she discovered nothing that would be useful for her research. On the chance that she had overlooked something, she went back to the department after the evening shift had come on. The dispatch, a youngish girl, Betty, of twenty-five or so, told her that a police blotter of each shift was maintained. Ria asked if they could talk privately, perhaps lunch, and they agreed to meet at the Fairmount.

Ria took the time in between to window-shop and then spent the last hour in the library reading magazines. Betty was sitting in the end booth having a cup of coffee when Ria arrived. She was pretty, in a tomboyish sort of way, and tanned from summer sun.

"May I order you something?" Ria asked, sliding into the booth.

"No, thanks. I haven't much time."

"Well, as I explained at the station, I'm working on some research for my degree in forensic psychology. In a word, I'm interested in the strategies police use in solving criminal cases."

Betty sipped her coffee and looked at Ria through the steam. "Cops are funny that way," she said. "I sometimes think they don't want anyone to know how disorganized things are."

"You thought you might be able to help me?"

"Maybe," she said. "I maybe could arrange for you to see the blotter. It's nothing official, really—the local newspaper uses it all the time."

"That would be greatly appreciated. I'm hoping it will turn up something that will help me finish my research so I can graduate."

Betty added a teaspoon of sugar to her cup.

"Well, I never went to college myself. Thing is, if someone were to find out about this, I'm not sure . . ."

"I can guarantee anonymity. I'll be using raw data for the analysis, and there's no need for any kind of names or such to be included."

"Well," Betty said. "Could you come back, then?"

"Sure."

"It's just little stuff, you know," Betty said. "Notes on times and calls and stuff like that."

"I'll get back with you, then. And thanks, Betty."

*****

That night, Ria sat in the parking lot of the Eastman for some time before going in, long enough to watch the first sprinkles of a storm run down the windshield. She was not convinced, even with Betty's help, that she could find the data she needed for her study. Anecdotal information did not hold much sway in the academic world. Perhaps it was time to call it off and go home. In the end, what could another semester or two matter?

160

She shook off the self-doubt and steeled herself for what lay ahead. Inside, the clerk motioned to her from the office. "Miss Wolfe," he said.

"Yes."

"There was a man here earlier looking for you."

"Oh? Do you know who?"

"A one-armed guy," he said.

"Thanks," she said.

She paused at the bottom of the stairs and then turned back for the car. As she drove toward the Quinlan spur, the rain deepened, and puddles gathered in the road ahead of her, mud spraying onto the windshield.

She pulled up to the caboose and shut off the engine. Lightning lit the windows of the caboose, and thunder rumbled as an afterthought. Slipping on her coat, she climbed the caboose ladder and knocked on the door. No answer. She looked about for Mixer but saw no sign of the dog.

Getting back into the car, she drove over to the foreman's shack. A dim light flickered from the backroom window. She knocked and waited.

Big Al opened the door with a blanket wrapped around his shoulders.

"Yes? Oh, it's you. What you doing out in this rain, Miss?"

"I'm looking for Hook," she said. "He doesn't seem to be around."

"No, he's gone to Fort Sumner, New Mexico. He had another one of them troll killings over there. He hitched out of here on a westbound."

"Oh, no, not another killing?" she said.

"I'm afraid so."

"Do you know when he'll be back?"

"He didn't say, Miss. He left me feeding that dang hyena dog of his, though. Thing is, I'm moving from job to job and can't be feeding no dog for long."

"Surely Hook will be back soon," she said. "If you hear something, would you give me a call at the Eastman?"

"Sure, I'll call, but you never know about Hook Runyon, do you? He might be gallivanting around Old Mexico and drinking tequila by now for all we know."

*****

Ria sat in the parking lot, the rain drumming on top of the car. Knowing Hook, he had probably taken on the investigation all by himself, and she worried that he did not have a full appreciation of the inherent dangers involved. Rounding up 'boes and seal busters was one thing, dealing with the calculated perversity of a psychopath—much less a repeat killer—was quite another.

Putting her coat over her head, she made her way through the rain to her room. She fixed herself a drink and tried to put aside her concern. She thumbed through her Moleskine notebook, realizing yet again how little information she had gleaned from her time with Hook. She had never known a person so reluctant to let anyone into his world.

In the end, she had little reason to stay in town any longer. Hook had gone his way and invited no intrusions in the doing. So they had shared a night together, a memorable night, and that had to be enough. Their worlds were disparate and would always be so. For her to stay longer invited only rejection and disappointment, so maybe it was time to get on with her life.

Chapter 24

HOURS LATER, HOOK WAITED for the freighter to slow at the bridge before he crawled out onto the grab iron. The cloudy night shrouded the world in darkness, and he hesitated. Jumping into the blackness never came easy, and he had seen his share of crippled 'boes as a result of it.

He counted off to three and bailed. Hitting the ground running, he veered off and commenced an uncontrolled slide down a steep embankment. Unable to stop, he tucked his shoulder and executed a roll, which degraded into a runaway tumble that sent him sprawling to the bottom of a ravine. He lay on his back, looking up into the clear black sky. The whole thing seemed a tad more difficult than he had remembered.

He struggled to his feet, picking the burrs out of his knees and examining the rip in the elbow of his shirt.

With his belongings gathered, he made his way to the river bridge, where he knew an active jungle existed. As he walked through the night, he wondered if anyone would recognize him on his arrival. He hoped not, but a one-armed man was not easily forgotten, and being a one-armed railroad bull walking into a hobo jungle could get downright dangerous.

He smelled the campfire first and then spotted the wink of firelight through the iron girders. Squatting in the darkness, he listened to the voices and to the men laughing. A shower of embers climbed skyward as someone dropped more wood onto the fire.

Hook worked his way toward the gathering with caution. The aroma of mulligan stew wafted through the night, and he could see the men gathered about the fire, five in all, enough to stretch him out if they took the notion. Taking a deep breath, he stepped out into the firelight. The voices fell silent, and the men stood.

"Brought a couple hocks to sweeten up that mulligan," he said.

A red-faced man, big as a water buffalo, stepped up. "You ride in on that green-ball freighter?"

Hook moved up to the fire and pulled out his smoked hocks. "Wasn't a green ball," he said. "She was a humpback job with a dozen hoppers out of Fort Sumner. I went over the side and joined the birds. Damn near killed myself, as you can see."

"My name's Duce," the big one said; Hook had passed the test. "Drop them hocks in. That mulligan's thin as spring grass."

Hook rolled the hocks into the pot. "When's the next run out of here?"

"Sunrise," Duce said. "There's a peanut roaster hauling ties to a job site. Comes through every day. She's faster than a walk, but barely so."

Duce pointed to the two men sitting side by side next to the fire, dead-ringer twins by the looks of them. "That one there is Pud," Duce said. "The other one is Punk. You get them mixed up, doesn't make a damn to no one, including them."

Pud and Punk grinned with picket-fence teeth. "I'm the oldest," Pud said. Punk ran his tongue to the tip of his nose. "I can pick up a pencil with my tongue and write my name," he said.

"I admire talent in a man," Hook said.

Duce reached for his cigarette makin's, folded the paper with his index, sprinkled in tobacco, and sealed it off.

"What happened to your arm?" he asked.

"Born that way," Hook said.

Punk studied him through the firelight. "Did it have a hook on it when you was born?"

"Not as big," Hook said.

Duce lit his cigarette, and the paper burned back in a curl. Suddenly a figure stepped from the darkness, a wiry guy with a tuft of hair growing out from under his bottom lip, lean as a greyhound. His hat was pulled down over his ears, and the toes of his shoes were scorched.

"Who comes there?" Duce asked, alarm in his voice.

"Why, I be the Reverend Dickey," the man said. "Just disembarked from that runaway freighter. I find myself in need of sustenance this night and am thinking an invitation to join in the festivities here would be much appreciated."

"You bring a contribution to the mulligan, Reverend?" Duce asked. "It's a common practice."

"And one I normally would honor, young man, but unfortunate circumstances have brought me up short this night. I found myself having to depart my last stop much sooner than planned. I bring a prayer for the mulligan, which will not go unheard by Him."

Hook remembered something Ludie had said about a minister being chased out of town. "Don't believe I've seen you around these parts before, Reverend," Hook said.

"I travel alone, you see, because a man's mind must be quiet to hear the voice of God."

"I hear voices from time to time," Duce said. "Most especially when I run out of liquor."

"You haven't been down Kiowa way, have you, Reverend?" Hook asked.

"Why, sir, your knowledge of my recent whereabouts intrigues me."

"Rumor has it that a Reverend Dickey has been attending to nearly every soul in that town, most particularly the women's."

The reverend looked up through his brows and smiled. "The folks of Kiowa were indeed a most generous congregation. I won't deny it. But God's work is never done, and a man's days are short."

"You a real preacher?" asked Punk.

"Marry and bury, all legal under the blessings of the U.S. government."

"I never knew a preacher what could hop a freighter," Duce said.

"Hopping freighters is easy," the reverend said, with a nod to Duce. "Needs a steady eye and a willingness to hang on, that's all. Saving souls is another matter altogether. Takes a particular kind of man to pry someone back from the jaws of hell and to do so without losing his own soul."

Duce dabbed the smoke from his eyes with his sleeve, while the other hand stirred the stew.

The boy sitting in the shadows said, "We let everyone who wants just walk in here and take our mulligan?"

"That boy over there is Hambone," Duce said. "He's new to the hobo ways, as you can see."

Hambone looked to be in his twenties. He sported a gold front tooth, and his cheeks were gaunt. His hair had grown long over his ears. He had eyes of steel, and he locked them onto Hook. "We been hearing about that bridge troll roaming about, killing 'boes and cutting 'em up," he said.

Hook knelt at the fire. "That's what they been saying, all right. Guess there's no way of knowing who it might be till he pulls out a hatchet."

Hambone threaded his fingers together, flexed, and cracked his knuckles. "Didn't hear your name," he said.

"Didn't give it," Hook said.

"I'm thinking that troll could be about anybody," Hambone said. "Somebody just drops in out of nowhere and starts slicing people up. But it's a sorry son of a bitch comes into this jungle on this night and tries anything like that."

"Like you say, could be anybody," Hook said. "Could be you or one of these other boys here, far as that goes. Still, no one says a man can't go home to his mama if he's too scairt to stay."

Hambone stood. "That killer troll could get his ass kicked too," he said.

Hook squared off, but Duce stepped between them. "Hambone's quick on the trigger, being young and full of heat."

"If it's a lesson he's looking for, he's come to the right man," Hook said.

"There ain't no trolls hereabouts tonight," Duce said. "And if there was, we'd have him well handled between us. Now, that mulligan's bubbling. Let's serve it up and be on our way come sunrise."

*****

That night Hook slept with his back to the abutment where the firelight cast between him and the others. He slept with his coat over him, which did little to keep the chill from his bones. He awakened in the night to a silent camp, save for the soft snore of Hambone lying in close to the fire. The others were scattered about the perimeter of the camp, men with no past and no future. From Hook's quick count, they were down a 'bo. The Reverend Dickey must have taken his leave sometime in the night, perhaps to celebrate the generosity of yet another congregation. Such was the way of the rails. There were seldom good-byes or "See you down the road." They had joined for a moment and no more. Men riding the rails shared little but a drink of whiskey or a pot of mulligan, that being the way it had always been, the way it always would be.

The next morning, Hook waited in the stand of locusts for the peanut roaster to come downline with its load of track supplies. He hopped an open flatcar stacked with new creosote ties, figuring the ride would be short and slow. He had never had a yen for closed-up boxcars, particularly those heavy with freight. He had seen too many men trapped and crushed under shifting loads.

The ride turned out to be slow and short as well. Within the hour, she slowed for a spur where crew cars were sided. Hook slid off early so as not to be detected and took up residence in a plum thicket. Sooner or later something would come downline, and he could move on.

Wasps buzzed about the overripe fruit, and locusts sawed their legs in the summer heat. Gnats whined in his ears, and sweat soaked his hat. He tried to rest without sleeping, not knowing when the next train might come through. He lay for hours in the sweltering heat, and his throat turned to dust. He ate wild plums, which only heightened his need for water. Within the hour, his stomach churned so loud he clutched his belly in fear of alerting the spike drivers working down track.

Dusk had set in when at last he heard a train braking in the distance. He could tell by the rumble, she had her tail over her back. Catching a hotshot could be tricky. For a man out of practice, it could be downright challenging. But laying up in a plum thicket had lost its appeal.

Hook squatted in the brush and waited for her glimmer to break. A highball artist had her by the throat, and she was closing in fast. Hook lit out in a hard run, but the cars raced by, spinning sand and dirt into his eyes. He shot a look back to see the louse box charging up. Coming downline in front of it, a boxcar with an open door presented Hook's last chance to leg up. He bore down in a fast clip, the hit and miss of ties throwing off his stride. When the car came up, he snared the door opening, which jerked him off his feet. Dangling like a spider, he pulled himself on board. He gasped for breath as the train charged down the high iron and into the evening.

He scrunched himself into the corner of the car and stared into the blackness. Wind whipped through the door as the train rattled down track. Dirt whirled in eddies and gathered in the corners of his eyes. The smell of stale bread and an amalgamation of past cargoes and question-able passengers gathered in his clothes and hair. The rattle and jerk of the car assaulted his bones.

Hook slept, awakening once to the sound of the engine whistle as the train labored through a crossing. The night grew cold, the chill seeping through his shirt, and he shivered and hunkered deeper into his clothes. Like so many before him, he savored the freedom of the rails, the escape they offered from the demands of the world. But freedom for a hobo came with a price, the relinquishment of even the smallest of decisions like when to go, when to stop, and when to eat.

Pulling his collar up against the cold, he struggled to sleep. The clack of the wheels beat in his ears, and he thought of Ria, her wit and intelli-gence, the way she deliberated alternatives and then chose one with solid confidence. He thought of the way she had come to him on the floor of the caboose with that same conviction. Such certainty sprang from an inner strength that he did not possess. His strength, if it could be called such, issued from instinct, from the prowl and stalk of the alley cat.

Sometime in the night, the train slowed to a crawl and then to a stop. She backed up, bumped in, and then cleared slack before moving out once again. Figuring they had picked up sided cars, he pulled his knees into his chest and for the first time since leaving, he slept soundly to the clack of the wheels.

*****

At some point, Hook sensed that someone stood over him, a shad-ow, black against black, but discernible against the starlit opening of the door. If he had any doubts that the figure was real, the cold blade of a knife pressed against his neck dispelled them. Hook struggled to make out the face of his assailant.

"Give me that gun 'fore I take off that other arm," a voice said.

"What gun?" Hook said.

"The one in your belt," the voice said, pushing the blade of the knife harder against Hook's neck. "And your billfold too, while we're at it."

Only then did Hook connect the voice to the disgruntled Hambone he had met the night before. "I don't have a billfold, and you best move on while you can," Hook said.

"I'm the godforsaken bridge troll," the voice said. "I'll cut you into bite-size pieces and feed you to the rats."

"I figure you for no more than a low-life bindle stiff and not long for the rails at that. Steal from your own kind, and life could get a tad lonely."

"I don't need no lecture. Now give me that rod and your money."

The clack of the wheels turned hollow as they passed onto the backwater bridge trusses. The engine bumped down with a lurch, and Hambone stuck his arm out to catch himself.

Hook took a shot at Hambone's kneecap with the heel of his boot. Hambone squealed and dropped his knife. Hook reached up and clamped Hambone's lip with the pinchers of his prosthesis. Hambone danced, and his arms flopped about as if they had been disconnected from his brain.

Hook dragged him to the open door of the boxcar. Hambone's eyes shone white and wet in the moonlight that now edged into the car. Sweat broke across his forehead, and his cheeks puffed.

The clack of the wheels deepened as the train slowed again for the river proper, and waves danced on the water below. Hook put his leg behind Hambone's leg and shoved.

"I don't much favor jackrollers disturbing my rest," he said to the empty doorway.

Chapter 25

QUIET AWAKENED HOOK the second time. He sat up and strained to hear beyond the chirp of crickets. The train had stopped, perhaps laying by for a hotshot to pass or to get clearance up track. He walked to the open door of the boxcar and looked out over the prairie. The first rays of dawn lit the clouds, and the smell of morning dew rode the breeze.

He leaned out as far as possible for a glimpse of the engine. But the engine was gone, having left behind his car and three other empties on a siding.

"Damn," he said, shaking his head.

He dropped onto the ground and peeked beneath the car. An old track, rusty from lack of use, wobbled off to the horizon. He could see nothing in either direction, not a house, not a tree, not a living soul. The bastards had switched off the high iron sometime during the night, cut loose the empties, and backed off again to the main line. How far that was from here, he hadn't a clue. He checked his sidearm and pushed his hat down against the morning sun. Blackbirds swept in over the cars and landed in the bedding rock to search for spillage.

Hook cursed under his breath. Just what he needed, marooned with no way back and nothing to eat. He couldn't just wait it out either. Sided cars could sometimes sit weeks waiting for orders. And he had a killer to stop. He figured the high iron lay to the east, and he had just about decided to walk out when the blackbirds suddenly lifted off and banked away against the sun. He stepped between the cars. Something had spooked them, maybe no more than the call of a distant hawk, but he could no longer be certain that he was alone.

Pulling his sidearm, he clicked off the safety before working his way toward where the birds had scattered. Now and again, he paused to listen or to check under the cars or to glance overhead, having been waylaid more than once from above. He was nearly to the end when he spotted the door ajar on the last car. Ducking down, he crawled underneath until situated below the open door. Something bumped overhead, and then rollers screeched as the door slid open.

Legs dropped down in front of him. He reached out, grabbed a pair of ankles, and jerked downward. A man spilled out of the car and onto his head. Hook waited a moment before announcing himself, just in case someone else might be following behind. When no one showed, he stepped out and screwed the barrel of his sidearm into the guy's ear.

"Who the hell are you?" he asked.

"I ain't nobody," the man said, half dazed. "Please don't shoot."

Hook rested back on his haunches. Something about the voice . . . and the manners. "Runt? Runt Wallace, is that you?"

The man pulled up onto an elbow and looked at Hook. "Who wants to know?" he asked.

"Runt, it's me, Hook."

"Hook who?"

"How many one-armed men named Hook do you know, Runt?"

"Not that many," Runt said, with a shrug.

"What the hell are you doing out here in the middle of nowhere?" Hook asked.

"I don't even know where 'out here' is, Hook. I thought I was headed north. Them bastards must have shuttled me off during the night."

"You bumming the rails now, Runt, drinking shine instead of selling it?" Hook asked.

Runt stood up and brushed off his elbows. "I lost most of the farm after the POW camp closed in Alva after the war. The army packed up and left overnight. Then I lost my wife, Amanda, what with dust pneumonia. I got the still more or less."

"I'm sorry for your loss, Runt."

"Every time I stood up, something kicked my feet out from under me. Just quit standing up after a while. You ain't going to arrest me, are you, Hook?"

"I haven't decided. You have anything to eat?"

"I finished the last of my baloney stick last night. I figured to do a little panhandle work in Clovis this morning. How far is it to Clovis, do you think, Hook?"

Hook holstered his P38. "Might be a block. Might be a hundred miles, for all I know."

Runt squared his shoulders and looked off down track. He had not grown an inch since Hook had seen him last.

"What we going to do, Hook?"

"Walk, I guess. No one's likely to come along with a taxicab."

"See these short pegs, Hook? I ain't big on walking."

"You big on starving?"

"Not particularly."

"Well, these empty cars might sit here till harvest before an engine comes back, and those legs of yours could be a damn sight shorter by then."

Runt pulled at his chin.

"Maybe you could send someone back to pick me up, Hook, you being a railroad bull and all?"

"It isn't the job of railroad bulls to arrange transportation for bums."

"You'd of thought the railroad would have a more generous attitude," Runt said.

*****

By late afternoon, the sun bore down in a blaze. Sweat soaked their shirts, and dust blew down the track. They stopped in the shade of a mesquite to rest. Runt rolled a cigarette and twisted up the ends.

"You gotta do that, I suppose?" Hook said.

Runt lit up and innocently looked at him through a cloud of smoke. "What am I supposed to do with it, Hook, park it behind my ear?"

Hook leaned against the tree and studied the hole in the side of his boot. He grimaced when he saw the white of his sock.

"The smoking habit demonstrates weakness in a man, Runt. It's clean living that gives a person peace and a sense of well-being. No one in his right mind turns his head into a stovepipe."

"Well, I ain't saying you're a hypocrite or nothing like that, Hook, but seems I recall you smoking plenty in your day."

"I'm just concerned about you, Runt. Smoking stunts your growth, something which I dare say you can ill afford."

Runt looked at the end of his cigarette and then flipped the ash off. "I quit growing about twenty years ago, so I guess I won't be worrying none about that. Anyway, I got the power of Samson right in these here hands, from milking cows, you know."

"Well, Samson didn't smoke those stinking cigarettes, that's sure. If he had, his legs wouldn't have grown either."

Hook turned onto his stomach, which had grown cantankerous in the absence of food. Heat waves rippled from the tracks, and the brown grass swept away in waves. He thought he saw something move. He squinted an eye to bring it into focus.

"Runt," he said. "I believe that's a rabbit out there. I favor fried rabbit almost as much as fried chicken."

Runt held his hand over his eyes as he searched for the rabbit.

"I've seen plenty of rabbits in my day, Hook, but seeing a rabbit and catching it are entirely different situations. I came upon an entire pack of coyotes laying dead on the ground one time. When I looked up, a jackrabbit was looking down from the top of the hill. It had run those coyotes clean to death, and you could see the disappointment on its face that they had given out so soon."

"I don't have to run it down. I have a gun."

Runt looked over at him. "That old P38 you carry? It's a rabbit, not a damn elephant, Hook."

"Well, I don't much care what it is," groused Hook. "I'm hungry."

Pulling the sidearm, he racked a round into the chamber, rested the barrel over his prosthesis, and took aim. He squeezed off a shot and watched rabbit fur explode ten feet into the air, the tufts drifting off like snowflakes in the breeze.

"I believe you got him," Runt said.

"Sometimes you just have to take action, Runt. I learned that hunting down dangerous criminals. Now, you see, there's fried rabbit on the menu."

They searched for the rabbit for fifteen minutes, turning up bits of fur and mangled body parts. The only clear evidence of it ever being a rabbit was the ear Runt found dangling from a soapweed. But in due course, everything was collected and put in Hook's hat.

That night, they camped in the right-of-way. Hook built a fire while Runt threaded bits of rabbit onto a stick. They fried it up black, ate it down, and sucked the grease from their fingers.

Runt threw more wood on the fire, and they watched the embers climb skyward.

"A quarter of rabbit hardly makes for a meal, Hook. I'm hungrier now than when I started."

"Well, I hadn't planned on having company for dinner," Hook said.

Runt sighed. "What brings you to be bumming again, Hook? Ain't you working for the railroad no more?"

"I don't want it widely known, but I'm hunting the bridge troll," Hook said.

"Hook, what's a troll?"

"Well, in this case, it's a killer taking 'boes right from their beds at night, cutting them up, and then rearranging their body parts."

"What for? Ain't no one in the world got less to give up than a 'bo," Runt said.

"According to fornicating psychologists, the bridge troll doesn't need a reason, not like you and me think of a reason. His head's haywire, like he doesn't even know himself why he's killing. He just is. And he likes it. That's what makes him so dangerous. In the trade, we call them psychopaths."

Runt looked at him through the firelight. "What kind of paths?"

"Psychopaths. They've got nothing left inside of 'em. They can't feel sorry for what they do or even happy about it. They're all torn up, kind of like that rabbit. Everything's all scattered about in their head, nothing fitting with anything else. The parts are there, but they can't be put together."

"That's right troubling, Hook. What's a troll look like?"

"That's the thing, isn't it? One could be sitting right next to you, and you wouldn't even know it."

Runt looked worried. "Hook," he said. "You ain't no troll, are you?"

"I do not believe that to be the case."

"Maybe you're just figuring it will come for you so you can shoot it with your P38?"

"Maybe."

"I sure hope it doesn't come tonight."

Hook searched out his coat. "We best get some rest now, Runt."

Runt lay on his back, put his toes closer to the fire, and watched the stars rotate overhead.

"Psychopaths is just people, ain't they, Hook? I mean, they ain't like that rabbit?"

"They're just people, Runt. There's no such thing as psycho rabbits."

Hook rolled his coat up for a pillow and stretched out.

"Far as I know," he said.

Chapter 26

HOOK AWAKENED TO RUNT talking in his sleep. Hook shook him by the shoulder. "What's going on, Runt?" Runt sat up, his hair tousled, and rubbed at his eyes.

"I was having the night terrors, Hook. There was this rabbit, see, big as a boar hog, and it was dragging me down track by the leg."

A spider ran onto Hook's foot and stopped on his toe. "Comes from a bad conscience, Runt," said Hook, kicking the spider off. "It's all the livers you poisoned over the years with that shine."

Runt slipped on his shoes, which appeared extra large for the length of his legs.

"It squealed like a baby crying," Runt said, shuddering. "And its pellets were the size of hen eggs."

Hook rolled his eyes. "Why didn't you kill it, and we could have had a real breakfast?"

Runt rubbed the stiffness from his arms. "I'm thinking I might go back to making shine, Hook. It's a hell of a lot safer than riding the rails."

"The price of store-bought liquor has put you out of business, Runt. Besides, making moonshine is against the law."

"Well, at least I didn't have to worry about no killer trolls or psycho rabbits."

"Come on, Runt. We got a ways to go, and it promises to be a hot day."

By noon, they had arrived at the high iron. Turning northward, they followed the track, which shone with wear. When a twist of smoke rose up from a distant house chimney, Hook pulled up. Runt dabbed at his forehead with his bandanna.

Hook said, "I do believe that's chimney smoke coming from a farmhouse up there."

"I was in hopes of a train and a ride to town," Runt said. "Every time I breathe, my belly squeaks like a wet inner tube."

"The situation presents opportunities for enterprising 'boes," Hook said.

"But houses got folks in 'em, with guns," Runt said.

"Don't be a pessimist, Runt. You see guns; I see food. Here's what we do: You go to the front door and ask for a little something to eat, setting up a diversion in the doing. Meanwhile, I'll slip in the back door and see what I can scour up."

"Why don't you go to the front door, Hook?"

"The inside man has to have experience. He has to know what to look for while under pressure and then be able to get out undetected. No offense, but that isn't for a greenhorn such as you. One mistake, and things could heat up pretty fast."

"But ain't it stealing, Hook?"

"It's more like hobo tradition. Anyway, a 'bo never takes but what's needed to survive. The community expects it."

"That sort of makes you Robin Hook, don't it?" Runt said, grinning.

"Yes, it does."

Runt scratched his head. "But don't it take more experience to talk to folks than to sneak in the back door?"

Hooked walked on a little farther before stopping again. "While that may seem logical to the uninitiated, it's replete with flaws. Suppose, while in the house, you come upon a barking dog or a husband bearing arms?"

"I'd hightail it out and go where it ain't so replete," Runt said.

"The difficulty of working the front door is not to be underestimated, Runt. Such requires a complex set of personal skills, none of which are similar to the house-entering specialty of the inside man. Front-door work is all about generating empathy, see. The more the owner feels it, the bigger the handout."

"What is it, Hook?"

"What is what?"

"Empathy."

Hook pulled at his chin. "Well, it's sort of like pity. They got to feel pity for the front man or they won't divvy up the grub. The more pitiful you are, the bigger the handout."

"You think I fit the bill, Hook?"

"I never knew a man more qualified."

Runt squared his shoulders. "I think you're pitiful too, Hook."

"I appreciate that. Now, I'll circle around. Wait about fifteen minutes before you knock."

"What do I say?"

"The lady of the house generally answers. Just act natural and say how you haven't eaten for three days and how you are trying to get home to your wife and kids. Make sure she sees the holes in your clothes. Let your hands shake a little but not too much. Dab at your eyes now and again and sniff like you're trying to hold something back.

"You can't expect much in the way of quality food out the front, mostly chicken necks or biscuits and lard. That's why I'm going in the back way to rustle up the better cuts. I'll meet you here soon as it's clear."

*****

Hook waited until he heard the knock at the front door before slipping the latch on the back door. He crouched in the shadows of the laundry room. The aroma of baked ham wafted from the kitchen. He peeked around the corner and could see the ham cooling on the oven rack, a glorious thing glistening with brown-sugar glaze and prickly with cloves. If he had had the time and a carving knife, he would have cut off just enough for him and Runt and left the rest. Unfortunately, he had neither, which would necessitate him taking the entire ham.

He peeked around the corner again and could see Runt through the living-room window, his shoulders drooping nicely. He could hear Runt's voice break as he related his litany of woes to the woman. It must have been a dandy list, for the woman soon left Runt as she retrieved something from the kitchen and in a few moments returned to the front door.

As for Hook, he was headed for the ham when he spotted a book lying in the magazine rack next to the washing machine, what appeared to be a copy of William Faulkner's *Soldier's Pay*. He dug it out and opened it, a 1926 first edition, Boni and Liveright, publisher. He flipped to the title page, and his heart pounded. There was Faulkner's bold signature, an uncertain mixture of cursive and print.

His hands sweating, Hook turned the book over and checked the condition, very good, maybe even fine—and it had been tossed in with a stack of *Capper's Weekly* magazines like trash.

He had wanted a signed Faulkner for years, and now here it was. How it came to be in this old farmhouse, he had no idea. Rare books showed up in the damnedest places sometimes, unnoticed and unappreciated by the uninformed. Hook looked over at the ham, his belly growling. Just as he headed out for the kitchen to nab it, he heard voices grow louder, and then the door shut. The woman's heels clicked across the living-room floor.

Slipping the book under his belt, he made for the back door.

*****

Hook waited in the bushes until he saw Runt walking down the tracks, counting ties as he went. He stepped out. "Runt," he said. "How did it go?"

Runt looked up at him, his face long. "All I got was this," he said, holding out a ham rind wrapped in newspaper. "It don't even have any fat on it."

"That's damn poor pickings," Hook said. "You were supposed to look pitiful."

"I choked clean down telling that woman about my ma dying and how she suffered and all. She just looked down her nose and says, 'Everyone's ma dies sooner or later. If they didn't, the world would be awash in 'em.' I never knew a woman more hard-hearted.

"She bawled me out for not working like everyone else and for not getting off my backside to earn a living. But I just stood there taking it, looking pitiful, 'cause I knew you were in the back snapping up the good stuff. Did you get it?"

"Get what?"

"I could smell that ham right out the front door, Hook. Let's have some now and save the rest for beans."

"Thing is, I ran into a bit of a problem."

"What kind of problem?"

"Time," Hook said. "I ran out of time."

"That old woman took my hide off for fifteen minutes, Hook. You had enough time to bake that ham yourself. Didn't you get nothing?"

"Sure I did. Just look at this," Hook said, taking the Faulkner out of his britches.

"What is it?"

"Hell, Runt, you don't know what a book is?"

"That's what you got, a damn book?"

"Nice, isn't it? Fine quality and signed too. Who would have thought you'd find a signed Faulkner out here?"

"My legs have gone numb walking this track," Runt said. "My ribs are poking through my skin, and you bring back a book instead of a ham?"

"Food for the mind," Hook said.

Runt headed off down track, his arms swinging. He stopped and turned. "It ain't my mind what's hungry, Hook. It's my belly," he said, stomping away.

*****

They had gone a few miles down track when a switch engine with a line of hopper cars came chugging along. They latched onto the end car and settled in over the wheel truck. Runt, still pouting over the loss of the ham, sat with his feet hanging over the side and his back to Hook. As the sun waddled onto the horizon, Hook spotted a crossing sign announcing the town of Hereford, Deaf Smith County, Texas.

"There's a jungle just this side of town," Hook said. "We ought to bail here and camp in the jungle. It's a fair ride on to Canyon, and the night can get cold on one of these old buckets."

"Maybe you could sell that book in Hereford," Runt said. "Buy some potatoes and onions for mulligan. Wouldn't that be a comfort?"

"That book is not to be sold for potatoes and onions or anything else. It's for posterity, a treasure to be passed on from generation to generation."

"I'm the one likely to be passing on," Runt said. "And you don't even have a wife, Hook, so I don't know why you're worried about offspring."

Hook swung out on the ladder. "Come on, Runt!" he shouted over the clack of the wheels. "And bring that ham rind."

Runt followed Hook down track to where an old trestle stretched over a dry arroyo. The moon looked like an ivory cue ball as it lifted into the sky, and ten-foot shadows moved along at their sides as they walked.

Hook scouted the jungle out first. Finding it empty, he motioned for Runt to come down. The trestle timbers rose above them, landmarks for those of their kind. They set about building a fire, Hook gathering wood while Runt broke sticks for kindling. Soon the smell of smoke filled the night, and firelight danced in the darkness. They threaded the ham rind onto a stick and browned it in the fire. Runt divided it in half with his pocketknife. With grease on his lips, he studied Hook through the firelight.

"You think that troll might be about tonight, Hook?" he asked.

"I didn't see any signs of it."

Runt tore off another piece of rind and chewed. "Maybe it's lying in wait. Maybe when we go to sleep it's figuring to cut off our balls like you said happens and stick 'em in our chests."

"It doesn't cut off just anyone's balls. It's particular about that."

"What balls does it favor?"

"Only hobo balls, from what I can tell, and only in jungles marked safe."

Runt looked out in the darkness, the firelight flickering in his eyes. "But we are 'boes, Hook."

Hook ate the last of his pork rind and wiped his fingers on his bandanna. "You're no real 'bo, Runt. You're just a moonshiner and farmer."

"You mean if a jungle's marked safe, it ain't safe?"

"Exactly. No sign. No troll. That's a one hundred percent guaranteed fact."

Runt said, "If we are 'boes and this jungle's marked safe, then we ain't safe?"

"This jungle is marked safe, but I'm a railroad bull. The troll isn't looking to take up with an armed rail dick, I can tell you that."

Hook no more finished his sentence, than a voice cold as ice came from out of the blackness behind them.

"You boys want to step into the light," it said.

Chapter 27

DUCE EMERGED FROM the darkness, his bloated face red in the firelight. Hook looked up and said, "You come for supper, Duce?" "Looks like mighty lean eating to me," Duce said. "Who's the little guy over there?"

"Runt Wallace," Hook said. "Hind tit stunted his growth, as you see."

"How you ever catch a train, boy? I've seen longer legs on a centipede," Duce said.

Runt's face, only moments ago slack with fear, turned hard. "I run faster than you might guess, if it comes to it. And I got arms like a mountain gorilla." He tightened his biceps, which bulged under his shirt. "I hefted a Ford coupe once while my pa changed the tire."

"That's a mighty feat for a runt," Duce said.

A breeze swept down the river bottom, and embers showered from the campfire.

"You alone, Duce?" Hook asked.

"Got others waiting for a come-up," he said.

"Send 'em in," Hook said. "Chow's lean, but the sleeping's free."

"Come on up, boys," Duce called.

Hambone moved into the light, his lip still swollen and purple. Behind him came Punk, and Pud. Hambone's eyes settled on Hook's. "You and me got unfinished business," he said.

Hook moved to the side so the firelight lit up the shadows. Duce said to Runt, "This here boy with the fat lip is Hambone. That there is Punk. He can sort peas with his tongue and flip 'em onto his hat brim. Double Ugly there is his twin brother, Pud."

"That's a right unusual moniker," Runt said.

Duce pulled out a pistol and leveled it at Hook. "I'll be taking that side-arm of yours now."

Hook studied him through the firelight. "What makes you think I have a sidearm?"

Duce leered and cocked his pistol. Hook handed him the P38. Duce pulled the clip, tossed it into the weeds, and set the P38 on a piece of fire-wood. "We found Hambone here floating downriver on a cottonwood log," he said. "Boy says you threw him off the train in the middle of the night."

Hook lifted his chin. "Your boy Hambone is a bindle stiff, stealing from his own. He's lucky we were over the river."

Duce moved in closer to the fire, training his weapon on Hook. "Us boys come up on a farmer building a barn. Landed a job pulling nails alongside another 'bo. I says, 'We been looking for a one-armed 'bo. You ain't seen one, have you?' He says, 'I ain't seen no one-armed 'bo, but I seen a one-armed rail dick once. His name was Hook Runyon, and he cost me thirty days in the Amarillo slammer.'"

"Jogged my memory too," Punk said. "I recalled having a fresh gump took right out of my starving hands by just such a bull one time. And I was needing that chicken plenty."

Hambone planted his feet. "A damn bull," he said. "That's going to make this all the more fun."

Hook spun around, kicking Duce's weapon away with his foot. The momentum threw him off balance, and he failed to ward off Hambone's roundhouse punch, which rocked him back on his heels. The world spun, and blood dripped from his nose.

He shook his head, slipped Hambone's uppercut that had already left the station, and smacked him hard with an open hand across the ear. Hambone's eyes rolled white, and his knees wobbled under him.

Runt had Punk's jaw locked in a hydraulic grip, and Punk was drooling and squealing like a pig as he danced on the end of Runt's arm, his prehensile tongue sprouting from his head. Pud, wary of Runt's trap, circled them both at a distance, like a hound treeing a coon.

By then, Hambone, who had regrouped, charged in and drove his fist into Hook's side, dropping him to his knees. Duce moved in for an opportune kick to the head, but Hook stuck him in the gut with his prosthesis. Duce honked and farted and sat back on his hindside.

Hambone grabbed Hook's prosthesis, stepped over it with one leg, and twisted the whole thing right off Hook's stump. Throwing it to the ground, he squared off again.

"Now, let's see how a real one-armed dick can fight," he said.

In the distance, the wail of a train whistle drifted in. Hook rolled to the side, snapped up his prosthesis, and cracked Hambone between the legs with it. Hambone howled in perfect harmony with the train whistle. He grabbed his testicles and teetered for a moment before plunging nose first into the dirt.

By the time Hook retrieved his gun and got to Runt, Pud had decided to call it a day. Hook searched out his ammo clip and shoved it into the P38.

"Come on, Runt," he said. "We got a train to catch."

Runt released Punk, whose crumpled face refused to unfold.

"Let's get out of here before these boys figure out what's going on," Hook said.

With his prosthesis clamped under his stump, Hook headed for the tracks, Runt close behind, his little legs working overtime.

The train's glimmer broke down track, and the ground rumbled under their feet. She came in slow, a blessing considering Hook's physical and mental state. They squatted in the bushes, and as the engine chugged past, Hook turned to Runt. "You take the next car. I'll pick up the one after."

Runt nodded and set a pace. Latching onto the grab iron, he pulled himself aboard.

Hook trotted alongside. "Catch this!" he yelled, pitching his prosthesis up to Runt.

Hook slowed for the next car, and then realized he had left his Faulkner behind. He looked at the bridge and then at the train, which had yet to power up. "Damn it," he said, turning back.

Sliding down the embankment, he made for the jungle. He could hear the train gaining momentum overhead on the bridge. He found Duce dusting off the seat of his pants.

"What the hell?" Duce said, his eyes wide.

Hook picked up a piece of firewood. "Make a move, Duce, and I'll loosen up your teeth."

Duce nodded and backed away. Hook spotted the Faulkner lying in the dirt. Sticking it in his britches, he ran for the tracks again, the clack of wheels growing ever faster above. He scrambled to the top of the embankment just as the louse box came wobbling downline.

He bent over to catch a quick breath before striking a pace. He looked over his shoulder to time the grab iron, knowing that failing a hop now would leave him dealing with those unhappy 'boes under the bridge. His lungs afire, he cranked up his speed, and as the caboose came by, he latched on. He struggled to pull himself up, his feet bouncing over the ties. In a final effort, he clawed his way onto the caboose deck.

He lay in the darkness, hoping all the while no one waited inside the caboose. When he had regained his breath, he checked the door, finding it locked. Climbing onto the roof of the caboose, Hook edged along to the end. The train had picked up speed, and the cars pumped up and down like pistons. The knuckle coupler below him creaked under the haul of the engine.

The wind sucked at his body, and his shirt collar slapped at his face. Jumping from car to car was like jumping from one boat to another in a hurricane. A man could never be certain what was going up and what was going down. To make matters worse, it had been awhile since he had jumped cars on the move. Counting to three, he bailed. Landing at an angle, he pitched forward onto his stomach to keep from sliding off the side.

One car after another, Hook worked his way forward, his confidence returning with each jump. A half dozen more, and he spotted Runt secured behind a flatcar loaded with new auto frames. Runt sat cross-legged, and he had Hook's prosthesis on his lap.

"How about giving me my arm back?" Hook said from above.

Runt looked up at him. "Dang, Hook, where the hell did you go?"

Hook dropped down next to him. "Forgot my book," he said.

Confusion washed over Runt's face. "I thought that Duce fella was the troll come to cut our heads off," he said, lighting a cigarette.

Hook moved upwind from Runt's smoke. "Those boys were just sporting, Runt."

"I guess we showed 'em, didn't we, Hook?"

Hook said, "You keep a lookout for trolls, Runt. I got to get some rest. Chasing trains ain't what I remember it being."

Finding a spot to stretch out, Hook lay down to the sound of the wind whistling through the car frames. Soon the pitch and sway of the car lulled him to sleep.

He woke once to the stars rolling overhead and Runt's sporadic snore. He woke again when the engineer lay in on the whistle at a crossing. He sat up and pushed on Runt's shoulder.

Runt rubbed at his face. "Sun's almost up," he said.

"That's 'cause it's morning. Sun comes up damn near every day that same way," Hook said.

"I sure am hungry," Runt said, blinking his eyes. "That ham rind's long since gone."

Hook yawned. "I don't have any food, Runt, as you well know."

"I was just thinking about breakfast is all. That ham sure would have made a fine meal about now. Course, it's a comfort to have that book in its place."

"Runt, would you just forget about the ham?"

Runt stood and hung his arms over an auto frame to watch the morning break.

"Hook?" he said.

"What?"

"It's going to be awhile 'fore we come to a town, ain't it?"

"Likely so at this speed," Hook said.

"Hook?" he said.

"What?"

"Why did you go back after that book?"

"You wouldn't understand."

"I would, if I wasn't so hungry."

"It's the owning of it and the ability to go where I otherwise couldn't go without it."

"Hook?" he said.

"What?"

"Would you read it to me?"

"Why?"

"I want to go there too," Runt said.

Hook retrieved the Faulkner and cleaned the cover off with his sleeve. "Okay, Runt, but I don't want to hear any more about no ham."

Chapter 28

RIA WAITED IN THE OUTSIDE office for the secretary to tell Dr. Wilson, her committee chairman, that she needed to talk to him. The decision to return to the university had been a difficult one, but Ria had failed to find an alternative.

"Dr. Wilson will see you now," the secretary said.

"Ria," said the professor from behind a desk covered in a slide of books and folders. "Have a seat. I'm surprised you're back so soon."

"I couldn't get the data I needed," she said, settling in a hard chair before him. "The whole law-enforcement thing . . . I mean, I found they've a problem with sunshine."

Dr. Wilson studied her over the top of his glasses. "I was afraid of that," he said. "You do understand that it's rather late to make significant changes in your program plan? Much more delay and you'll have to wait and then reenroll in dissertation hours next semester. You'll need an entirely new hypothesis, perhaps even a new topic. The delay won't look good to the committee either."

Ria sat up straighter. "It's not like I haven't tried, sir. The trip gave me a front-row seat to thieves and killers. I just found the law as dished out by a rail-yard bull to be unconventional at best. The anecdotal records were of little use as well."

"If you're having problems finding hard data in the field, you could always do a survey."

"I'd hoped to avoid surveys altogether. No one answers them truthfully, if at all. I fear my results would be biased by the inherent weaknesses in that sort of research instrument."

Dr. Wilson picked up a folder. "I tried to dissuade you from this at the outset, Ria, but you were determined."

"I just wanted my study to make a contribution to the field. Isn't that what's important?"

"In the end, that's what it's all about, of course. But there are always compromises that have to be made in the real world. Law enforcement has an entirely different perspective, and conflict with academia is probably inevitable.

"You have to realize, Ria, that your railroad detective is operating on a very different level. It's called survival, and he probably doesn't know or appreciate the importance of research to that very end."

He looked at his watch. "Look, I've a class. Can you come back in an hour or so? We can talk this out." He walked to the door. "By the way, I saw a couple of your classmates, Susie Bliss and Ross Carson, in the student union a while ago. Perhaps you should talk with them, though I can't say they've exactly shaken the academic world themselves."

*****

Classes were changing as Ria made her way to the student union. Students poured from doorways with briefcases and books in hand. They chatted and laughed as they made their way to their next classes.

Ria's stomach tightened. That time for her had begun to slip away, the excitement, the curiosity, the sudden passion for learning that somehow morphed out of the milieu of adolescence. She suspected that it happened only once in a lifetime, at least with the same intensity.

She found Susie and Ross sitting at their usual spot by the bay window. Susie rested her chin in her hand as Ross held forth. Ross, a frail sort, with his mascara-black mustache, waved his finger in the air. He favored conversation with the opposite gender, but his conversations had a way of becoming monologues.

Both friends looked up at the same moment as she approached. "Will you look at that?" Ross said. "It's Ria Wolfe back from the Wild, Wild West."

"Hello, Ross," she said. "Susie."

Susie slid over for her to sit. "Jeez, Ria," she said. "What are you doing back here? I thought you were out turning over stones, looking for data that would rock the world of law-enforcement forensics."

"Let's just say I ran into some problems," Ria said.

Ross poured sugar into his coffee. "I never understood why you went out West in the first place. There are easier ways to get data."

"Exactly what have you been doing?" Susie asked.

"I've been working in the field with a railroad detective, with a Santa Fe bull, to be exact. I'd hoped for access to municipal law enforcement, but it didn't work out."

"Research is all about getting the numbers," Ross said, "but they need to be the right numbers. I can't see that happening with one detective."

"I thought it a place to start," she said, "but Dr. Wilson seems to think it's too little, too late as far as my original proposal. I'm not sure I can salvage it."

"What are you going to do?" Susie asked.

Ria shrugged. "Dr. Wilson wants to see me about that very thing after his class."

"So what has this railroad detective had to offer, if not material for your paper?" Ross asked, with a sly smile.

"Just stop, Ross. He's an honorable man, unlike some I know."

"Does he have anything you could use for your study?" Susie asked.

"That's the problem. He's involved in a serious case at the moment, but he keeps everything close to the vest. And it's become pretty clear to me that he has no system for how he's approaching it."

"Sounds kind of seat-of-the-pants," said Susie, "and I can see the challenges in that for you. But I know you, Ria, there's something else bothering you. Come on, it's us."

Ria frowned, hesitated, realized she had Ross's attention now as well as Susie's. She took a deep breath. "He's investigating a brutal murder, well, a series of murders, all strikingly similar, both in setting and method."

Susie gasped. "You mean, like a repeat killer?"

"Possibly, we're still not sure. But from what I remember, I'd have to say yes."

"My God, an actual psychopath repeat killer," Ross said. "That's a once-in-a-lifetime case."

"Yes, and that's all well and good, Ross, but I need to finish my research, and one case—no matter how fascinating or gruesome—is not exactly helpful."

Ross set his cup down and looked at her. "And why not?"

"Why not what?"

"Why not just one? It's called a case study. It's not common, but it has been done. We talked about it in class. Done right, it can be of real merit."

"And knowing you, it would be done right," Susie said.

"Would your railroad bull approve?" Ross asked.

"I don't think he would disapprove," Ria said uncertainly. "The profession could learn a lot from him, you know. His powers of observation are remarkable and his courage too. He operates over hundreds of miles of remote territory alone. No one to call if he gets into trouble."

"You might want to work on your objectivity if you're going to do this case thing," Susie said, winking at Ross.

Ria rolled her eyes. "Really, Susie, you're no better than Ross."

"I like the whole idea of it," Ross said. "Not everyone gets the chance to study a repeat killer, you know."

"Do you think Wilson would go for it?"

"There's one sure way to find out," he said.

*****

Dr. Wilson pulled his chair up to his desk and parked his chin in his hands. "A killer who mutilates and poses the corpses? Are you certain?"

"I've seen the victims," said Ria. "And as for whether whoever is doing it is a repeat killer, well, everything points to it."

"If found to be true," he mused aloud, "this would be a first for the department, possibly the field, but I must warn you, Ria, it's not without danger. I hope you realize that."

Ria squirmed in her chair but answered without hesitation. "I do, sir."

192

"We're not talking studying the average criminal, Ria. We're talking a killer with some deviant ritual tendencies. By definition alone, there is nothing more unpredictable or dangerous. If something happened . . ."

His voice trailed off.

"If something happened to me, you mean?"

He nodded. "It's a risk that can't be ignored, Ria."

"I see."

Dr. Wilson got up from his desk and walked to his bookshelf. He turned. She could tell he had made up his mind.

"I'm sorry, Ria. If something happened to you out there, I could never forgive myself."

Ria stood and nodded. She knew the professor well enough to know to argue would be futile.

"Thank you, Dr. Wilson. I'll get to work on my request for postponement."

••••••

Ria sat in her car and watched the students walking to and fro across campus. For a while, she had lost sight of her goals, had let her situation defeat her. But despite Dr. Wilson's decision, she knew what she had to do, and this time she would see it through to the end, no matter what.

Better to ask forgiveness than permission.

Hook had taught her that.

Chapter 29

HOOK AND RUNT BAILED OFF just as the train slowed for the Canyon depot. Runt pitched forward into the ditch, removing a patch of skin from his chin in the process. Hook helped him up and picked the burrs out of his elbows. "You're supposed to run when you hit the ground, Runt. It's a damn sight easier on the elbows."

"I was running, Hook," Runt said.

"I've seen wiener dogs run faster."

Runt shook off the dirt like a dog would water. "We going to find something to eat or we going to talk about wiener dogs?"

Hook looked up and down the track. "Let's split up here," he said. "There's an eastbound comes through about six. See if you can chase up a little grub and meet me back here."

"What if you ain't here?"

"Then I'll meet you in Pampa. There's a jungle not far from the first crossing into town. And remember to look pitiful when you're asking for food. Shuffle your feet and bury your hands in your pockets. Don't make eye contact."

"I ain't supposed to look at 'em?"

"Womenfolk don't like eye contact. Makes 'em nervous. Just shuffle and mumble like you're scared. Make 'em lean forward to hear you, and put a little quiver in your voice."

"This begging is a lot more complicated than I thought, Hook."

"It's got to be done right, but you'll get the hang of it. Being pitiful has got to come from the inside of a fella, see. You got to feel it or it won't ring true. If it doesn't ring true, they won't give you even their crumbs. You could starve to death right before their eyes, right there on their front porch, and they wouldn't care."

"I don't know how to be as pitiful as you, Hook. I just keep thinking about that food and how good it's going to taste."

Hook lowered his head in thought. Pretty soon, he said, "Your ma ever send you out for a switch, Runt?"

"Oh, sure. 'Runt,' she'd say, 'I've had enough of you. Go to the shelterbelt and cut a switch. Cut a big one and bring it back here. I'm going to tan your hide.' "

"And you remember how you felt cutting that switch?"

"I sure do. It's the worst feeling in the world. Sometimes I'd have to go back three or four times to get a switch big enough to suit her. She could sure make you dance with it too."

"Okay, so every time you go to the door to beg for food, just think about how it was going for that switch. You'll have so much pity seeping out of you, they're likely to empty their kitchens right at your feet.

"Now, I'll take the west side of town. You take the east. Don't eat it all up, either. This is a share-and-share-alike deal."

Hook watched Runt walk away. He could tell by the slump in his posture and how he hung his head that Runt was already thinking about the switch. Circling back, Hook soon found himself in a modest neighborhood not far from the tracks. He knocked on the door of a small frame house and waited. An old woman answered the door. Her glasses were thick and dusty and hung far down on the end of her nose. She had sparse gray hair, and he could see her pink scalp through it.

"Who are you?" she asked, peering at him through her glasses.

"I'm looking for work, ma'am, without much luck," Hook said, making certain she could see his prosthesis. "A bite of food would be mighty nice."

"That so?" she said. "You haven't found any work?"

"Work's hard to come by," he said. "If you could spare a little something, I'd sure be grateful."

"I never found work hard to come by," she said. "Work is everywhere I turn, and I've been doing it for eighty-odd years. Funny you can't find none nowhere, ain't it?" The wattle under her neck shook. "Now get off my porch 'fore I call the law."

"It's the arm," Hook said, holding up his prosthesis. "Folks won't hire a fellow with one arm."

"You don't get off my porch, you're going to have another arm looks just like that one," she said, slamming the door.

Hook made for the road, looking back over his shoulder. "Old bitch," he mumbled.

By late afternoon, he had managed to land a job mowing an old man's lawn for three dollars. The old man sat on the front porch drinking ice tea with lemon and sugar and watching Hook work. The man's white socks gathered about his ankles, and varicose veins twisted under his thin skin. Finished, Hook mopped the sweat from his forehead and pushed the mower into the garage. The old man met him at the drive.

"Here's your two dollars," the old man said, handing over a pair of bills from his pocket.

"But the deal was for three dollars."

"You heard it wrong, mister," the old man said. "I can get a boy for one dollar any day of the week."

"But you said three."

"Three was for a prime job. Damn lawn looks like a set of bad teeth."

Hook snatched the bills out of the man's hand and stuck them in his pocket. "You married?" Hook asked.

The old man spit onto the ground. "I'm old, not crazy. Why?"

"There's an old lady down the street who's looking for an old tight-ass son of a bitch just like you."

*****

Hook deliberated on what to buy with his two dollars, deciding in the end that it would be a mistake to purchase perishables such as fresh fruits, meat, and eggs, given the harsh climate and the lack of refrigeration. What he needed was something with a long shelf life, something he could tote in his pocket that would not be adversely affected by the elements. A bottle of Old Crow whiskey fit the bill, and he found it in the liquor store on Main. He tucked it safely into his hip pocket and headed for the meeting spot. Runt, being a connoisseur of fine whiskey, would no doubt appreciate the thought Hook had put into his selection.

He found Runt taking a half dozen scrawny potatoes out of a paper bag and laying them out in a row. The scrape on his chin had scabbed over, making him look like one of the Three Musketeers with a goatee. He looked up at Hook. "I got some spuds for a mulligan. Last season's by the looks of 'em, but they will boil up. What did you get?"

"Money," Hook said.

Runt's eyes grew large. "Money? Oh, man, we can buy a ham bone, maybe even a ham, something to go with the spuds."

"I spent it," Hook said.

Runt's face fell. "You bought a damn book, didn't you?"

"Course not. I bought this," Hook said, pulling the bottle out of his hip pocket. "Something for seeing us over the rough spots."

Runt looked at the bottle and then at Hook. "You bought whiskey?"

"Not just any whiskey. Old Crow."

Runt's cheeks puffed in and out, as he paced in a circle. "I'm near starved, Hook. Whiskey ain't what I had in mind."

"Sustenance is of no avail to a disturbed mind. This here Crow will settle out any nervous thoughts you're entertaining."

Runt shook his head. "My mind is in my stomach looking for food, and it ain't finding any. That's as unsettled as you can get and still be alive."

"Well, that's fine," Hook said, heading off down track. "You don't want any Crow, that suits me just fine. I swear, I don't remember you being so uppity."

"All right, Hook," Runt said. "I ain't so uppity I can't have a drink of Crow now and then."

"Had I been thinking, I'd a-picked up an onion," Hook said. "Maybe we can shake one loose somewhere."

They had gone only a few hundred yards when a railroad half-ton truck pulled up alongside them. The man driving appeared to be in charge, having on a clean shirt and such, while the passenger, a darkskinned fellow, was dressed in overalls and had grease under his fingernails. A sweat ring encircled his hat.

The driver said, "Where you boys headed?"

"We're with the Santa Fe," Hook said. "Checking for bad ties."

"That a fact?" the driver said, looking over at the other fellow. "Well, I'm the wheel monkey, been inspecting some cars back there on that siding. This here is Joseph. He don't speak much English, but he don't have much to say anyway."

Joseph turned briefly, his black hair falling over his pale blue eyes. He flipped his mane back with a toss of his head but said nothing. For a moment, Hook thought he recognized him, but then, he looked hard and worn, looked like a lot of men working the rails.

"You boys finishing up the job, are you?" the driver asked.

"That's right," Hook said.

"Hop in the back. I'll give you a lift."

Hook looked at Runt. "Okay," he said. "Need to get to a bug line to call in this job. Maybe you could drop us off in the yards?"

"Sure. You boys help yourself to the water jug."

Runt and Hook crawled in the back and waved off the driver. They took pulls off the Old Crow, chasing it with ice water from the jug.

"You know these fellers?" Runt asked.

Hook shook his head. "Can't know everyone on the railroad, Runt, though they seem right accommodating, I'd say. We'll hop something out of the yards. It's a damn sight easier to hop a train what's sitting still, particularly when your legs are sawed off like yours."

The old truck bounced and rattled, and Hook could smell the smoke of the driver's cigarette as it drifted back from his window. Pretty soon they turned, and dust spiraled up behind them.

"Sure is a long ways to the yards, Hook. It's on a dirt road too."

"Maybe they're taking a shortcut."

Runt checked his potatoes and pulled his hat down over his eyes.

Fifteen minutes passed, and he said, "Why ain't we there yet, Hook?"

"I don't know," Hook said, "and I must say, I don't remember a dirt road neither."

Just then the truck pulled over, and the driver stuck his head out of the window. "Here it is, boys," he said. "Climb out."

Hook and Runt jumped out. Hook looked down the road, and all he could see was an old spur track running parallel to it.

"Wait a minute," he said. "This isn't the yards."

"It ain't?" the driver said. "Well, you ain't no damn tie-checkers either. Have a nice walk, boys."

And with that, he rolled up his window and pulled away.

Chapter 30

HOOK AND RUNT WATCHED IN SILENCE as the taillights of the truck disappeared down the road. Runt spun in a slow circle before turning to face Hook.

"Where are we?" Runt asked.

"How the hell should I know?"

"You don't know where we are?"

It was Hook's turn to take a spin before frowning and saying in a voice that sounded a lot like he was bluffing: "We'll just walk out, that's all."

"I feel swoony from lack of food, Hook."

"Maybe we can stir up a gump. There's bound to be farms out here. And if there are farms, you can bet there's chicken to be found."

"If you'd bought chicken instead of Old Crow, we'd be eating about now," Runt said.

"Well, if I had, we wouldn't have any Old Crow, would we?"

Runt fell in behind Hook, and Hook could hear Runt breathing and his little legs swishing as the fence posts passed by one by one.

"I hadn't thought about it that way," Runt mumbled.

"That's the difference between you and me, Runt. There are layers and layers behind my thinking. Layers that run deep 'cause I've got experience. Being without a gump for the pot isn't half as bad as being without Old Crow for the spirit."

As they walked on, darkness fell, and the night sounds tuned up. Runt struggled to keep up with Hook's pace.

"Hook," he said from a ways behind.

"What?"

"You think that troll might be following us?"

"No," he said. "No self-respecting troll would be caught dead without a bridge."

"Hook," he said.

"What?"

"Maybe we ought to tap that Old Crow again, you know, to keep the spirits up."

Hook stopped. The moon broke on the horizon, casting their shadows across the tracks. "Have you ever heard of delayed gratification, Runt?"

"What does that have to do with having a drink of Old Crow?"

Hook rolled his eyes, pulled out the Old Crow, and opened it. He gave it a smell test.

"It isn't Runt Wallace shine," he said. "But it will pass."

He handed it to Runt, who took a swig and passed it back to Hook. Runt wiped his mouth on his sleeve and watched as Hook tipped the bottle.

"Hook," he said, checking the level.

"What?"

"My gratification is still delayed. Maybe I ought to have another."

"I never knew a man had so many nervous tensions," Hook said.

They walked some more, passing the bottle back and forth while deliberating on the troublesome aspects of hobo life. Suddenly Hook pulled up and pointed to a small yellow light shining back in the trees.

"If I ain't mistaking, that's a farmhouse," he said.

"I'm all pitied out, Hook."

"They likely have a chicken house, and you know what that means."

"A gump," Runt said. "But they're likely to have a shotgun too."

"You don't become an experienced lawman like me by being afraid of shotguns, Runt. Now, I'll sneak in and pick us up a fat gump."

"What about me?"

"You wait here. Fella as nervous as you might get us both shot. And you might save a little of that Crow for camp tonight, if you don't mind."

Soon, Hook emerged from the darkness with a white leghorn tucked under his arm.

"Well, I'll be," Runt said.

Hook reached in his coat pocket and pulled out a sweet onion. "Found the cellar too," he said. "Next time through, I'll leave those folks a little money at their door, though I doubt they minded helping out the law like this. Now let's find us a place to settle in. The world will look a lot brighter when we get this chicken to cooking."

*****

Hook and Runt ducked under the old wooden spur bridge, sending a flurry of pigeons airborne, dropping small bombs on their way up.

Runt yelped and covered his head. "Damn," he said

"Have another pull of that Old Crow," Hook said. "This appears to be a jungle, though a tad neglected. See if you can't rustle up something to cook the mulligan in. Check up in those beams over there."

Hook built a fire and gathered up wood for the night. Runt returned with an old enamel pot that had been squashed down on one side.

"Found this," Runt said.

"It'll do," Hook said. "Now wring that gump's neck and then dress it out. Go down on the creek so the guts don't draw coons."

Runt looked at the chicken, which cocked its head and looked back at him with blue eyes. "Ma always whacked off their heads with an ax. I never wrung one's neck before. The thought of it makes me swoony, Hook."

"Chopping or wringing is all the same to a gump, and you were raised on the farm? Oh, for Pete's sakes, let me do it."

Picking up a stick, Hook laid it over the chicken's neck, placed a foot on either side of its head and yanked, popping the head off and sending it rolling right between Runt's feet, its blue eyes blinking. Over by the fire, the headless chicken flopped about, blood spewing from its neck.

"Hook?" Runt said.

"What?"

"I think that chicken head is looking at me."

Hook took a slug of Old Crow and handed the bottle to Runt. "Just don't look back."

"I can't help it."

"Crimey," Hook said.

"Hook?"

"What?"

"You think that chicken knows its head's pulled off?"

"I don't see why not."

"Does the head know or does the body know?"

"They both know."

"But how could the body know without a head?"

"It's a matter of perspective."

"I thought so," Runt said.

Soon Hook had the mulligan boiling, the savory smells of chicken and onion scenting the night. They took turns adding wood to the fire and sipping Old Crow.

"Hook," Runt said.

"What?"

"Suppose that troll is hiding out there waiting to cut our heads off just like that chicken's."

"There's no troll waiting."

"Would both us and our heads know our heads were cut off, you think?"

Hook focused on a wood tick crawling into his sock. "Yes, but there's no troll waiting out there," he said, digging the visitor out and squashing it with his fingernail.

"Why not?"

" 'Cause there's no point in cutting off someone's head if no one knows you did it."

"We would know," Runt said. "We've got perspective like that chicken."

"I'm a railroad bull, and I got a gun, Runt. You couldn't be safer sleeping in a church. Just eat the damn mulligan, and I don't want any more talk about cutting heads off."

After eating, Hook curled up under his coat and read awhile from his Faulkner. The fire crackled, and the crickets tuned up. The old bridge timbers creaked as they cooled in the night, and the chill of night air rushed in on the wind.

"Hook?" Runt said from the other side of the fire.

"What?"

"That chicken head just winked its eye at me again."

"Oh, brother," Hook muttered.

He lumbered to his feet, picked up the chicken head by its comb, and tossed it into the darkness. "It's gone, okay? Now go to sleep."

Hook pulled his coat over his shoulders and soon dozed off. Sometime later in the night he woke to Runt nudging his shoulder. Hook rolled over, focusing in on Runt, who stood between him and the fire.

"What?"

"I'm having the night terrors again," Runt said.

"Just go back to sleep."

"I dreamed that troll was standing over my bed. He had a big stick and was going to pull my head off."

"I'm thinking that's not such a bad idea, Runt. Now, go back to bed."

"But then he did."

Hook raised himself up on his elbow. "Did what?"

"Pulled my head off and threw it in the dirt. I could see his feet standing next to the fire, but I couldn't do nothing because I didn't have no legs."

"You've never had any legs worth speaking about. Just build that fire up good and high. Trolls are scared of fire. And don't wake me again."

"Even if that troll comes back to take me?"

"Especially for that," Hook said.

Hook turned over. He could hear Runt gathering up wood and tossing it onto the fire. The warmth and crackle soon lulled him back to sleep.

Hook woke to the bottoms of his feet burning. It was still ink black, and he smelled smoke. He sat up to find the bottoms of his shoes melting from the blazing fire. He shot to his feet. "Holy damn!" he hollered as he stomped his feet while circling the fire.

Runt jumped, up looking like a madman. "He's here! He's here!" he screamed.

Hook drew his sidearm, realizing that the bridge timbers above him were ablaze, that the entire structure was enveloped in flames. The timbers creaked overhead from the intensity of the fire.

"We gotta get out of here now!" Hook yelled. "This thing is coming down any second."

They scrambled up the embankment, the night sky glowing with flames behind them. The smell of smoke followed them on the wind.

Runt said, "Hook, I forgot to put on my shoes."

"What? Where are they?"

"Under the bridge. I can't hardly walk barefoot in these burrs."

"Oh, for Pete's sake!" Hook said. "Stay here. I'll see if I can get them."

Hook dashed full tilt toward the burning bridge. Holding his prosthesis over his eyes against the heat, he worked his way under the seething timbers. He scoured the ground for Runt's shoes, spotting instead his Faulkner, which lay precariously close to a burning timber. "Damn," he said, snatching it up. "I nearly forgot it."

Just then a timber, flaming hot with burning creosote, broke loose above and crashed before him. Hook made a run for safety just as the bridge collapsed upon itself behind him. He climbed the embankment, gasping for breath.

"Well, did you find them?" Runt asked.

Hook pulled out the Faulkner. "Just in the nick of time," he said. "She was within an inch of burning to a crisp."

Runt looked at Hook and then at the Faulkner.

Pulling up the collar of his coat, he turned, and without a word, headed off down the road, barefoot.

Chapter 31

RUNT, REFUSING TO ACKNOWLEDGE Hook, walked down the road a good ten yards ahead in silence. As dawn rose, he would stop now and again to examine his feet and to grumble. They were nearly into the city of Canyon before Hook could get him to stop.

"I'm sorry, Runt," Hook said. "All this has been my fault. I spotted that book, and I just clean forgot why I went back."

"You'd sell your own mother out for a dang book, Hook."

Hook sucked at a tooth and looked back down the road. "I can't explain it, Runt. It's like a disease what takes me over."

"Well," Runt said, wiggling his toes, now black with dirt, "I guess what can't be helped can't be helped. I feel the same way about eating."

"There's a culvert over there, Runt. You hole up, and I'll walk on into town and rustle up some shoes."

"But what if you come upon a book or a pint of Old Crow?"

"You take the Faulkner, just so you know I'm coming back. And here's my sidearm. Don't shoot yourself with it."

"But what if you don't come back, Hook? They'll just find my bones holding a gun and that dang book," Runt said with a sigh.

"We can always meet up, Runt. There's a jungle this side of Amarillo."

Runt checked the bottom of his left foot, which looked similar to a pincushion. "All right," he said. "I'll wait."

Hook nodded and turned to go.

"Leave the book," Runt said.

"Oh, right," Hook said, handing him the Faulkner. "Don't be turning the corners down or making notes in the margins."

"I take a size nine," Runt said.

"Eight through ten should do it," Hook said.

"And something to eat too."

By the time Hook reached town, the day had warmed. He cut through the park in his search for the local Salvation Army and spotted a newspaper lying on a bench. The headline "Bridge Troll Strikes Again" caught his eye. He picked the paper up, took a seat on the bench, and started to read:

> *The killer, known among the hobo community as "the Troll," has reportedly struck these parts once again. The mutilated body of an indigent by the name of Roy Bissel was discovered under a bridge not far from the Pampa, Texas, rail yards. According to local police, as with previous victims, a blow to the back of the head resulted in Bissel's death.*
>
> *Police likened the crime scene to a Frankenstein movie but declined to go into details for fear of compromising the investigation. The police chief said the hunt for the killer was being hampered by both a lack of clues as to the attacker's identity and the hobo community's reluctance to cooperate when it came to police inquiries.*
>
> *Railroad security declined to comment on the killing, stating only that the matter was under investigation by Mr. Ludie Bean, an experienced railroad detective, and that the public would be notified as soon as any further details became available.*

Hook rolled up the newspaper and stuck it in his coat pocket. He considered calling Eddie, but realized he would then have to tell him where he was. Eddie would insist that he return, which would put his plan in jeopardy, and since Eddie had no idea that he had seen the article, Hook figured to keep it that way.

He found the Salvation Army thrift store near the edge of town in a dilapidated building that appeared to have been a warehouse in days gone by. He tried the front door, finding it locked. He tried the back door, where the donation bin was kept, and found it locked as well. He unrolled the newspaper and looked at the date.

"Sunday," he said. "Damn it."

He looked down the alley in both directions. Not a soul in sight. No way would he return without shoes for Runt. The poor guy's feet were raw and bloody, and it was all Hook's fault.

He tried the donation-bin door and found it open. Leaning in, he spotted a pair of old black dress shoes in the far corner sitting on a stack of magazines.

Try as he might, however, he could not reach them. Taking off his coat, he climbed into the bin. He checked the shoes—size twelve, a bit large, but they would do. He was about to climb out when he heard a car pull into the alley. Lowering the door, he hunkered down in the darkness. The car pulled by, slowed, and then went on. Hook waited until he could no longer hear the car or anything else. The Salvation Army frowned on taking stuff from the donation bin without the obligatory sermon that accompanied its usual dispersal. The bin, smelling of musty clothes, had become awfully hot.

When Hook finally dared a peek, he lifted the lid to an eye-level view of a cop's gun belt and holster.

"Come on out of there," the cop said.

"Yes, sir," Hook said, crawling out.

The cop, an enormous specimen with great jowls, held Hook's coat up by the collar. His nose lay to the east and was red as an apple. "This might be yours," he said. "I found it on top of this here donation bin."

"I was in bad need of some shoes," Hook said. "I didn't think anyone would mind."

"Looks to me like you have passable shoes already," the officer said.

"These are for a friend."

"Right," he said, taking the cuffs off his belt. "This here's private property and not yours for the taking. Now turn about so's I can cuff you."

Hook held up his prosthesis. "I only have the one arm, as you can see."

"No problem," the officer said, cuffing Hook's right arm. "Now climb in and we'll hitch you up."

The cop snapped the other cuff around the partition that separated the prisoners from the front seat. "There," he said. "That ought to hold you."

He got in the front and worked the keys out of his pocket. Hook could hear him breathing through his swollen nose and could almost smell the sweat in the creases of his neck. "Where you taking me?" Hook asked.

"Jail."

"What's the charge?"

"I ain't worked it out just yet. Consider yourself the guest of Texas for a couple days while I think it over."

The jail, in the basement of the courthouse, smelled of tobacco smoke and burned coffee. The cop led Hook back to a cell and unlocked the door. A blast of heat slapped Hook in the face.

"You damn bums think you can waltz in here and take what you want. It ain't that way in Texas. No, sir," the cop said, pushing Hook into the cell. "It ain't that way at all."

Hook looked up to find himself face to face with the Reverend Dickey. On the bottom bunk, Punk, Pud, and Duce had a game of cards going.

"Well, I'll be," said the reverend. "It's that one-armed rail dick you boys was talking about come to visit."

Duce stood. "Where's your stick of firewood today?"

"Take it easy, boys," Hook said. "Fact is, I'm a railroad bull just like you figured, but I'm incognito and on the hunt for that bridge troll what's been cutting up 'boes. My name is Hook Runyon, and I'm just trying to clean up the jungles for you fellas, so maybe we could put our little misunderstanding aside."

"Well, why didn't you say so sooner?" Duce said. "I ain't in no hurry to have my nuts cut off and put in my belly like a cookie jar. Anyway, we was just funning you."

"Where's that Hambone fella?" Hook asked.

"Turns out he was a damn bindle stiff, just like you said. Last we saw, he was under a bridge looking for his ass."

"Probably still there," said Pud.

Punk looked up. "I can unzip my britches with my tongue."

"Seems right handy," Hook said.

The Reverend Dickey slid away from Hook and into the far corner of the cell. "The cops here got small ways of thinking," he said. "I was fixing to baptize a young lady down by the river when they come running out the trees shouting as to how I was violating her. She comes up saying, 'No, no, no, the Reverend Dickey was laying me down in the water to save my soul.' "

"Damn," Hook said, wiping sweat from his brow. "How is it then that you came to be in here with these common criminals?"

"I'd already broke that cop's nose by the time she got around to saying it," the reverend said, rolling up a sleeve.

Hook caught the flash of a sawtoothed tattoo on the bared skin, and wondered when men of the cloth had taken to ink. Dickey followed Hook's gaze and gave his arm a shake, letting the shirtsleeve fall back.

Before Hook could say anything, Duce said, "Me and the boys could take offense at being called common."

"No offense meant," Hook said. "I'm thinking you could well qualify as uncommon criminals."

"We're victims of injustice just like the good reverend here. We've been eating beans three days now, counting today, for panhandling at the crossing signal. The cop tells me to hold out my hands, that he's going to cuff me up. I says, 'This here is railroad property, and I'm standing on it. You got no rights to arrest me.' He kicks my feet out from under me and says, 'You ain't standing on it no more, are you?' The rest of these boys surrendered without a struggle, as you can see."

"It's Sunday," the Reverend Dickey said, combing back his hair with his hand. "Not a day for holding grudges. It's my way to say a prayer on Sunday, no matter how brief the stay or unfortunate the circumstances.

"Now, Hook Runyon, as a rail dick maybe you'd like to join us? Or maybe you see yourself above the perils of man?"

Hook found himself a place on the opposite wall. "I don't have much taste for religion, Reverend, having had more than a fair dose of it in my youth. That said, the option of leaving does not seem to rest with me."

Reverend Dickey lifted his arms. "Lord," he said, "what you see here today is the cream of the crop, far as thieves go. And we ask forgiveness for those who trespass against us, including this rail dick here. If Lazarus could rise up from the dead, then even such as a misshapen rail-yard bull as this can be made anew.

"And as for these other sinners, I'm recommending a general reprieve. Their sins are a matter of ignorance and of little consequence one way or the other.

"Oh, and you might forgive me too for having broke that cop's nose. Had that young lady been a little quicker on my defense, it likely would not have come to that. Amen."

"Amen," said Duce.

"Amen," said Hook.

Duce rolled a cigarette, sealing it off with his tongue and sticking it in the corner of his mouth. "It's a power the reverend has got, all right, a right particular power when it comes to the well-being of women. Say, where's that little guy what follows you around like a wiener dog?"

"Lost his shoes," Hook said. "I was picking up a donation pair when I got the invitation to come visit you boys here. Course, I hadn't planned on a revival or I'd have dressed for it."

"That boy don't hardly need shoes," Duce said. "A couple of skids under his ass would do just as well."

"Runt likes to be uptown, when possible."

Smoke curled upward into the sunlight that shot through the window. Hook moved to the cell door.

Duce said, "You figure to catch that troll soon?"

"Soon enough," Hook said.

"He have a name?" Pud asked.

"Some, like Duce, call him 'Troll,' " Hook said. "Me, I have him figured for just another 'bo."

"Maybe he's that Hambone boy," Duce said.

"Hambone's just a thief. He's not got the grit for cutting folks open," Hook said. "The troll is a mean son of bitch of a different order, some would say a psychopath."

"A what?" Punk asked.

Hook sat down on the bunk. "I was advised once by a person what knew that a psychopath is someone who kills for no reason, least not one anyone can figure out. He just keeps killing because that's what he wants to do. He's got no remorse, no conscience, no feelings like normal folks. When he isn't killing, he's thinking about killing. He's a mean son of a bitch inside and as dangerous as any man can be—mainly because he can look on the outside as friendly as your best friend."

"You can't always know what's in a man's mind and heart," said the reverend. "You got to remain forgiving for the least of men."

Hook nodded. "True enough, Reverend. You can't know a man's mind, but you're a fool if you don't learn from what he does."

"How you figure on catching this devil?" Duce asked, squashing out his cigarette.

Hook studied the cigarette butt smeared across the floor. "Can't say that I have a plan as yet. But he's working my line sure as I'm stuck in this hole. In the end, I figure a man who can't stop killing is going to wind up under one of my bridges sooner or later. I aim to be there when he does."

*****

Forty-eight hours later, Hook stood at the culvert. He could see the cold ashes where Runt had spent the night and his barefoot tracks in the mud near the entrance. But a thorough search turned up no sign of Runt Wallace.

When a whistle blew downline, Hook stepped back out of sight and waited for the freighter to make the bend. The engineer powered her down as he hit the town limits. Her bell clanged, and her whistle screamed. Hook spotted an open car door, set a pace, and pulled himself inside. It smelled of old cardboard boxes and dust. He leaned against the wall, closed his eyes, and listened to the hum of the wheels.

Soon the engineer powered up, bringing her to speed. The ride to Amarillo would not be long, and Hook only hoped Runt had gotten there okay without his shoes. Most of all, he hoped that the troll had not.

Chapter 32

THE ARTICLE IN THE *Boston Herald* about the recent troll killing in Pampa, Texas, moved Ria to leave at once. She got more funds from her father, packed her car, and headed across country. Three days later, the weariness of the road had settled into her shoulders and neck. By the time she pulled into the Eastman Hotel parking lot at last, she had a throbbing headache.

The clerk signed her in, and within moments of entering her room, she was asleep. Twelve hours later, she awoke to the whistle of a train pulling into the Waynoka yards.

Unpacking her bags took the morning because each item had to be once again arranged in its proper location and sequence, the childhood ritual that she had continued to observe to keep her life in order. When she came to her Moleskine notebook, Ria sat down on the bed and flipped through the pages. Most of what she had recorded had little to do with the theoretical constructs of anything. Instead, entry after entry addressed her observations of one Hook Runyon: the way he had refrained from comment when she had failed to get off the boxcar and had to be rescued; the way he had secured the loyalty of nearly everyone who knew him, including a half-wild mongrel dog; the way he had risked his life to save a train crew and never spoken a word about it to anyone, even her.

She turned to a new page and entered the date, promising herself that this time she would be more objective. With luck, she should have a significant amount of data collected by summer's end, complete her case study, and return to the university with her head held high. With everything in hand, she just might tie it altogether and finish this thing on deadline.

When she had completed unpacking, Ria checked her watch—too late in the day to drive to the courthouse. Perhaps she should go out to the caboose and see what Hook had discovered on the Fort Sumner case.

*****

Lit by the setting sun, the road to Quinlan twisted through the hills like a red ribbon. The expanse of the countryside gave way to a sky exploding with rainbow colors. The air smelled clean and scrubbed, and crows watched from their perches in the mesquite as Ria passed. She slowed as she passed the foreman's shack but saw no one about. The caboose sat on the siding like a red Christmas package, its ladder hiked in the air from the pitch of the spur. She shut off her engine and waited. The lonesome call of a mourning dove came from the locust grove beyond.

She knocked on the caboose door and waited. No answer. Mixer's food dish sat empty on the porch, and the water had long since evaporated from his bowl. She knocked again and then opened the door.

Hook's blankets lay on the floor, and books were scattered across the table. She picked one up and thumbed through the pages. The thinking processes of a man at once creative and practical must hum in his head like a swarm of bees. She sat at his table and listened to the silence, wishing that she might hear him climbing the ladder outside.

Finally, she stacked his books in a neat pile, took one last look, and then closed the door behind her.

Nearly to the car, she heard something rush from the dusk behind her. Whirling about, her heart racing, she exhaled in relief at the sight of Mixer emerging from the tall grass near the tracks. She gathered him up and hugged his neck. "You're getting skinny, boy," she said. "Where's the boss?"

Mixer sneezed and dropped his paw into her lap. "Well, he'll be back soon, I'm sure," she said. Sliding into her car, she started it up. Mixer, perched on his haunches, watched her with his head cocked. Ria sat there for several moments and then rolled down her window. "It's okay, Mixer," she said. "I'll tell Big Al that it's time for a feed."

He wagged his tail, his front feet poised. Ria beat a rhythm out on the steering wheel with her thumb. She leaned over and opened the door. "All right," she said. "You can ride to the store with me."

Mixer sprinted over, jumped in, and made three full turns on the seat before lying down.

At the local grocery, she rolled down the windows while she went in to buy dog food. When she came out, Mixer, having jumped out the window, was just completing marking all four tires on the black Cadillac parked next to her. The driver stared at the process with his mouth open.

"For heaven's sake," Ria said, opening her door. "Get in there."

Pulling away, she shook her head. "You don't even know him."

Back at the caboose, she fed Mixer and filled his bowl with water from a jug she had gotten at the store. She sat on the steps to watch him eat. When finished, Mixer jumped off the caboose porch and worked his way toward the locust grove. He stopped once, looked back, and then disappeared into the trees.

That night, she lay in bed and listened to the eastbound light up the crossing as it came into town. Tomorrow, she would go back to the sheriff's office in the basement of the courthouse and talk to Betty about getting access to the blotter. Maybe there was something there she could use to bolster her data. She wondered about Mixer, his lack of food and water. Big Al must have moved on to another job. Hook gave Mixer his freedom, but it did not seem like him to leave the dog unattended for so long.

*****

Ria found Betty sitting on a park bench on the courthouse lawn, having just finished her lunch and moved on to a doughnut.

"You never showed, hon," Betty said.

"I'm sorry. I had an emergency trip home. Do you still think I could get access to the blotter?"

Betty sucked doughnut glaze from her fingertips.

"Thing is," she said, "the blotter is open to the public. I mean, it's law-ful to look at it and all that, but they don't like it much. I work the evening shift, three to eleven. Maybe if you could come to the office around six. The jailer goes to dinner about then, and he takes a nap at home before he comes back. I've got the place to myself."

"He leaves you there with the prisoners?"

"Look, hon," she said, licking frosting off the wrapper. "It's the ones *not* behind bars that you have to worry about."

"I'll be back at six, then," Ria said.

"Come to the back door and ring the buzzer. I'll let you in."

*****

Ria rang the buzzer as a squirrel sized her up from the branch of an enormous mulberry tree. Betty opened the door and motioned her back to the dispatch room. "Coffee?" she asked, pointing to a chair.

"Thanks, no," Ria said.

"Don't blame you," she said. "Tastes like crankcase oil."

Ria took a seat and tucked her purse under the chair. "How long have you worked here?" she asked.

"Seems like forever."

"You know the deputies, then?"

"In the biblical sense, hon, if you get my drift."

"Oh," Ria said, sitting back in surprise.

"It's like watching the same black-and-white movie over and over," Betty said, checking her hair in the reflection of the window. "I mean, you done one, you've done them all, what with their little guns and badges."

She turned. "Just between us girls, you know who is the best lover in the courthouse?"

"I couldn't begin to guess," Ria said.

"The janitor. Lordy, I mean it took me thirty minutes to work up enough strength to get the closet door open. You think it's from working that mop all day?"

"About the blotter?"

"Oh, that. It's in there," Betty said, pointing to a small anteroom off to the side. "The boys don't enter anything in the log until their shifts end."

"Maybe I should get started?"

The radio crackled, and Betty stepped over and read off an address into the two-way. The transmission complete, she dug through her purse, pulled out a cigarette, and lit up.

"Why do you want this blotter stuff anyway?" she asked.

"I'm completing my degree in forensic psychology—this is data for my research."

"Foren . . .?"

"Forensic psychology. The psychology of criminal behavior."

"I could tell you a thing or two about that."

"I'm guessing so."

"Sometimes I go upstairs to the jail when the jailer's off at dinner. Give the boys up there a little treat, you know."

Ria's ears warmed. "You mean . . ."

"Oh, lordy, no. Not that," Betty said. "I'd never let them out of their cages—that would be against the rules."

Ria tried not to smile. "Then what?" she asked.

"I just give them a little change of scenery, picking stuff up off the floor, emptying the trash, things like that. Give them a little something to think about."

Ria checked her watch. "Isn't that dangerous?"

"I figure, what the hell? What can it hurt? Anyway, why should the deputies get all the fun?"

"But you could be caught?"

"What are they going to do? I mean, all I have to do is make a few calls to a few wives, and we have a new force by morning."

"Not to mention custodial staff," Ria said. "You could shut down the jail."

"You bet I could," Betty said. "And as for those boys up there in the cells, well, they're grateful for whatever they can get, even if it's just a peek."

"The blotter?" Ria said.

"Oh, right. It's back there in that anteroom. Those blotters don't tell half the story, not half, hon. They're just arrest records, you know, 'the subject this' and 'the subject that.' You want to know the real deal, come talk to me."

"I'll keep that in mind."

"And if you hear Fred, the jailer, buzz in at the front, just go on out that side door. There ain't nothing he can do but bitch, and I'm about bitched out, if you know what I mean."

"Can I come back again?"

Betty snuffed her cigarette out in a rubber ashtray shaped like a miniature tractor tire.

"Oh, sure. Just make it about the same time, okay?"

In the anteroom, Ria found the blotters, what looked to be old courthouse ledgers, stacked on a table, the years written in ink on their spines. Taking out her Moleskine, she started with the most recent and proceeded to work her way through the entries.

Most were just as Betty had described, little more than a perfunctory listing of time and location, with a one- or two-word description: *11:02 p.m., loud music reported, Benson Apartments, manager said he would take care of it; 11:45 p.m., domestic disturbance, John Rebel residence, 830 Church St., fighting in the driveway, husband taken into custody; 1:00 a.m., 412 Elm St., cow in the road, 4 miles south of town; 2:00 a.m., someone reported to be down behind bowling alley, person taken to the emergency room; 4:00 a.m., barking dog, 300 Cherry St., dog could not be located.*

Ria noted the entries in her Moleskine and had no sooner leaned back in her chair than she heard the front-door buzzer. Slipping out the side door, she circled around to her car. She sat there for some time watching cars pull in and out of the grocery parking lot across the street. Considerable time and money had been invested in her being there, and she was determined to see it through. She had been warned that there would be little useful information, but yet here she was. So she would just try again tomorrow.

Chapter 33

HOOK SLEPT, HIS HEAD LEANED against one of the cardboard boxes. At some point, he realized that the train had stopped, and he sat up in the darkness to listen. Some sort of switching was in progress, busting up a cut probably, adding on empty wheat hoppers at the Honey or Zita spurs outside Amarillo, Texas. The shuttling of wheat cars went on endlessly in the summer months.

He rubbed at his face, the stubble having grown soft on his chin. The car bumped back, and he could hear the air compressor kick on somewhere upline. For a brief moment he thought he saw something move—and then he saw it again, the profile of a man. The man turned, and the light that filtered through the open door lit his face. Hook recognized him, even with broken teeth.

"Hambone," Hook said, struggling to stand.

He never made it up; a packing crate crashed across his shoulders. Pain flashed up his spine and settled in the glands under his ears. He reached for his sidearm, realizing too late that he had left it with Runt.

"You messed with me, and now I am sending you to the company croaker," Hambone said, his voice hard.

The second crate struck Hook across the side of his head. He could smell the pine pitch, and his ear began to ring as his world flipped upside down.

*****

He awoke with one eye searching the darkness, the other swollen shut, Hambone's parting shot. The boxcar creaked in the heat. But there were no other sounds to center him in the blackness, no engine throb, no compressor, no voices.

Climbing over the jumble of boxes, he searched for the door, finding it closed and locked. The reality of the situation rushed in, suffocating and impenetrable, and he fought to regain his composure. Sweat stung his eyes and raced into his beard. He searched for his bandanna to wipe it away.

That bastard Hambone had clobbered him straight up, bailed out, and then locked the door, leaving him to die in the heat. Hook had seen more than his share of melted bodies trapped in train cars, and he would just as soon not become one.

He put his ear against the door, hot against his cheek. Who knew if anyone would show up? Even if someone did, they wouldn't know he was in there, and pounding on the massive door would do little to alert anyone. His breath shortened at the prospects. He had ridden rattlers his whole life, but this one just might become his tomb. He slid down the door onto his haunches.

At first he could not process the slit of light in the darkness, could not fathom its significance. But then it came to him, the crack between door and car. If only he could get something through it, a way to signal his whereabouts to the outside world. Searching his pockets, he found his bandanna, tore off a piece of cardboard box from behind him, and wrapped the bandanna over it so that he could work it through the crack. The red bandanna just might catch someone's eye, stir up enough curiosity to make 'em come for a look.

He waited then, lying in the blackness with his head against the wall of the car.

*****

The thump-thump came from far away as if in a dream. Hook sat up, turning his ear into the sound. The noise traveled down the rails like a distant telegraph signal, a thumping familiar yet foreign.

When it came again, he recognized it for what it was, a hammer against the iron wheels of the cars, the sound of a car toad checking for wheel flaws. Slowly, the thumping grew louder, and Hook, more confident that it was in fact the doing of a real person. The car toad had probably driven in on a company truck to clear the cars before they were short-hauled to a grain elevator someplace.

Hook worked his way back into the boxes just in case it was Hambone returning to finish him off. When the door slid open at last, a shaft of sunlight blazed into the darkness. Hook held his hand against the blinding light long enough for his eyes to adjust before he swung out and dropped to the ground. The car toad yelped, but Hook just ducked his head, slipped under the car, and took off down the high iron.

His eye throbbed, and the cuts on his head burned from perspiration, but he did not slow down. He was out. He was alive, and he had a two-pronged mission ahead: first, to find Runt Wallace and second, to track down Hambone and kick the son of a bitch into unconsciousness.

*****

Hook spotted Frenchy's old steamer getting a drink at the far side of the Amarillo yards. She towed a salvage engine and two flatcars of scrap iron on her tail. Frenchy was one of a few old-timers still operating teakettles for the railroad. He spent most his time gathering up bobtails, smaller units used for switching in the yards.

Hook stepped out of sight between the flatcars. If he hitched a ride with Frenchy, his cover as a 'bo could be blown. If he didn't, he could wait hours for another hop, and even then, he might not be able to bail at the proper jungle. A ballast scorcher at the throttle had a way of changing one's travel plans. Maybe he should just take his chances with Frenchy. He had known him a good many years and trusted him as much as he did any man.

Hook waited until the engine water had been topped off and the steam brought up. Before stepping out, he looked upline and downline to make sure it was clear.

Frenchy lay in on his whistle and bumped her back into the switch. Hook swung up on the engine ladder about the time Frenchy stuck his head out the window. Frenchy looked down at him, chewing on his cigar.

"Hand me that jay rod," he said over his shoulder to the fireman. "There's a damn cyclops climbing up my ladder."

Hook swung into the cab. "I need a hitch, Frenchy. Maybe you can give me a slow at that jungle north of town?"

Frenchy looked at the bakehead. "Who is this, anyway?" he asked.

The bakehead pushed back his hat and gave Hook the once-over. "Danged if I know," he said.

"Voice is familiar, though," Frenchy said. "Kind of looks like that Hook Runyon."

"He's only got one arm too," the bakehead said.

"That's a fact," Frenchy said. "But this fella's also got only one eye, or maybe it's three. Right hard to tell, ain't it?"

"Looks a little like that old mongrel dog what lives in that caboose over to Quinlan," the bakehead said. " 'Cept older and uglier."

"You bastards through yet?" Hook asked.

Frenchy lit his cigar, and the cab filled with smoke. Hook fanned his face. "That troll catch up with ya?" Frenchy asked, pulling onto the high iron.

"No, he hasn't. I ran into a 'bo carrying a two-by-four," Hook said.

"I hear that troll don't leave no tracks behind," Frenchy said. "Like he drops down out the sky, pokes a hole in a 'bo's skull to let the air out, and flies away again. I hear there ain't hardly a 'bo left between here and California with his damn head still in one piece."

Hook gingerly touched his eye; a pain settled in under his eardrum. "I counted five dead 'boes just this morning," he said. "Might have been more had I another hand for counting."

Frenchy grinned and eased the throttle forward. The old bullgine dug down, and black smoke boiled skyward. They were soon clipping down the high iron. Frenchy lit the whistle and then leveled out the engine stroke.

Frenchy turned. "Ain't for me to say, Hook, but them clothes is getting a bit gamy. Don't you work for the company no more?"

"Can you boys keep a secret?" Hook asked.

"Oh, hell, yes," the bakehead said. "If I told everything I know, Frenchy here would never see the light of day again."

"Fact is, I'm incognito," Hook said.

The bakehead looked over at Frenchy and then back at Hook. "I think my cousin died from that," he said. "One eye swelled plumb shut just like that before the Lord took him home."

Hook looked up through his brows. "Undercover, you bastards," he said. "I'm living in the jungles undercover, pretending to be a 'bo. I figure sooner or later, that troll is going to come looking for me and make the mistake of his life."

"Wouldn't it help if you had your gun?" Frenchy said, pointing to Hook's empty holster.

"I loaned it to Runt Wallace. He used to run shine over near Alva, you might recall."

"That little guy with the short legs, what looks more like an orangutan than a man?"

"There's some family resemblance," Hook said.

"Why's he on the bum?"

"Times are hard for moonshiners, Frenchy. Thing is, I've lost track of him. We got separated and what with this troll lurking about. . . . "

"Well, I bet he's got a gun," Frenchy said.

"You boys know Ludie Bean?" Hook asked.

"A sweet man, ain't he?" Frenchy said.

"You think you could get hold of him? Tell him to keep a lookout in the jungles for Runt Wallace. That damn troll could be anywhere."

"What do you want with Ludie? All that bastard ever does is sleep in that crew car of his," Frenchy said.

"If you could wake him up and tell him, I'd appreciate it. I don't want to blow my cover."

"You couldn't look more like a 'bo if you was one," Frenchy said. "No, wait. You was one."

Frenchy brought her down as they approached the curve outside of town. Hook climbed to the ladder, the wind whipping at his hat. Frenchy set the brakes, and the old steamer huffed down to a crawl. "She's just ahead," Frenchy said.

Hook stepped out on the ladder. "Thanks, Frenchy."

"You might want to keep that gun yourself in the future," he said. "It works better that way."

*****

The bridge turned out to be the wrong bridge, and Hook had to walk three miles in the dark. He could smell the wood smoke drifting in before he arrived. Dark clouds shuttled overhead, and the distant smell of rain hung in the air. Heat lightning flashed on the horizon.

He paused at the approach to the bridge to get his bearings and the lay of the land. He could see the wink of a campfire through the timbers. He wondered if Runt had found shoes and made it on in. If not, he'd better steel himself; Runt's temper might be a little short by now.

He worked his way down the riprap, pausing now and again to listen. He figured Runt to be alone since he could hear no voices. More than one 'bo in one spot nearly always resulted in a bull session of one sort or another. He peeked around the corner but saw no one. The fire had burned down to embers that throbbed red and grew brighter with each gust of wind.

When he spotted the body lying behind the campfire, his heart sank. He knew poor Runt's eyes, once so bright and full of mischief, now carried only all the sorrow and regret of a shortened life.

He heaved a sigh and stepped into camp. As he reached the body and turned it over, he shuddered. The chest had been opened from belly button to neck. Shriveled testicles filled the gaping wound. But it was not Runt who stared back at him but Hambone, his eyes ringed with grass and dirt, his gold front tooth missing. Hook turned the body back over. Sure enough, there was a hole in the back of his skull. "You were a son of a bitch," Hook said, "but no one deserves to die like this."

He pulled the body away from the threat of the campfire but otherwise returned it to how he had found it. The local law would want to see the place as discovered.

Hook searched the area looking for tracks, but like the other killing sites, everything started and ended within the bridge itself. He walked down to the creek, a small stream but with an expansive floodplain. He splashed water on his face and wished the hell for a cigarette. He stood and looked back at the bridge that loomed like a skeleton in the night. He was getting close, he knew, but would it be in time?

Chapter 34

WHEN THE PHONE RANG in Ria's room, she jumped up from her chair in hopes that it might be from Hook. "Hello," she said.

"Ria, this is Betty."

"Betty?"

"Betty from the courthouse. The jailer called in with Saturday night flu, and I've got the place to myself. Thought you might like to know."

"Oh, right," Ria said. "What time?"

"Anytime, hon," she said. "I'm already at work. Just buzz in."

"I'll be there as soon as I can get around, Betty. And thanks."

"No problem," Betty said. "Us girls have to stick together, don't we?"

Ria showered, dressed, and gathered up her Moleskine and pen. As she made her way to the car, the clouds, the color of red grapes, gathered overhead, and the smell of rain drifted in on the breeze. She wondered if Mixer would be safe and dry but decided that he had taken care of himself long before she arrived on the scene and could do so now.

After stopping for gas, she headed for the courthouse. Fat drops of rain splashed against the windshield and then abruptly stopped. Lightning cut through the clouds and danced on the horizon. Thunder rumbled off, and then the rain commenced to fall in earnest. She slowed, her wipers struggling against the deluge.

By the time she reached the courthouse parking lot, the storm had raced off into the prairie, and a rainbow arched through the sky. The air smelled clean and washed, and the colors of summer were scrubbed bright.

She parked the car, made the short walk to the front door, and rang the buzzer. Betty, dressed in jeans and flouncy blouse, let her in.

"Hi, hon," she said. "Come on in. I've got the coffee on."

Ria took up a chair in the dispatch room and waited as Betty filled a cup with black coffee.

"Thanks," Ria said, taking the cup.

"Sunday morning," Betty said. "Not much happens around here on Sunday morning."

"I appreciate the call," Ria said. "But the truth is, I'm not getting much useful information from the police blotter."

"Well," Betty said, pouring sugar into her coffee. "If I were you, hon, I'd go straight to Saturday-night entries and skip all that other stuff."

"Why do you say that?"

"Nothing happens in this burg except on Saturday night. Then the jail is chock-full. Good citizens work their collective asses off all week, see. Come Saturday, they're ready for a little diversion, whether it be getting drunk, getting laid, or beating up the wife and kids. And there's Sunday just around the corner for whatever redemption is required, not to mention time enough for an afternoon nap before going back to work on Monday."

The two-way crackled, and Betty jotted something down in her log. Ria leaned in and smiled.

"What?" Betty said, looking up from her notepad.

"Do the Saturday-night parties include you?"

"Why, no, hon," she said. "I get my diversions during cleaning hours at the courthouse, if you get my drift."

"Oh, yes, how could I forget."

"And I have a hobby too."

"Hobby?"

"Trash," Betty said.

"Excuse me?" Ria said, squinting her eyes as if to better understand.

Betty grinned. "I know the trash schedule for every street in town. I go diving every chance I get."

"What do you do with all that trash?"

Betty checked a chipped fingernail. "Some I keep. Some I sell. Some I read."

"Read?"

"It's like looking in someone's window, 'cept legal. You'd be surprised what stories you can read in a dumpster."

"Like?"

"Like bills, for instance. Who owes whom what and for how long. Empty bottles give a fair account of the night's events. Panties show up in the damnedest places. I know more about the folks in this town then all these deputies put together."

"And what about redemption?"

"Redemption?"

"Do you seek it out come Sunday?"

"Not so much. I figure sin can be salted away like coins in a jar. Redeem it all at once during off-hours. Saves time for me and God both.

"So yes, it's best to work weekends, hon. Just sit here in my little cage and watch these fools trying to make their boring lives less boring. I tell you, there ain't one life in ten thousand worth living."

"You're a born cynic, Betty."

"You're not the first to notice," she said.

Ria finished her coffee and dropped her cup in the trash can. "About that blotter."

"The room is open. Remember, hon, it's all about Saturday nights."

Ria picked up with the ledgers where she had left off the day before, but by the fourteenth entry on reported loud music and barking dogs, she decided to try Betty's suggestion. It wasn't long before she had made some significant finds for her notebook.

Betty was right. Crime and violence swept in like a black storm on Saturday nights, the same people arrested by the same deputies, often for the same crime, and it all happened on Saturday nights like some tribal ritual.

After a long afternoon of picking black pearls from the blotter, Ria was winding down for the day when an entry name suddenly jumped out at her. She ran her finger across the ledger. *Sat., June 4th, 2:00 a.m., reported rape in parking lot of Mick's Bar & Grill. Ludie Bean taken into custody at the scene.*

Ria leaned back in her chair. Could this be the same Ludie Bean of railroad fame that she knew? It had to be, the name being too uncommon for mere coincidence.

But rape? Who would hire a rapist, much less to serve in law enforcement? Perhaps the allegations had been proved false. Or perhaps they had been true but were covered up. She drummed her fingers on the desk, closed the ledger, and went looking for Betty.

"Yeah, I remember the incident," Betty said, pushing the two-way to the side. "They brought her in here that night. She was a mess, drunk, sick, and beat up. She didn't get that way by herself."

"Is this the same Ludie Bean who works for the railroad as a security agent?"

Betty nodded. "Look, hon, are you sure you want to get into this?"

"I'm sure," Ria said.

"He's the same Ludie we all know and love," she said. "The bastard's knuckles were raw from beating on that girl's head."

"So what happened?"

"To him? Nothing happened to him. They gave her a public drunk and sent him home. Charges were eventually dropped."

"Because?"

"Insufficient evidence." Betty scooted her chair back. "Look, Ludie's law enforcement. These guys get accused of this and that all the time. No one's going to believe he was guilty without a hell of a lot of evidence. They didn't have it."

Ria got up and walked to the window. From there, she could see one of the patrol cars parked in the parking lot.

"Tell me about Ludie Bean," she said.

"I don't know much about him, but drunk or sober, I wouldn't want to meet him in a parking lot," Betty said.

Ria turned. "Do you know where he's from? This could be important, Betty. People's lives might be at risk."

"Well, I know how to find out," she said. "But if anyone asks, I'll deny everything. Understood?"

"Understood," Ria said.

"Give me a minute," Betty said, pushing back her chair.

When Betty returned, she handed a piece of paper to Ria. "His home address is in Wichita," she said.

Ria tucked the paper into her pocket. "Thanks, Betty."

When she reached the door, Betty said, "You be careful, hon. It doesn't pay to cross some folks."

Chapter 35

HOOK SQUINTED HIS eyes and spit, the smells of carnage and death like syrup in the air. His head still throbbed from the blow Hambone had delivered not so long ago. But unlike Hambone, at least he still had a head without a hole in it.

He widened his search for clues, finding deep tracks at the base of a bridge piling where someone had dropped from above. He spotted a safe-haven symbol scratched in the abutment and what appeared to be a small owl, its head cocked to the side.

Circling the fire, he looked for evidence of where the culprit might have exited the scene, but found none. It looked to have all happened quickly, with great force: a spew of blood into the grass, a sprig of hair caught on a thorn bush. Hambone appeared to have been taken from behind, a swift and violent blow to the head. He had not had a chance.

A breeze swept down the valley, and the embers of the fire briefly flared, shadows dancing in the timbers. Hook debated what to do. If he were to report the killing, his cover would be blown, his chances of catching the troll ruined. And then there was Runt, a guy with plenty of grit but damn little experience on the rails. He was in a dangerous situation out and about alone with the troll lurking in the area. Hook leaned against a bridge piling and dabbed at the perspiration stinging the wound on his head. The faraway rumble of an approaching train traveled from the piling and into his bones. The Dumas jungle was not that far away, and he figured Runt to have headed there for the night. Ludie Bean, having been alerted by now, might well have found Runt and got him off the rails and to safety. But Hook could not be sure, so pushing on was still the best choice, the only choice that made sense. Hook, scrambling up the embankment, made for the high iron. By the time he reached the top, the train's glimmer broke in the distance, and the shrill whistle of a diesel cut through the stillness.

He sprinted down track, putting distance between him and the bridge so he could set a pace. Drawing back into the shrubbery, he waited for the approach. She was coming fast, a ballast scorcher making time in open country. The ground trembled under his feet, and the smoke of the diesel engine blacked out the sky as she charged toward him. When she passed, a gust of wind nearly knocked him off his feet. The engineer was walking the dog, the cars careening from side to side, their wheels screeching like death.

She was batting the stack, and with no time to wait, Hook ran as best he could over the rough ground. He could hear the bouncer coming up behind way too fast, but he was desperate to catch the hop. Taking a quick look over his shoulder, he spotted the grab iron on its way up. Reaching out with his prosthesis, he snared the iron as it passed and knew in that instant that he had made a big mistake.

The prosthesis made a whishing sound as it tore away. Hook lurched forward into the night, hitting the ground hard. He sprang to his feet and watched the caboose race off into the distance.

*****

The call of an owl lifted from out of the plains with its lonesome refrain. His ma had always said that the hoot of an owl was a man's name being called from the roll of death. Hook hoped that it was not his name come up just yet.

Still battered and weary, he walked as best he could. Now and again, he took a seat on the rail, still warm from the day's sun, to rest. His shoulder burned where the harness of his prosthesis had been torn away.

He had retrieved the wooden arm from the bar ditch and cobbled everything back together. But nothing worked as it should any longer. When his shoe came untied, he struggled mightily to retie it, finally giving up with a swear of frustration.

Hook walked for hours through the night. He walked until dawn lit the morning and until his legs ached with fatigue. Any other time, the rails would have been alive with freighters, but not on this day. Hooding his eyes with his hand, he looked down the rails, morning heat now quivering up from them in waves. He could see someone in the distance sitting in the shade of a switch signal. When he approached, the man stood.

The whiskered stranger wore a suit or at least what had passed for a suit at one time, now soiled and torn. A tie, the knot dark with oil and dirt, hung from his neck like a diseased tongue.

Hook approached with caution. "Hey," he said, pulling up at a proper distance.

The man pushed his hat back, revealing a face bedraggled with the weariness of the rails. "Pass in peace, mister. I'm just taking my rest."

Hook stepped in closer. "How far to the Dumas bridge?" he asked.

"Too damn far," the man said. "You riding rails?"

Hook shook his head. "Walking rails."

The man rocked up on the toes of his shoes and stuck out his hand. "Dr. Armstrong," he said.

"Hook," Hook said.

"I got a pot of tater soup going down under that tree. Care to join me?"

"I'd be pleased," Hook said, "but I don't have any contributions at the moment."

"Well," the man said. "Can't guarantee the taste. Them taters were shriveled up like nuts in a snowbank."

Hook fell in beside his host as they walked toward his camp.

"Doctor, is it?" Hook asked.

"That's right, M.D.," the man said. "Specialist."

"That so? What kind of specialist would that be?"

"Gynecology." And with that, the doctor let slide down the embankment toward his camp with an agility that belied his age.

"I wouldn't have thought there would be much demand for a gynecologist out here."

The doctor came to a halt and looked at Hook straight on.

"You ain't that troll, are you?"

"No," Hook said. "And you ain't no gynecologist, I suspect."

"I'm an artist."

"What kind of artist?"

"Painter."

"What kind of painter?"

"A painter painter," he said. "You ain't never heard of Armstrong the painter?"

"No, I haven't, but then I'm not up on my painters like I ought to be."

"Well, I'm Armstrong the painter. I got paintings in the Louvre."

Armstrong picked through a gunnysack, coming up with a tin cup, which he handed to Hook. Hook dipped out some tater soup and sucked at the lip of the cup. He looked over at Armstrong.

"What's your medium?" Hook asked.

"Medium what?"

"You know, pencil, oils, pastels?"

"Oh, that," he said. "I've done hundreds of mediums, all kinds."

"You don't have a little salt, do you?" Hook asked.

"Salt ain't good for you," Armstrong said. "Learned that in medical school."

"I thought you were an artist?"

"Painter," he said.

"What's a painter doing in medical school?"

"You can't be no gynecologist without going to medical school," he said. "Everybody knows that."

Hook finished off his soup and leaned back against the trunk of the mesquite. "That was fine soup," he said.

Armstrong pulled out his makin's and rolled himself a Bull Durham. "Learned it in cooking school," he said.

"You went to cooking school too?"

"Oh, hell, yes," Armstrong said. "I worked as a chef in the finest restaurants. Five years in Tuscany."

"You've lived an interesting life," Hook said.

Armstrong flipped the ash off his cigarette. "What happened to your arm?"

"Car wreck," Hook said. "Damned harness is broke."

"Why didn't you sew your arm back on?"

"Didn't occur to me at the time."

"Been me, I'd have sewed that son of a bitch back on. You'd be good as new right now. Sewing is my specialty. Learned it in surgery school. I can fix that harness."

"I figured," Hook said. "Well, give it a go, will you?"

Dr. Armstrong dug out a little packet with needle and thread in it and worked over Hook's harness.

"There," he said. "Good as new."

"Damn," Hook said. "That works just fine now."

"Yes," he said. "What you doing out here without no taters?"

"I'm looking for a fella."

"You sure you ain't that troll what puts holes in people's heads?"

"I'm pretty sure."

Armstrong kicked dirt on the fire and picked up the cups. "What's his name?" he asked.

"Who?"

"That fella you're looking for . . ."

"Runt Wallace," Hook said.

"Is he a gynecologist?"

"Yes," Hook said.

"Why do they call him Runt?"

" 'Cause of his size, I suppose."

"A little guy, sawed-off legs, looks something or other like a spider?"

"Yes," Hook said.

"Don't wear no shoes and reads Faulkner?"

"That's him, all right. You seen him?"

"No," Armstrong said.

"Right," Hook said. "Well, thanks for the soup. I better get on down track."

"Yeah," he said. "You ever need a gynecologist, just let me know."

Chapter 36

RIA FOUND THE ADDRESS in the older part of Wichita, a neighborhood of bungalows mostly, with overgrown yards. As she walked up the driveway, a man emptying his trash at the next house over pushed back his hat.

"Morning," he said.

"I'm looking for the home of a Mr. Ludie Bean," she said. "Do you know if this is the correct address?"

He pointed at the house. "His mother lives there. You'll have to knock loud. She can't hear nothing," he said.

"Thank you," she said, nodding.

Cemetery roses, at the end of their bloom, clung to the rickety lattice that had been wired across the end of the porch. An old rug, blown into the yard at some point, lay half-buried under leaves.

Ria knocked on the door and then knocked again with more force. She could hear the door chains falling away inside, and then an old woman with missing dentures peeked out at her.

"Yes?" she said.

"Hi. Would this be the Ludie Bean residence?"

"Who wants to know?" The woman asked.

"My name is Ria Wolfe," she said. "I'm trying to locate the home of a Mr. Ludie Bean. It's an insurance matter."

The old woman opened the door. She wore a plain cotton dress with an apron tied high up under her considerable breasts. One of her house shoes, pink rabbits, had given way to a big toe, which now peeked out of the hole where a bunny ear had once been.

"What kind of matter did you say?" the woman asked, holding her hand behind her ear.

"Insurance," Ria said. "Mr. Bean has a small amount of cash coming to him, I believe. May I come in?"

"Ludie don't live here no more," she said, "but I'm his ma."

"If I could visit with you a moment," Ria said. "I promise not to take up much of your time."

"Well," she said. "Come in, then. I'll go get my teeth."

The living room was nearly bare of furniture, save for a rocking chair and an old couch darkened from wear. A windup mantel clock ticked in isolation from its perch on the wall. The pattern on the linoleum floor was all but erased in the heavy traffic paths. There were no curtains, only yellowed pull-down blinds to keep out the world.

The old woman returned from the bathroom and dropped into the rocking chair. She pointed to the couch, and Ria took up a corner.

"You say Ludie has money coming?"

"Yes," Ria said. "I need to clarify a few details first, if you don't mind."

The lady of the house ran her finger under her nose. "What kind of details?"

"Well," Ria said, "first, are you related to Mr. Bean?"

"Like I said, I'm Ludie's mother. Has Ludie done something? Is he in trouble?"

"I need to make certain of his residence so he can receive his money."

"This is where Ludie grew up, if that's what you mean," she said. "He don't come around no more."

"I'm sorry to hear that," Ria said. "Are you his only parent?"

She reached for a cup of cold coffee. "His daddy's dead. His real daddy took off when Ludie was a boy. Went bumming on the rails."

"I see, and do you know where his father is now?"

She looked up from her cup, her eyes like sparks of fire. "If there's a hell, I do," she said. "He left me with three kids and a mortgage. Got himself killed in the process."

"Oh?"

"They said he got drunk and passed out under a boxcar. The switch engine backed it over him."

"He was killed?"

"Pretty much. It cut his body clean in half. They said his eyes never closed, and he was still holding his whiskey bottle. They wanted me to go down and identify him, but I wouldn't do it. Why should I look at something like that?"

"I'm sorry for your loss," Ria said.

"Well, we didn't have nothing when he was here. Had just as much when he was gone."

"Must have been a hard thing for a boy," Ria said.

"Not much difference between Ludie and his daddy when it came to it. Always one thing after another. Quitting school. Trouble with the police."

"Your son went to jail?"

"Not no real jail. He was just a kid, though he looked more like a grown man. He never had no real record, but there's something hard inside Ludie, always has been. They gave him tests once at the asylum, but it didn't come to nothing. One day he was gone, and I ain't heard from him since."

"The other children are home then?"

"They left too, soon as they could. You think you have a family, you know, folks who will care about you no matter what, but it ain't that way. It ain't that way at all. I figure to die alone right here in this house, and who's to care? Now, about that money?" she asked.

Ria dug a fifty from her purse. "Maybe you can see he gets it."

The old lady folded the money into her pocket. "Ludie shows up, I'll see he gets it right off," she said.

Ria was halfway down the drive when the neighbor stepped out from behind the shrubbery.

"I overheard," he said. "That old lady won't give that money to no one."

Ria stopped. "It doesn't matter."

"And that boy of hers was no damn good. I'd stay away from him if I was you."

Ria turned and looked at the man. "What do you mean?"

"He kilt my dog sure as I'm standing here," he said. "I'd had that dog near fifteen years."

"What makes you think it was Ludie Bean?"

" 'Cause some things you just know. I hope Ludie Bean don't never come back," he said. "I hope Ludie Bean's gone forever."

Ria walked to the end of the drive and turned. "I was told there's a mental institution somewhere around here?"

"Sedgwick County Psychiatric Hospital," he said. "Take a left at the stop sign. It's five miles straight south to the front gate."

*****

Ria parked her car and looked up at the red stone bell tower that adorned the entry to the hospital. A security fence walled in the campus proper, and a guard sat in a checkpoint shack at the entrance.

Ria approached the shack, and the man stood, an older man in uniform. He had a receding hairline and a fresh sunburn on his nose.

"May I help you, Miss?" he asked.

Ria smiled. "Yes, perhaps. I'm a forensic psychologist out of Boston and was wanting to check the medical records on one of your patients."

The guard pulled in his paunch and threw back his shoulders. "This is Sunday, Miss. There's only the staff working today. It takes a doctor to get into the records. Law, you know?"

"Oh, and I've come so far."

"Well, maybe you could come back Monday."

Ria pushed her hair back from her face and smiled. "Oh, I wish I could, but I must get back."

"I'm sorry for your trouble, Miss," he said.

"Well, it's not your fault," she said. "You've been very helpful. Have you worked here long?"

"About a hundred years," he said. "I guess I've seen about everything there is to see."

Ria said, "You can't be that old, a nice-looking man like yourself."

"Not quite a hundred years," he said.

"Well, I just needed some general information about a Mr. Ludie Bean.

242

It's my understanding he was a patient here a few years back. But I'm sure you wouldn't remember him."

The guard pulled back his shoulders. "It's a rare patient I don't remember," he said. "Part of the job, you know. You'd be surprised how many of them try to get off campus, hiding in the bushes and what not."

"Then you do remember him?"

"Big son of a bitch for his age," he said. "Excuse the French. Mean too for just a kid. He used to sit under that big tree over there hours on end watching the squirrels. Ludie Bean wasn't one to forget easily."

"Well, thanks," she said. "I guess I will just have to come back some other time."

"Sorry I couldn't help," he said.

"Oh, that's all right," she said. "I understand. . . . Procedures and all."

Ria sat in her car and listened to the tower bells strike out the hour. She took a deep breath and exhaled. She had to get to Hook fast, to tell him what she had learned. She had no evidence of anything per se, but Ludie fit a pattern, a pattern that concerned her deeply.

Chapter 37

RIA DROVE STRAIGHT TO Hook's caboose. A cobweb ran across the ladder, and Mixer's water bowl was dry. Taking a stick, she cleared the web and climbed onto the caboose landing. She knocked first and then eased the door open. The air smelled stale, and everything lay on the table just as she had left it. After closing up, she walked to the locust grove and whistled. Mixer came bounding out of the trees. She knelt and hugged his neck. He had lost more weight, and his fur was matted and full of sticks.

"So where is he?" she asked.

Mixer wagged his tail.

"Okay, you're coming with me."

She made for the Waynoka depot, where she found Banjo sitting at his desk humming "The Water Is Wide" through his nose and keeping time with his pencil.

"Excuse me, I'm Ria Wolfe," she said. "I was here once before with Hook Runyon."

Banjo laid down the pencil and looked up at her. "I decided to add percussion. What do you think?"

"Percussion is always nice."

"I thought so," Banjo said, leaning back in chair with a pleased look on his face. "So what can I do for you, young lady?"

"I'm looking for Hook."

"I ain't seen him for a spell," Banjo said.

"It's important that I get hold of him right away. I think he might be in danger."

Banjo pulled at his chin. "There ain't much trouble he hasn't already seen, you know. What kind of danger you talking about?"

"I can't say just yet," she said. "I have to talk to him. Can you tell me where he is?"

"Not exactly," he said.

"Look, Banjo, I'm sure you don't want anything to happen to him."

"No, I don't, but he said not to say nothing unless . . ."

"Unless?"

"Unless he didn't show up."

"It's important. And he isn't here."

Banjo stood. "Well, I guess technically, then, he didn't show up, so maybe it's okay."

"What's okay?"

"Hook told me he'd be sending a package, and he did. But he said to keep it for him, to open it only if he didn't show up. I reckon we've established that this is that time."

"What kind of package?"

"Right over there," he said. "It was posted out of Fort Sumner."

"Open it, please," she said.

Banjo nodded, took out his pocketknife, and slit open the package. He laid the contents out on his desk: Hook's clothes, his billfold and badge, and a railroad-systems map.

"I don't understand," Ria said. "Why would he send all this to you?"

"I overheard him on the phone talking to Eddie Preston about that troll. Sounded like maybe he was figuring to flush him out."

"By setting himself out as bait? By going undercover as a hobo?" Ria's voice seemed to rise with each word.

"I reckon," Banjo said with a shrug. "I don't know why you're so upset. Hook knows his way around that world better than most."

Ria opened the railroad map and spread it out on Banjo's desk. "These places marked with an 'X,' what are they?"

Banjo studied the map. "Can't say for certain," he said. "But they look like bridges to me. See the rivers leading in. My guess is that they are jungles, hobo jungles."

"Yes," she said. "He's marked out places he intends to check out. He's marked them out just in case."

"Hook knows them jungles, every one of them," Banjo said. "I figure he can take care of himself."

"You can't defend yourself if you don't know who the enemy is," she said. "Sometimes it's what you don't know that can be the most dangerous."

She went to the door and opened it. Mixer sat on his haunches outside waiting for her. She turned back to Banjo. "Do you know where I can find Ludie Bean?"

Banjo shrugged. "Rail bulls keep their schedules close to the vest, but I did see an order come through to move that crew car of his."

"Where?"

"I don't rightly remember. South, I think."

"How could I find out exactly?"

"Frenchy picked the car up with that old teakettle of his. I guess he'd know."

"And how would I find Frenchy?"

"He's out in the yards greasing the pig. Now, the public ain't supposed to be in those yards, though, Miss. . . ."

The door slammed behind Ria before he could finish his sentence.

*****

Frenchy waited at the bottom of the ladder as Ria and Mixer walked across the rail yards.

Ria smiled as she approached, stretching out her hand. Frenchy reached down to shake it, a questioning look on his face.

"We don't get many fillies out here," he said. "Who might you be?"

"My name's Ria Wolfe. I'm an associate of Hook Runyon. Banjo said you moved Ludie Bean's crew car recently. I wonder if you could tell me if that is correct?"

"Isn't that Hook's old dog?" Frenchy asked.

She nodded. "I'm a friend as well. Hook and I are working together on a research project. Could you tell me about the crew car? It's important."

"Left it on a siding outside of Dumas," he said. "You need a rail bull, I'd suggest you call Eddie Preston."

"Dumas, Texas?"

"That's right. While it ain't the end of the world, it's damn close."

"And would you happen to know where Hook is?" she asked.

"You're the one with his dog," he said.

"I'm taking care of Mixer while he's gone, but I'm worried about Hook. There have been some recent developments."

"So you're looking for Ludie Bean and Hook Runyon both, are you? That's two more railroad bulls than most folks would ever want to find."

Steam shot out of the side of the engine, and Frenchy stepped down and took her arm, shuttling her to the side.

"These yards can be hazardous. That 'Keep Out' sign is there for a reason. I suggest you move on now."

"I think Hook could be in danger," she said, shaking off his hand. "My guess is that he's working undercover somewhere."

Frenchy frowned. "Hook don't need no one running shotgun for him," he said. "And Ludie Bean is best left to hisself. He ain't one you want to go poking with a stick."

She took the systems map out of her pocket and showed it to Frenchy. "This was in Hook's things that he sent back to Banjo. He's marked these spots—Banjo says they are all where a bridge crosses a river, and I believe them to be hobo jungles. I believe that he's staying in them hoping to flush out the bridge troll. And I believe you know more than you're telling me. Your loyalty to Hook is misplaced here."

"You ain't one to hold back on what you believe, are you, Miss? And if I did know more, why would I tell you?"

Ria pushed her hair back from her eyes. "I believe that Hook's real danger comes from within the ranks, and I need to get to that crew car," she said. "Can I drive there?"

"No," he said. "You'd never make it in a car. There's no proper road."

Frenchy took his pliers out of his overalls and banged on the engine ladder. The ash cat stuck his head out of the cab window.

Frenchy called up to him. "The pig's greased. Bring up a head of steam."

The fireman nodded and turned back to his work. Frenchy walked to the front of the steamer before returning to where Ria waited. "When a man tells me something in confidence, I'm prone to keep it to myself," he said. "But if Hook's in danger. . . ."

"He's out there alone somewhere," Ria said.

"Hook's working undercover just like you figured," Frenchy said. "I dropped him off at a bridge outside town in the Texas panhandle, and I ain't heard from him since."

"What town?"

"Amarillo. He was on the hunt for a friend of his at the time, a Runt Wallace. Thing is, he wanted me to put Ludie Bean on Runt's trail for him, which I did."

"Runt?"

"An associate you might say."

Ria crossed her arms over her chest. She could feel her heart pounding. "I see."

"When we moved his crew car, Ludie said he'd be in the area and make it a point to check things out."

"Could you take me there, Frenchy?"

"It's against the rules for anyone to ride this here train," he said. "I could get fired. Anyway, the rails are no place for a lady. Hook's probably moved on by now. 'Boes don't hang in one jungle long, you know."

She opened the systems map. "The next one marked is outside of Dumas," she said. "Maybe he's gone there?"

"Maybe," Frenchy said. "Maybe he hopped a hotshot and found himself in Kansas City. There's just no way of knowing for sure. Why don't you just call the police?"

Ria glanced down at Mixer. "Without any evidence? They'd laugh me off the phone."

Frenchy climbed the ladder. "I'm running late," he said. "We're towing this short haul to Amarillo. We'll be going by Ludie's crew car on the way."

"Take me with you, Frenchy."

"We've got an empty louse box on the tail. Sometimes 'boes hitch a ride without us ever knowing. And there's a slow signal not far from that crew car. We'll be coming back through early the next morning. The rails ain't no place for a lady on her own. She wouldn't want to miss her ride back. Course, hitching a train is against the rules, and I'd never allow it, not if I knew it."

*****

Ria and Mixer sat in the shadows inside the old caboose, which rocked back and forth with every dip and sway of the tracks. Now and again, Frenchy's whistle would rise up like the lonesome call of a wolf as they drove south into the prairie.

The more Ria thought about her actions, hopping a train into the middle of nowhere in pursuit of a possible psychopathic killer, the more she began to doubt her sanity. She was a student, an academic, and had not the least experience in actual crime fighting or hopping trains. When had she become the kind of woman who defied her adviser and broke the law, much less played Sherlock Holmes? She couldn't say, but she suspected the timing coincided with meeting a certain rail-yard bull.

The hours passed as they rumbled southward. She dozed alongside Mixer in the caboose for a good while and then went out on the porch for a breath of air.

Soon they passed a work crew aligning rail. Spike drivers swung their mauls in perfect synchronization, a dance timed by a sixth sense and the beat of their hearts, as their muscled arms rose and fell. They paused and watched her pass before bringing their mauls to bear once more, with the faultless timing of New York Rockettes.

When she awoke, the sunset had turned the windows orange. Mixer stirred, scratched at his ear, and settled back in for another nap.

Ria had just dropped off again herself when three short blasts from Frenchy's whistle jerked her upright in the darkness. Wheels, metal against metal, screeched as the train slowed.

"Come on, boy," Ria said. "I think this is our stop."

Ria waited on the caboose landing until the train was down to a crawl before boosting Mixer off the side. She dropped from the ladder and moved into the right-of-way, where Mixer soon fell in beside her.

Frenchy's glimmer lit up the rails down track, and when his whistle sounded, uncertainty flooded her once again. The cars bumped out slack, and the train soon wobbled off into the darkness, leaving her and Mixer standing in the night.

Ria could smell the dampness and hear the crackle of locusts. She soon spotted the crew car sitting on a siding off in the distance, a converted sleeper by the looks of it, its windows small and well shuttered.

She eased up on the wooden step just as the moon slid behind a cloud. The night grew dark and silent. There were no lights, no signs or sounds of life within the car. She paused. Mixer whined and looked up at her.

"Okay," she whispered. "Here goes nothing."

Chapter 38

S HE STEPPED INTO the darkness, the air still and damp and smelling of stale hamburger grease. Mixer leaned against her leg, trembling with excitement. Feeling her way through the darkness, she lifted a blind. Moonlight flooded the room. An old skillet sat on the stove, and on the table next to it lay an empty whiskey bottle. Clothes were strewn about the area, and a pair of work boots, covered in mud, sat next to the door.

She began with the overhead luggage racks, searching each as best she could in the dim light. Mixer circled the room, sniffing out trails that only he could detect. It was not until she got to Ludie's closet, an area walled off from the room proper but without a door, that she made her first discovery.

The keg, an old wooden nail keg by the looks of it, had been shoved to the far back of the closet. She worked it forward into the low light. For a moment, she thought she heard something bump, a movement somewhere outside the car. She held her breath and waited, searching the car for a quick exit, but there was none. The minutes passed, and she heard nothing more, nothing beyond the distant bay of a lone coyote.

She tipped the keg and found it empty. Climbing onto the keg, she searched the top shelf with her hand and discovered newspaper articles that had been cut out and saved. She read them by the light of the moon shooting through the cupola. Each dealt with some aspect or detail of the bridge troll murders. She pushed aside Ludie's clothes, the smell of him still lingering in their folds.

The door suddenly opened, and a dark shadow stepped in. Ria's head whirled as the blood drained away.

"Who—who are you?" she cried, her voice trembling.

"Dr. Armstrong," the voice said. "Who are you?"

*****

After they had walked a safe distance from the crew car—far enough away not to be seen if someone else should return—Dr. Armstrong built a small fire and offered Ria his suit jacket to ward off the chill.

"No, I'm fine," she said. "A little shaken is all."

"Tater soup or coffee?" the doctor asked.

"Coffee," Ria said. "You're a doctor?"

"That's right," he said, poking the fire with a stick. "You ain't that troll, are you?"

"No. I'm not. I'm a woman, and history would say the troll isn't."

Armstrong pushed his glasses back up on his nose. "I hear the troll pokes holes in the heads of 'boes and then gouges out their eyes. A painter sure needs his eyes."

"You're a painter?"

"I paint paintings and put them in the Louvre. That's a fancy French art museum in Paris."

"Yes, I know. But I thought you said you were a doctor?"

"That's right." He took the coffee off the fire. "I don't have no cream."

Ria held out the tin cup he had provided earlier and waited for him to fill it. "You're a doctor who paints?"

"A painter paints. Doctors don't," he said, stirring the grounds.

Mixer sniffed Dr. Armstrong's shoe, working his way around the heel.

"What's this here dog's name?" he asked.

"Mixer," she said.

"Does he drink coffee?"

"I don't think so," she said.

"What you doing in Ludie Bean's crew car?" he asked.

"What were you doing there?"

Armstrong took a sip of his coffee, looking at her over the cup. Firelight danced in his glasses. "Ludie Bean don't like nobody in his crew car," he said. "He threw me out of a baggage car once at road speed, so I came to steal some of his stuff. I didn't know there would be no woman in there."

"Oh, my, were you hurt?"

"It cut open my head, but I put in a hundred stitches."

"A hundred stitches?"

"I learned to sew in surgeon school."

Armstrong poked at the fire, and embers raced up into the blackness.

"How you going to get out of here?" he asked.

"I'm catching a train at sunrise," she said, taking a sip. "That's good coffee."

"I used to be a chef. Frenchy's short haul comes through at sunrise."

"You know Frenchy?"

"I ride his louse box all the time. He don't never check. Sometimes he comes through before I'm awake, though."

"Are you catching it in the morning?" she asked.

"If I'm awake."

Mixer sat down next to Armstrong who gave the dog a pat. Mixer licked the doctor's hand. Ria relaxed. Any friend of Mixer's was a friend of hers.

"Do you know Hook Runyon?" she asked.

"I know him. I know almost everyone."

Ria's attention kicked into high. "And have you seen him?"

"I've seen him. He don't have no left arm, just a hook. I sewed his arm harness up for him."

Ria stood and moved around the fire. "Where did you see Hook?"

"The Amarillo jungle," he said.

"Is he still there?"

"I don't know. I ain't there no more. I'm here now. Most don't stay in the same jungle long. People take your stuff."

"Did he say where he might be headed?"

Armstrong shook his head. "He ain't no troll, though. He was just looking for that little guy, what don't wear no shoes."

"Is that all you can tell me about Hook?" Ria eyed him, looking for clues.

"Yes. I'm going to bed now."

After the fire had simmered down, Ria curled up next to it. Mixer slept at her feet. Armstrong had retreated to the edge of camp, and she could no longer hear his movements. He was a lonely and confused soul, and she wondered how many like him slept tonight under the stars.

For now, she needed to find Hook to warn him that Ludie might be dangerous, that he had been traumatized as a boy, so who knew what he might be capable of as a man? But she had no way of finding Hook, no way of getting to him even if she knew where he was.

There was nothing to do except go back.

*****

Ria and Mixer waited at the track's edge by themselves. She had awakened to a cold campfire that morning. Sometime in the night, Dr. Armstrong had left and not returned. Now golden rays streaked into the flat-bellied clouds. She was not certain when Frenchy would be coming, but Hook had told her that a train could broadcast its arrival through vibrations down the rails. A steamer, he said, pulls and rests, while a diesel hums like a hatful of bees.

She got on her knees and put her ear against the rail. "I can hear it. Mixer," she said. "A steamer, I think, and not far away."

They moved back into the bushes to wait. Frenchy didn't like to see 'boes riding his train, and for now, she figured she fit the bill.

Soon, she could hear Frenchy laying in on his whistle, and then his glimmer broke on the horizon like a morning star. The whistle screamed again and again as he came steaming in. The wheels screeched as he brought her down to a crawl. When the engine passed them, she could see Frenchy's elbow sticking out the cab window and the red tip of his cigar.

She moved closer to the track to await the bouncer. The cars rumbled, and the smell of heat filled the air. How she was to get both Mixer and herself on board with the train moving, she wasn't certain. Maybe she could toss him up first and still have time to board before Frenchy cranked her up.

The caboose came lumbering up the track, rocking and pitching like a ship at sea. She gathered Mixer into her arms, and just as the caboose reached her, she pitched him up onto the platform.

She broke into a trot just as Frenchy's whistle blew, but the caboose was moving much faster than she thought. The ties threw her stride off, and the turbulence, stirred by the passing cars, held her back. She realized that she might be left behind, and her adrenalin surged. She burst into a hard run and at the last second, reached up blindly for the grab iron.

Someone took her arm, someone with a grip of steel, and hoisted her onto the caboose platform. She gasped for air and tried to focus. She could see his shoes, frazzled and worn. He lifted her onto her feet. He wore his hat to the side and had a tuft of hair under his lip, a tall man, with a sinewy, tattooed arm. Only then did she realize that he still held her arm. She struggled to get loose.

"Sister," he said, "it ain't often I meet such a pretty lady on the rails."

From behind him, Mixer growled and bared his teeth. The man looked over his shoulder at Mixer and then back at Ria. Releasing her arm, he said, "Another day, perhaps, when there's more time."

Tipping his hat, he swung out on the grab iron and was gone.

Chapter 39

HOOK CAMPED IN THE OPEN, too exhausted to go any farther. Sometime in the night, he had heard the distant wail of a steam engine but had been unable to force himself to chase the hop. He figured Doc Armstrong, crazy though he was, had probably managed the hitch and was halfway to Kansas City by now.

Hook climbed from his nest of leaves and scratched at his beard. Dawn was breaking, and mosquitoes whined in the morning dampness, helping themselves to the tops of his ears. His stomach knotted with hunger. He thought about the many Harvey House breakfasts he had eaten over the years. No better existed on earth, sunny-side eggs coddled in milk, crisp bacon, sourdough toast with tomato marmalade, chicory coffee black as tar.

He banged his shoes against a rock to release any critters that might have taken up residence inside during the night. Taking stock of the neighborhood, he saw an old barn down in the draw. It leaned leeward, long ago having given up any semblance of color. A couple of Holstein milk cows, with hipbones like hat racks, stretched their necks through the corral fence.

Below the corral, a melon patch had been coaxed out of the sand. A creaky windmill pumped a trickle of water into the tin pipe that led to the patch. Farther up the hill sat a farmhouse, unpainted like the barn and not much for style, given that the front porch sagged and a gutted tractor sat in the yard.

Hook considered going to ask for a little grub, but the house appeared to be asleep. Even though he ranked high on the pitiful list this morning, he doubted that much fare was to be found there. He craned an ear for the sound of any trains that might be coming down track. Missing the one last night had been a mistake, one he hoped did not cost anyone his life, particularly his running mate, Runt Wallace. The troll, having only recently struck in Pampa, could be anywhere on the line by now.

He washed up at the windmill, splashing the cool well water on his face, and then took a look in the barn, finding only a half-empty bucket of feed hanging on a nail. More than once, he had heard Runt Wallace talk about milking cows. If Runt could do it, surely a certified railroad security agent could pull it off. He peeked through the planks of the barn to check the house once again before taking down the bucket.

He dumped the feed onto the ground and stepped back as both cows headed for it. When they were fully engaged, he squatted next to the nearest one, set his bucket under her, and reached for a teat. She stopped eating and swung her head back for a good look at Hook, her eyes bulging, her black tongue rolling up and over the top of her nose.

"Easy, ol' girl," Hook said. "All I want is a little milk."

Her hoof cracked like a gunshot when it hit his shin. Hook yelped and jumped, his bucket clattering off under the other cow. Cussing under his breath, he limped around the corral, rubbing his shin.

Undeterred, he eased up to the other cow, a critter clearly more tranquil and sweet natured. Grabbing and setting his bucket again, he squeezed, and a single drop of milk formed on her teat. He squeezed harder, but nothing happened. Runt, having two hands, obviously had the advantage in this situation. The fact that his legs were short only served to make the whole process easier for him.

Unaccustomed to such inefficiency, the cow swished her tail and danced back and forth from one foot to the other in a sort of ritualistic cow dance. But Hook stayed with her, realigning his bucket each time she moved. Suddenly, she butted the cow next to her in the side, a vicious butt, which caused the adjacent cow to back over the top of Hook, trampling him and his milk bucket into the cow manure.

Getting up, Hook threw his milk bucket at the cow, bouncing it off her back. She simply turned back to her feed once again. Afraid that he might have awakened the house with his tantrum, Hook peeked through the barn planking to check for movement. All was quiet. He washed yet again at the windmill, picked a melon from the patch, and carried it back to his camp, where he cut it open, only to find it was green.

He had walked a short distance up track when he spotted an old shunting boiler at a siding gathering up boxcars for a short haul. The switchman had just coupled on the last car and was walking toward the engine. He was taking his time, running out the clock, no doubt, so they would not have to make another run before the morning shift.

Hook slipped down the right-of-way, testing each car door as he went. All had been secured, and the train was too short for a top ride. They would have spotted him sure.

That left the rods underneath the cars, sometimes truss rods, sometimes brakes, sometimes air. Any way it was cut, no 'bo rode the rods unless driven by desperation and madness, which described Hook's state of mind to perfection. He had hoof-padded about as far as he cared to go. Combine that with a bellyful of green melon and the rods seemed less dangerous than they otherwise might.

The shunt boiler blew her whistle, three short blasts, signaling departure. Moments later, she bumped out the slack. Hook looked at the rods, one on each side of the car. He would have to stretch over the two like a hot dog on a grill. He would be only inches from the railbed, with no way of knowing how far, how fast, or how slow he would be moving or when—if ever—he would be able to get off. God forbid he fell asleep, for the slightest mishap could turn him into sausage in a matter of seconds.

The cars creaked and inched forward. Hook looked up track and then down track, seeing nothing but miles of open country. Latching onto the side of the car, he slid his legs under and across the rods, where he hung suspended like a spider in a web.

The shunt boiler blew her whistle, a long and forlorn blast, as the engineer brought her up. The wheels screeched only inches from Hook's head, ringing in his ears, and the ties below commenced to clip along faster and faster, gaining speed until they were little more than a blur beneath him.

The wind whipped under the car, his shirt collar slapping his ears. Dust and gravel stung his face, and the pitch and sway of the car threatened to dislodge him from his roost. He could have been going two miles an hour or two hundred, he had no idea, his notion of speed having given way to worrying about the proximity of the ground. Nor did he any longer have a grasp of time. It could have been eons, centuries even, before the short haul finally came to rest.

When it did, Hook struggled to move his legs, which had gone dead back somewhere in the second century. He rolled out from beneath the car, his eyes full of grit and the hide worn off his neck from the constant sand-blast from the wheels. He pulled himself into the weeds, his legs trailing behind him, where he waited until the shunt boiler pulled out once again.

When it had disappeared down track, he looked around to orient him-self. It was later than he had thought, the sky already darkening with sun-set. Down track, he could see a bridge abutment and a single black-and-white sign that read "Dumas."

Once the feeling returned to his legs, he worked his way down track, where he came upon a bridge. Taking a wide swing downstream, he re-turned up the draw, where he knelt in the grass to assess the situation. He had no doubt that this was the Dumas jungle. He had spent a cold winter night here once, a night a man did not easily forget.

He soon spotted a fire but no signs of life. Perhaps they had heard him approach or perhaps they had caught the shunt boiler out.

Hook stepped into the firelight. Shadows danced through the bridge timbers. No food had been prepared, no mulligan, no coffee, and no fire-wood had been collected for the night. Whoever had been here had left in a hurry.

He stoked the fire and when it burned high, the blaze revealed a safe-haven "U" carved in the abutment and what looked to be an owl with its head cocked next to it, drawn in fresh charcoal.

Something in the darkness beyond the firelight moved behind him, and he turned.

"Ludie," he said. "Ludie Bean."

Chapter 40

HOOK STEPPED BACK INTO THE firelight. He was startled when he recognized his P38 stuck in Ludie's belt. "You found Runt?" he asked.

Sweat trickled off the end of Ludie's nose. He twisted his mouth to the side. His eyes, large and round like a pig's, sat deep under his heavy brow, and his lungs rattled when he breathed.

"Gathered him up," he said. "He was carrying this here sidearm at the time. So, I arranged a vacation in the county jail. I got little patience with 'boes carrying sidearms."

"I gave it to him, Ludie. He was running with me, see, and I figured he might need the protection, what with this troll murderer about."

"I can see that, him being a close friend and all, but you should have taught him to use it while you were at it, Runyon. Got himself in a heap of trouble, didn't he?"

Hook took a deep breath, thinking to whip this guy's ass if it came to it. But charging Ludie Bean head-on was not a particularly good idea in the best of circumstance. Charging him when he held a firearm in his hands was nothing short of madness.

"I seen how you look the other way, Runyon, giving these 'boes free rides, helping them along. I seen it, and I don't like it. They don't need no help, drinking, stealing, riding for free. Ludie Bean don't allow it on his railroad."

"They're just men like you and me, Ludie, 'cept they're down on their luck. They've been through the Depression and the Second World War, and it's knocked them to their knees. They probably got families somewhere, folks who care, a gal who stays up nights wondering where they might be. Most of these men just need a chance, that's all, a chance to take a breath and start over."

Ludie shook his head. "They don't care about no family," he said. "They care about the next bottle, the next free meal, the next hop on Uncle John's train. There ain't a one out here wouldn't cut you open and eat your liver for breakfast given a chance."

"They ain't worth saving," he said, more to himself than to Hook. "Just like that Runt guy. Someone should have pinched his goddang head off when he was born."

Before Hook could protest again, from the darkness came the faint hoot of an owl, and Ludie turned. Hook prepared himself to charge, to seize the moment. Ludie was unpredictable and mean, and Hook had no intention of letting him keep the upper hand. But before either of them could move, something dropped from the darkness behind them.

Ludie spun about. "Who the hell?" he said.

"Dickey," the man said. "At your service."

The reverend had a maul spike at his side, like a knight would carry a saber, and his old jacket was tied off about his waist. In his hand was a side arm with a barrel as big as a rail tunnel pointed at Ludie's head.

The reverend did not wait for a welcome.

He fired.

Ludie fell back into the fire, dead before he hit the ground.

Hook took a step back into where the shadows began.

Dickey faced him, his eyes little more than slits like knife cuts, and what firelight remained flickered in them from under his brows. His shirt-sleeves were rolled and cuffed. His thin arms were knotted like strands of steel, and his hands were gnarled and tense. And there on his forearm, clear as day, was the tattoo of an owl.

With his gun on Hook, Dickey loosened the jacket knot and spilled the contents of its pocket near the campfire edge: a butcher knife with curved blade, a man's wedding band, a Case XX pocketknife, a torn photo of a little girl dressed in white, and a gold tooth, freshly scrubbed from its mooring. He slipped the butcher knife into his belt.

Hook took a deep breath and considered a head-on charge. But the element of surprise was gone, and the odds of beating a slug out of the good reverend's sidearm seemed untenable. An alternative strategy escaped him at the moment, but the one thing he did understand with some clarity was that he was finally standing face to face with the bridge troll murderer. "Looks like you been collecting a few souvenirs there, Reverend," he said.

"These are no souvenirs," Dickey said. "These here are relics of the dead, remnants of souls saved that would have otherwise been lost."

"I suspect their previous owners would disagree," Hook said.

"Sinners and filth," the reverend said. "Drunkards and fornicators and thieves."

"I've known a few of them and can't say you're wrong, and the dead man there would surely agree with you if he still could, but I can also recall some who were more than that."

The reverend shook his head. "There wasn't one among them wouldn't take a man's life for a drink of Thunderbird or a sack of Bull Durham tobacco. I saved them. I transformed them, gave 'em a second chance at paradise."

"Strikes me as a bit harsh, I have to say, what with them being hacked open that way."

"Some things are too evil for saving outright," Dickey muttered, more to himself than to Hook. "They got to be killed off and brought up new. Got to make 'em fresh as newborns. Unleash the bird of death upon them and then free their souls for the glory of God."

He paused and looked at Hook as if it was the first time he had seen him. "You're one of them your own damn self, rail dick. You always been— no job, no title, no desk could change that."

The sound of a train whistle drifted in from above, and for a moment, Dickey looked up. Being a creature of opportunity, Hook slammed his prosthesis down on the reverend's gun-wielding arm, and the weapon spun off into the weeds.

The reverend pulled his knife from his belt. Stepping in, he delivered a searing swipe across Hook's chest. Hook flung himself backward, then righted himself and squared off.

A bolt of pain shot through Hook's chest like lightning. A knife fight was not the best option in the world, but it was decidedly better than staring into the barrel of a sidearm, especially one aimed by a madman.

The reverend seemed to also recognize that his situation had changed and determined that the new odds were considerably less favorable. He slipped the knife back into his belt, grabbed an overhead bridge timber, and lifted himself up.

Hook held tight against the wound that now oozed blood into his shirt.

The distant rumble of a train rode down the track and amplified in the timbers of the bridge. Her whistle rose as she bumped out slack somewhere in the distance. He could tell by her voice that she was an old teakettle, and she was moving slow. In all likelihood, she was shuffling short hauls somewhere downline. But she would still be a sight faster than Hook could run. If the reverend hopped her, there would be no chance of catching him.

Hook rolled his shoulders, and a flash of searing pain fired across his chest. Although the wound was painful, there appeared to be no muscles or tendons severed. He looked up into the bridge again and saw the reverend climbing steadily upward. He was nimble and fast, a practiced climber who would be difficult to catch in the best of circumstances.

At that moment, as Dickey approached the riverbank, he stopped and looked back at Hook. And then he was gone into the shadows.

When the clouds broke, Hook spotted him again, already in the highest part of the bridge. At this rate, he would soon be out of reach. Even now, it would be hard to close the distance between them.

But letting Dickey escape seemed a poor choice, given his penchant for murder and mayhem. So Hook gritted his teeth and hoisted himself up into the timbers. The climbing was treacherous and slow, and his wound burned like fire. Time and again, he was forced to lean out into space to secure a new grip. Such climbing would be challenging for a two-armed man. For Hook, it required a dangerous expenditure of energy.

As Hook worked his way upward, he at times caught a glimpse of Dickey as he ascended ever higher into the bridge beams above. Below, the river twisted like a ribbon in the moonlight.

Hook paused to catch his breath. Sweat ran into his eyes, trickled down his neck into his collar. Blood had caked on his shirt, and the wound had tightened like a cable around his chest. Many times in his life he had wished for two arms; never had he wished it more than now.

He stepped up, and his foot slipped from under him. He swung out into thin air, hanging there by one arm. He shifted his weight from side to side, pegging his legs to gain a little momentum until at last he snagged a timber with his toe and pulled himself back on board. For several moments he clung there to regain his breath and calculate his next move.

Overhead, Dickey continued his climb, an ephemeral shadow in the moonlight. For Hook to lose him now might well cost lives, because this much Hook had learned from Ria: Such a man as this would never stop killing until he was killed himself.

Hook worked his prosthesis between the timber bracing above him, levering it in as tight as he could. The rumble of the train rode in once again like a distant thunderstorm. He leaned back to catch a glimpse of the reverend, who had nearly reached the top deck of the bridge.

Hook glanced down, and his stomach tightened. To get higher, he would have to let go with his good hand and put his entire weight on the prosthesis. It was something he never did, and for good reason. The harness was simply not sturdy enough to bear that kind of weight. To make matters worse, his confidence in Doc Armstrong's sewing job was something less than one hundred percent.

His arm trembled and burned with fatigue, and his fingers were numbed and bleeding. Sooner or later, he would lose control of their movement. He had to act, and it had to be now.

Shutting his eyes, he opened his hand, and his body fell away. His weight caught hard against the prosthesis, and the harness bit into his flesh. But it held, giving him the few seconds he needed to snare the bracing above him.

He climbed higher then, his lungs burning. If the reverend managed to get on deck, Hook would never catch him. He paused to reconnoiter, the bridge deck above him like piano keys.

Dickey was a fast climber and with a substantial lead. Whether he was smarter remained to be seen, but at this point, he had the edge. One thing Hook was pretty certain about, an encounter with this madman while hanging from a bridge timber with only one good arm was probably not the best idea in the world. But the alternative was worse. The last thing Hook wanted was for the reverend to catch that hop, only to reappear under some bridge a thousand miles down track with a spike maul in his hand.

Above him, Dickey abruptly stopped and drew his knife from his belt. Hook fell back. The reverend looked up at the bridge deck, which was now within his reach. The engine whistle lifted once again in the distance, but there was still no light, no sign of an approaching engine.

Suddenly, the reverend, having made up his mind, shoved the knife back into his belt, pulled himself up between the ties and into the bridge deck. The fit was tight, and he struggled to squeeze his shoulders through the ties. His legs dangled in midair as he fought to worm his way through.

The train whistle blew again, and the bridge shuddered under its weight. But there was still no glimmer. Overhead, the steel wheels of the boxcars shrieked like the screams of a dying man. Dickey's legs jerked back and forth instinctively, as if to run to escape some awful terror.

And then he yelped, as if suddenly startled, and a moment later, his headless body fell away, crashing and careening through the timbers and into the river below.

The boxcars atop slowed and then stopped. A ripple rode down the train's length as it pulled forward once again. Only then did Hook realize that the train had been backing onto the bridge, that the cars had rolled from out of the darkness, taking with them the severed head of the bridge troll murderer.

Chapter 41

THEY FOUND RUNT OUT OF JAIL, barefoot, and sound asleep in Banjo's baggage room. He was still carrying Hook's Faulkner. Hook introduced Ria and after declining to listen to Banjo's latest rendition of "Victory in Jesus," they drove back to the caboose, where Hook made a pot of coffee and fed Mixer a can of tuna.

Hook set a pair of his shoes on the table in front of Runt.

"Aw," Runt said. "Those are your Sunday best, Hook."

"Take 'em," Hook said. "You saved my Faulkner. Anyway, I can't remember the last time I had cause to wear them to church."

Runt slid back his chair and worked on the shoes. "I figure to grow into 'em," he said. "Hell, Hook, I don't have no money to pay you, and here you don't even have a mattress to sleep on."

Ria stirred her coffee. "You going back on the rails, Runt?"

Runt looked out the window of the caboose and down track. "No, I guess I'll be going home. Jungle living strikes me as a bit too exciting. Course, there ain't much left at home for making a living, 'cept shine. Then again, I just happen to know where there's a good still."

A whistle sounded down track, and Mixer lifted his ears.

"That would be Frenchy," Hook said. "I'll flag him down while you circle around and hop the louse box, Runt. Frenchy don't like 'boes hopping his train, as you well know."

Runt tied off his new shoes and dusted the toes on his pant legs. He opened the door and turned. "You ever want any goods, Hook, just let me know."

Hook and Ria stood near the edge of the track, while Runt circled out through the locust grove. Hook waved Frenchy down, and the old steamer sidled in, hissing and blowing steam. Frenchy leaned out the cab window, his cigar stuck in the corner of his mouth.

"If it ain't Hook Runyon and his sidekick, Miss Ria Wolfe."

"Hello, Frenchy," Hook said.

"I hear that bridge troll tried to baptize you, Hook."

"Yes, sir," Hook said, holding his hand against the knife wound on his chest. "You might say he lost his head over it. Anyway, takes more than a rogue preacher to get me in a pew, Frenchy."

"Word is they're thinking a whole passel of 'boes could be missing up and down the line."

"We'll never know, Frenchy. A man has to be missed to be missing, don't he?"

Frenchy pushed his hat back. "You suppose that boy's climbed aboard my louse box yet?"

Hook said, "I don't know what you're talking about, Frenchy."

Frenchy gave a nod, brought up steam, and eased the old teakettle off down track. Hook and Ria waited for the caboose to come waddling by. Runt was out on the deck with the caboose mattress hiked up on the porch rail. He waved and pushed it off with a grin.

Hook walked Ria to her car and waited at her open window.

"I guess my research here has come to an end," she said.

"What lies ahead for you, Ria?" he asked.

Ria shrugged. "Back to Boston. There are people waiting, hypothetically, but I'm not so sure about the case study anymore. I can't be certain what I've learned matters much in the real world."

"Don't be in too big a hurry to give it up, Ria. No one but you understood what was behind that troll's thinking. That's no small matter. It was you right there in his head all along."

"But it was you who did what had to be done to stop him," she said.

Hook reached through the window and kissed her on the cheek.

"Guess you could say we were a team."

Ria started the car and dropped it into reverse. "And a damn good team at that."

Acknowledgments

Thanks to Jeanne Devlin, my editor, and to her staff for guiding this project through the process and to my loyal readers who lift me up. You are great fun.

About the Author

Sheldon Russell taught at the University of Louisville and the University of Central Oklahoma. He is the award-winning author of nine novels, including *The Yard Dog* and *The Insane Train*. He lives in western Oklahoma.